Perseus
by
Scott Rhymer

Copyright 2011 Scott Rhymer
All rights reserved. No part of this publication may be reproduced or transmitted in any form or by any means, electronic or mechanical, including photocopy, recording, or any information storage and retrieval system without the permission of the publisher.

Requests for permission may be submitted via email to theblackcampbell@gmail.com or online at scottrhymer.wordpress.com.

Cover art *Medusa* by Carvaggio, 1595.

A novel is never written in a vacuum. I would like to thank my wife Susan for spelling me from baby duty when I needed to get some words spat out, to Susan for her work on the proofreading.

This one's for wee Sofia -- welcome to the world.

PROLOGUE: EFFRONTERY

Nix had provided a particularly lovely setting for their tryst. The moon had yet to rise, but the sky blazed with stars, so many that the young woman winding her way along the seaside path could see her surroundings plainly. Her heart was already beating in anticipation of her lover's touch, excitement and lust mixing with the too-wise fear of who – what – she was to couple with. The ocean washed along the rocks, singing to her. She swore she could hear a chorus of sea nymphs, accompanying the shush of the water. She had always been a romantic soul. Her sisters might have inherited their parent's longevity, but she had been born with the kindest gift the gods could bestow: she was staggeringly beautiful. Coupled with her light, happy nature, she was intoxicating.

Happy steps. Happy breath. Her eyes wide and searching for her lover. She was on the crest of a series of rocks, not far from the small temple to Athena, where she was pledged to the priestesses. Looking out over the black sea, she saw phosphorescent foam battered against the land, transmitting the sea god's power through the rock. The Shaker of Earth, Poseidon was sometimes called. Salt spray and the pungent scent of sex caught in her nostrils, wind played along her chiton and sent luscious caresses along her body.

He was here! Naked, dark-skin over powerful muscle, his black hair and beard wild with curls. He moved with a swiftness she did not expect, taking her into his arms. Strong hands played along her skin, gentle but unshakeable. Kisses on her face, her mouth. She could smell the sea on him, taste the brine on his lips. With a fluid motion, she was lifted from her feet and carried along, up the rocky hill from the sea's edge. She could feel urgency in his embrace, the cool breath on her face, like an ocean breeze before a storm.

She barely noted the building, simple and stately. Columns and a simple frieze, inside braziers threw enough light to make out the pastel hue to the walls. Her lover's skin reflected the light, almost blue, his eyes still a dark blue, almost black. He was laughing lightly, but the humor did not reach those eyes. He was on top of her, seemed to surround her, and she could feel him inside. He surged against her, forceful, enveloping, and she was transported! Pleasure rolled through her rhythmically. She called his name aloud.

"What. Is. This?" The voice shook the building, a strong mezzo-soprano that nearly split the ear with its violence. While loud, the speaker seemed preternaturally calm. The girl was suddenly very aware of her surroundings, the familiar interior of the temple to that goddess she was to serve, the one who was to be forever chaste...

He was off her in a flash, almost seemed to flow away into a ready stance. She could see in the doorway of the small temple and the Woman that accompanied the Voice. She was tall and lithe; a slim frame that might give the appearance of youth and femininity, but her muscles played under the surface of bronzed skin and her stride into the temple evinced terrible power and authority. Her chiton was an elegant linen of Ionic cut. The light from the fires around them caught her face, not beautiful, but handsome. The eyes gleamed in the light, greenish-gray, like the color of storm clouds before a tempest. "You dare to defile my house, uncle? You seek to mock me in my own temple?" Her voice rang clear and the anger suppressed in her tone nearly stopped the poor mortal girl's heart.

It was only then that she realized she was lying on the plynth for the offerings, those gifts cast aside by her lover in their haste. She shuddered in terror – she was not, like her sisters, immortal, and she knew the goddess whose house this was on sight, as if her image had been burned into her very brain sometime before she was born, that she (or any mortal) would know her when revealed.

"Harmless sport, little one. I think you take your vow of chastity far too seriously. There's no need for the rest of us to resist our natural inclinations to salve your desire to remain...above us." The god's tone was mocking and playful, but there was an undercurrent of fear. Could a god feel fear? And if the creature advancing slowly, confidently toward the larger man could instill fear in a god, what hope did she have of surviving this night?

"This is the last time you wrong me, uncle," she said

coldly.

He rose up, seeming to fill the space. "Third Born, you forget yourself, who you talk to."

"A coward, and a lecherous one at that. One who would steal his brother's rightful throne, had he only the courage to do so. A sniveling wretch who cannot satisfy himself with the greatest of realms, but would seek to own the sky, also."

"You would know theft of one's prerogative. An olive tree? Better than a spring?"

The goddess laughed, "Take it up with the Athenians who chose me of their own will, uncle, if you've the courage. You insult me for the last time, Sea God. And you..." She glanced at the mortal girl, who had slid off of the offering table and was hastily gathering her clothing while edging away from the two giant figures that were circling each other in the faintly lit space.

"She's done nothing."

The goddess' eyes bored into the other Olympian. "You like this one, do you?"

Oh, no! Zeus preserve and protect me! She made to run, but the goddess boomed, "STAY WHERE YOU ARE!" Collapsing to the ground, the young girl slapped her hands over her ears. The eardrums had burst, she was sure of it, and her head swam from the force of the deity's shout. Her war cry, it was said, could unman whole armies; even Ares himself feared this apparition in front of her. So, apparently, did the Master of the Waves.

Athena's voice rumbled through the masonry, dislodging dust from the mortar joins. "You will pay for this insult, Poseidon. Now."

"You cannot war on me. Your father forbids it." As if to punctuate the statement, a peal of thunder rolled outside the temple. Through the doorway, she could see clouds swirling in toward their location, flashes of lightning accenting their approach.

Poseidon's words, however, did not match his actions. He continued to move cautiously, trying to flank the goddess and – the girl realized – escape through the door. Athena, almost casually, had advanced on him, catlike, until he was nearly pressed to the wall. "I will best you. I will bind you with the best net my brother the smith can provide. And I will hold you in your watery kingdom, captive, until such time as I have undone all of your works, everything you love."

Poseidon stomped his foot and the earth shook with convulsions. The earthquake rippled through the structure, toppling the statue of Athena at the end of the space, cracking columns and collapsing a section of the roof. The girl shrieked and bolted from the temple, staggering across the heaving earth. Behind her, she could see the goddess unbalanced for a mere instant. In that moment, her lover had lashed out and tossed Athena across the temple and into the opposite wall.

Naked, the girl toppled out onto the dirt outside of the temple, then dragged herself to her feet and ran for her life. Over her shoulder, she could see the temple half collapsed and a section of wall burst outward, as her lover was tossed through it. He rolled to his feet, but it was too late. The goddess had leapt onto him with stunning speed and was pummeling him expertly with short, deliberate blows to the vital sections of his body. Staggering into a collection of juniper bushes, the girl hid and watched as the Olympians tore at each other.

Poseidon was strong, and his blows could have won the day, but his opponent was fast, her movements smooth and calculated, using his movement to pivot and throw him, or run him into her outstretched arm or sweeping fist. Their violence exploded across the hillside, ripping the earth itself. The sea was frothing and slamming into the coastline, and overhead the stars were extinguished by low clouds, glowing with internal lightning.

STOP! NOW! the sky commanded. It was delivered as thunder, accompanied by a lightning stroke that blasted a nearby lemon tree into flames and splinters. The goddess paused to look up.

"He has insulted me, father! Again and again he taunts me! Will you not allow me to avenge myself?" she wailed, her fist balled, chiton torn from her one shoulder and exposing a small, but finely shaped breast. "I demand justice for this infraction!"

That was when the sea rose up and battered the war goddess to the ground. As the wave retreated, the girl watched her lover sink into it, become part of the water, which swept him away from the furious incarnation of war, and out into the sea and safety.

Athena screamed in anger, and her voice burst rain from the clouds and drew a single lightning bolt from the sky into the ocean. The discharge illuminated the angry green sea for stadia[1] upon stadia in every direction.

YOU WILL HAVE YOUR REVENGE, MY DEAREST. I PROMISE YOU, the sky said. BUT NOT NOW.

Defiant, she shook her fist at the sky. "This is not over!" The sky crackled and rumbled in response, but no bolt of lightning struck. Athena glared at the sky, at the sea, then seemed to deflate some. With increasing panic and terror, the girl watched as the goddess stalked across the wrecked, smoking ground, the rain wetting her until her gown was translucent and the muscles of the goddess rippled with undisguised potency. "Come out." The order was simple, quiet, and while the fury in her voice was barely contained, it was unmistakable.

The girl stood, shivering, her blonde hair matted to her head by the rain. She swore she could hear a sigh from the sky, whether disgust or resignation, she could not tell. "Please..."

"My temple: it is my home, a very extension of my body, you understand?" The voice was almost gentle now, still angry, but the rage had been contained. What terrible will could hold back rage so strong it could call lightning from the sky? "And you...you invoked his name. In my house."

She attempted to explain, but her voice caught in her throat. She dropped to her knees, imploringly, hand stretched out in supplication. The goddess did not hesitate. She did not move to invoke her curse, but the girl could feel the changes

---

[1] Nine stadia are roughly a mile.

sweeping through her body. Her skin felt too tight, her face...wrong. Her hair – that lustrous airy mass of blonde curls that has so enticed the Sea God himself, rose from her shoulders, whipping in the wind. Out of the corner of her eye she could see the movement, as the blonde hair twisted and wove itself together, losing its color and shine, darkening into frightening masses of asps. Their cold eyes stared back and a few of them lunged threateningly at her face, only to recoil at the last minute.

      The goddess was impassive. Quietly, she whispered the answer to the girl's unspoken question. "Until death release you, Medusa."

1. THE BOY WHO WOULD BE A HERO

The sun beat down on the fishermen at their work and stripped the sky of its color. The ocean around their boat was a deep cerulean blue and flat calm. About forty stadia distant, the island of Serifos was visible. The groves of olive, almond, and fruit trees lined the shore and made patches of green around the small city, and the dusty hills were brown from the summer heat. There had been no trace of wind for the last few days, and the summer heat ashore was oppressive much of the day. People would doze through much of the afternoon, spending all of their efforts during the morning and evening hours. The fishermen considered themselves lucky. They could enjoy the cool of the sea while at their labors.

The boat was a fine thing. This was to be expected when the owner was the brother of the king. Larger than the other fishing craft bobbing nearby on the serene waters, *Okeia* – "Swift" – was fifty feet from stem to stern, designed along the lines of a warship. Her crew, in time of war, could be as high as sixty men, but for the everyday work of feeding the people of Serifos, only ten men would row her out to sea, if they could not sail. She was painted shining white, with cobalt blue gunwales and prow. On either side, stylized blue eyes gazed out to sea, looking for dangers that could harm her crew. Her mast and spar were blue, as well, but accented with a rust red series of bands where her rigging connected. Inside, white benches for the oarsmen clashed with the red-stain on the deck works.

The nets were out, and the men were relaxing under the sun. Most were naked. There was no need for modesty out here; the women were all ashore. The captain lounged under a sunbreak at the stern, a strong man with skin burned to brown and dark hair that had been bleached to a pleasing auburn by the sun. He was eating figs and laughing easily at his crew's gossip. Nearby, sitting on the gunwale and watching the nets for signs of their catch, was a young man – barely old enough to have the fuzz of an early beard on his face. The captain shot the youth a look, proudly.

Perseus was not his son, but might as well have been.

The youth was just an infant when he and his mother had been cast adrift in an ark by his grandfather, Acricius, the King of Argos. The ark was barely that...it had been an oceangoing coffin, really. Dictys, the captain, was sure that was Acricius' intention when he placed them in that casket-like vessel: that his own daughter and grandson would die at sea. However, one does not kill the son of a god so easily. That was Perseus – son of Zeus, if his mother was to be believed. And Dictys believed it. The day he found them had been extraordinary. The sea had been as becalmed as ever he saw it, the water like a board when it should have been heaving under a frothing, cloudy sky that crackled and thundered. In the midst of this, he could see the ark, carried along, just under the surface, until it popped aloft next to his boat. Dictys knew the will of the gods when he saw it and rescued them, stunned when he opened the casket to find the woman and child alive and well, despite their submergence.

According to the mother, the boy had been sired by Zeus, who had come to Danae as a shower of golden rain. At least that was her story. After fifteen years of raising the boy as if he was his own, and providing a home for the both of them, Dictys knew Danae to be a truthful girl.

Dictys had raised this demi-god from an infant to the fine young man he was now. He taught him the art of sailing – the intricacies of knots and navigation, how to gauge the mood of the sea and sky by the smallest hints, and how to command men as well as catch fish by net or spear – and he taught him the arts of combat, how to wrestle and to use a sword and javelin. More importantly, he taught him how to be a good man; to be humble but brave, honest and true to his friends, his people, and the gods. He never shied away from the subject of Perseus' divine birth, even though Dictys' brother King Polydectes believed neither the story of his birth, nor that it was a good thing to fuel hubris in the boy with tales of his parentage.

His brother had never taken to the boy. Dictys knew this was because his brother desired the mother, Danae, and more to the point, the throne of Argolis, which he hoped to have claim to by marrying her. For years, Dictys' ruse that he was having Danae for himself had worked to fend off the monarch's advances for a while, but he was never meant to be a "great" man; he strove to simply be a good man. Besides, the true nature of the captain's desires was no real secret on the island, and after a few years, his brother had begun to sniff about Danae like a dog. By that time, Perseus had become old enough to recognize Polydectes' intentions and he stood like a rampart between the king and the object of his desire. The boy was of royal (if not divine) stock, and it was only right that he control access to his mother. With Dictys' aid, they had prevented Polydectes from his desire to take the woman into his bed.

Dictys knew his brother's character better than any, and while he loved him dearly, he knew that Polydectes was often as selfish and cruel as he could be a delightful companion. There was a hunger to his attraction to Danae that Dictys mistrusted, and Great Men...men of power, he found liked to exercise it on those who had been previously mistreated. The woman had suffered greatly at the hands of her father. Not just in his attempt to drown her and her son, but for years he had locked her away to stop the fruition of a prophecy he had learned at Delphi: that his grandson would be the death of him. Before that, her uncle Proetus had seduced her to trying win the throne of Argolis away from Perseus' grandfather.

Bits of these stories Dictys had plied out of her over the years. Much of it sounded outrageous, far-fetched, but the fisherman believed her. This was because he had seen enough of the world to know a simple truth: Power had a way of twisting a man -- the "great" man -- up inside, of making a person monstrous in intent and action. He had seen it in his brother's dealings with other rulers from larger kingdoms. All were warped by their strength and the extent of their control over their people. This was why Dictys fished.

Perseus noticed it even before he did. "The air is shifting. We'll have weather tomorrow." The youth shielded his eyes and scanned the burnished white sky. To the Northwest, there were a few high, wispy clouds. "Tomorrow afternoon, I think..." Dictys followed his gaze and judged his prediction good.

"You've got a fine sense, my boy." Dictys rose to his feet and nudged the boy's shoulder with his fist. "Gifts from your true father, I think."

"I sail with my true father," Perseus said lightly. The boy was a delight to the captain. Tall and well-muscled, he possessed a keen sense of balance and was fast – so fast! – in his reaction time. As a simple boy, he had quickly learned his way around the sword. Dictys had to handicap Perseus now when they sparred. Dark curly hair and deep gray eyes made the girls of Serifos go weak at the knees. His voice had not fully changed yet, and occasionally would still break. He was a gentle one at heart, but brave. He had handled himself well in foul weather on these very decks, even diving into the violent sea to rescue a shipmate a year ago.

Dictys couldn't be prouder of him were he his own child. If anything, it was Perseus that made him occasionally consider Danae as a wife. He was sure she would accept his offer, and he thought that she would please him, but it was always a passing notion. He thanked Zeus that he had the opportunity and happiness to raise the boy.

"Check the nets, you flatterer. It's hot, I'm feeling tired, and I've a feeling we've got all the fish we're going to catch today." Perseus jumped off of the gunwale and motioned for the other, older men and boys to aid him. Dictys climbed onto the gunwale and scanned the horizon quickly, returned a wave from Hippo over on a rival boat, and cracked a smile as the nets were hauled up to the side of the vessel, then up over the side into the ship. He could see fluttering, silvery movement in the nets. A good catch – more than enough to feed his brother's guests tonight.

"Ha!" shouted Pirithis, one of the older mates. "We'll eat well tonight, my lord!"

Dictys had them secure the netting and catch forward, then the men took to their oars and took *Okeia* back to the shore. As they rowed home, the sky in the East began to regain its blue hue as the sun rode its fiery chariot toward sundown. By the time the ship was pulled ashore and staked down, some of the local men had sidled down to aid them in taking the catch into town. Some of the men, Dictys included, quickly wrapped themselves in their clothing as the townspeople began to come out to greet them. Dictys left the apportionment to the crew to Pirithis, and ordered the rest taken to Polydectes' home. He then threw his arm around Perseus and they headed for home. A few of the local girls were lurking along the pathway into town, casting looks at the naked boy and giggling to each other.

Perseus flashed them a grin and nodded. Dictys chuckled, and Perseus shot him an amused look. Dictys nodded toward him, "You should cover up. Wouldn't want to disappoint them, would you?"

"Hey!" Perseus took the insult in stride and the two walked along the beach to the path through the olive trees and up a slight grade to where their house waited. It was a simple structure. A single story that was a single rectangle, viewed from above, with a central courtyard dominated by a reflecting pool. Only a few windows looked out of the world, most were directed inward at the courtyard. The stonework was thick and strong, made to repulse any violence it might meet, but was covered by a thick stucco to make it look more domestic than it was. Fine terra cotta tiles covered the roof. Like many here, it had a simple wooden door painted blue, but with twin fetishes hung on the door. Zeus and Poseidon, those holy brothers, held their totems – lightning and trident, respectively – to ward off evil.

Inside, the heat of the day was held somewhat at bay, and the light in the alcove came from inside the courtyard. A few of the servants were bustling about, making a show of working for the master of the house. In the courtyard, reclining on a couch and fanning herself lazily, was Perseus' mother. If anything, the years had made Danae more attractive as she matured. Her figure remained shapely and pleasing, and her face might have lost some of its youth, but had gained a delightful maturity. At only thirty-four, Dictys thought Danae was still gorgeous enough to move a god. At the sight of them, she rose and came to give Perseus a hug and peck on the cheek.

"A decent catch today," Dictys told her, "and it looks

like we'll finally have some rain tomorrow."

She responded, "Good. This heat is unbearable."

Perseus smiled, "It was pleasant enough out to sea. I am going to wash up before we leave."

"Wear something tonight, showoff. We don't want the guests mistaking you for one of the servant boys," the captain told him. Perseus, smiling, waved him off. Dictys told her, "He's definitely coming of age. Some of the girls were out to see us come in."

"He's been asking about home, again," she added. "I am keep telling him to forget about Argos, but he seems intent on returning."

Dictys nodded. "He had a destiny. He knows it. I think that Zeus fathered him on you to punish your father for his treatment of you."

She shrugged, feigning disinterest. Dictys knew she was uncomfortable with the notion that her son was some force of vengeance, fated to kill his grandfather. Despite her imprisonment by Acricius, despite his attempt to drown them at sea, he was still her father. At some level, the little girl she used to be was still in there, hoping that somehow she could win her father's love.

"I'm simply saying that he has a course set for him. Perseus might not know the route, precisely, but he knows a few of the navigational points. He's old enough to be able to make the journey. We can't hold him here or protect him forever."

"I don't want to hold him forever..."

"...and we shouldn't try," he interrupted. "We've raised him the best we can. I'm confident of his abilities. And if his father is looking out for him, I think he'll be alright. I'm more worried about you, once he's gone."

She smiled slightly and hugged the captain. "So am I."

*****

Torches lit around the palace of King Polydectes painted the walls of the grand house in golden hues. Guests had already arrived and the sounds of revelry spilled out into the night. Overhead, the stars were incredibly bright, and the moon – while still behind the hills in the East – was beginning to light the night. The house was a grander version of Dictys' home, with the wings of the house being larger, and more well-appointed. The central court of the house was closed to the revelers, who were packed into the sitting room near the entrance. The room was full of guests, some local, some from the ships that had been passing by on their way to elsewhere. Couches had been placed around three of the walls and some of the elders and the guests lounged, chatting volubly. The younger men were seated on the floor and on small stools here and there. The house servants were hustling about, pouring wine cut with water from the house *krater*, in this case a spectacular bronze jug with the visage of Medusa on it (to ward off evil spirits), and delivering food to the guests.

Polydectes was a slightly older, fatter version of his fisherman brother, with graying hair and the slightly enlarged nose of an inebriate. Where Dictys was brown from the sun, Polydectes was fair-skinned, and while he still was respectably strong, he was not used to work as his younger brother was. He was wearing a pale yellow chiton with a black border wrapped around the waist and thrown carelessly over the right shoulder. On seeing Dictys, he burst into a grin. "Here he is!"

The other guests glanced around and caught sight of the captain, draped in a bland white muslin wrap, and Perseus. The sovereign bade his brother to sit beside him, but the smile on his face slipped for a moment at the sight of Perseus. The boy had done a simple wrap, like the captain, around his waist and was a glowing picture of health and youth. He could see the town pederast grinning at him and ignored the old fool. Instead, he bowed slightly to Polydectes. "Thank you, king, for the invitation."

"You are welcome in this house, grandson of Acricius." Neither meant a word, and only the locals were likely to catch onto the subtle jabs taking place. Perseus took a stool near the door, across the room from Dictys and his royal brother. A moment later, a bowl for his wine was brought, and charged from the *krater*. Perseus looked at the grotesque visage in the bronze, fascinated.

The symposium was an interesting affair. Perseus had been to one at the palace before, a few months back, but this was his first time meeting people from outside Serifos. The ship captain, Telephemus, was on his way through the Cyclades chain, doing trading. Perseus thought he detected a trace of falsehood, of obfuscation in the man's tales, but he seemed harmless enough. Fishermen, like soldiers, understood the importance of a little creative license in the telling of tales. A twist here, an exaggeration there, was forgivable if it made the story that much more enjoyable for the listener.

Tales of strange people, places, monsters, and the gods wove through the night, along with poems, singing, and general revelry. Perseus enjoyed the camaraderie, and was pleased when some of the men included him in the discussions. He could feel the wine flowing through him, and he felt with each bowl more at ease, and more confident in his talk with the older men. Each time the bowl was charged, the glaring face of Medusa seemed even more idiotic: why would someone use a monster to ward off monsters? Wasn't that the purview of the gods? Zeus and Poseidon defended his home, not some snake-haired harridan that had offended Athena.

"Perhaps young Perseus can regale us with the story of his birth," joked Polydectes. While he laughed, but the mirth did not reach his eyes. It was a challenge, meant to embarrass him in front of these men. Dictys leaned in to say something to his brother, but the ruler waved him off, still smiling at the boy.

Perseus could feel his blood burning and his ears felt hot. "As you wish, oh king!" and he leapt to his feet. Heart pounding, he glanced around the room. Nearly everyone had stopped to watch the strangely bronzed young man. Dictys was nodding, but Perseus could see he was worried for him.

"Those of you from Serifos already know this tale. It is one of woe and hardship, and destiny, but like all the best stories it is a true story!" Perseus cried. He grinned, playing the imp to the hilt, while stalking around the room dramatically. "My mother, the noble Danae, told it to the man who has been like a father to me: Dictys!"

With that, Perseus raised his bowl to the sailors, and the company did likewise – more from the joy of shouting his name than any real salute. Argus, an older hand from the ship cocked his head to the side and examined Perseus carefully. "Danae? Your mother is the daughter of Acricius, the King of Argos?"

"She is, sir," he acknowledged. "Granddaughter of the fearsome Abas, whose prowess in battle I think few here would contest." There was a murmuring from the gathering and some nods.

"I have heard the very sight of Abas' shield could break whole armies," encouraged Argus. Perseus felt buoyed up, He had another supporter in the crowd.

"It is true," agreed Telephemus. "My father used to tell me of the army of Argos!"

The prederast giggled, "Isn't this your story, young Perseus?"

"It is!" he enthused, trying to regain control of the room. "As you know, Abas – like Ares, himself – was a terrifying figure, but at times he could be...less than understanding of human nature..."

"Oh, well put!" said Argus. "Very true!"

"...and in an effort to put his kingdom at ease after his passing he thought to allow his twin sons to both rule, one after the other, over Argolis. You see, his sons – Proetus and Acricius – had, from their time in the womb, been at odds with one another. In their very blood, there was a need to compete with each other in everything, in sports, in war, and in love. Even for the love of their parents! We all here know the special bond between twin siblings, how close they can be, like the Dioscuri, Castor and Pollux, two halves of the same soul."

"Those fine boys! They protect us now that they are placed among the stars by all-mighty Zeus!" Telephemus cried. "Castor and Pollux!" The assembly lifted their cups again and roared the names.

Perseus persisted, "But in Proetus and Acricius, this filial bond was twisted around, and their rivalry could know no bounds. On the death of my great-grandfather, Acricius took his turn as ruler of Argos. Five years he was to reign, before his brother would take up the burden and vice-versa. Already, Acricius had managed to make himself better than his brother with his fortuitous marriage to Eurydice, a daughter of Sparta, (we all know those Spartan women to be the most willful, intelligent, and strongest example of the human woman!), and they had the fortune to have a beautiful daughter, Danae.

"Proetus, not content with waiting for his turn as ruler, and seeking to gain a better claim to the throne, made to seduce Danae and hoped to father a son on her, even though she was barely old enough to know the touch of a man. This selfish man would ply her with soothing words and seemingly innocent caresses until one night he made his way into her bed. Caught in the act by a servant, Proetus was forced to flee my grandfather, who pursued him to the edge of the sea. However, with good fortune, Proteus was able to escape by ship to the land of Lycia and the court of Iobates."

Perseus glanced about the room, gauging the crowd. They were suitably horrified by Proetus' lack of filial piety, but also were waiting for judgment on Danae for her part in the story. "Danae had barely understood what it was her uncle was offering until it was too late, and now she was faced with her father's righteous anger over her indiscretion. Now, I'm sure some of you fine men are fathers yourself, and some of you have daughters. When faced with the tears of your beautiful child, who has been ravaged without understanding her part in the debacle, what would you do, I ask?"

"Lock her away!" and "Sell her!" were some of the quick responses, but Argus replied, "Try to forgive her." This met with a shower of derision until the old man rose to his feet. Suddenly, the elder seemed taller, fuller in statue, and he pointed at some of the other men, "You say that this is a flaw of the woman, yes you! – and in this you are wrong. It is a condition of youth to make mistakes, and stupid ones, at that. The young do not think; they react, they emote. They allow their feelings to guide them in their inexperience away from a path that wisdom would sketch out for them. Even Wisdom herself, Athena, has trodden this terrible road, allowing rage or grief to overwhelm her reason. Do not so sharply judge the foolishness of youth, you who have *all* done something regrettable in your past!"

The symposium was silent for a moment, staring at Argus in a mixture of surprise or admiration. Slowly, the old man sat, the spirit seemingly gone out of him, waving to Perseus to continue.

He picked up the story once more. "Another three years passed, and on the day that he was to take over the throne, Proetus returned to Argos at the head of a Lycian army, with his new wife, Sthenaboea. 'Give to me my kingdom!" he demanded of Acricius, but the king of Argolis would not submit.

"These two brothers, who could never live in peace with each other, drove their armies into each other on the beaches near the harbor of Argos. They fought for a day and a night, again and again, retiring only to bring their exhausted troops together once more. In the end, neither side could force the other to concede. While they gathered their strength, it is said a wise man wandered across the battlefield, and suggested the obvious solution. They would split the kingdom of Argolis between the brothers. Acricius would retain the portion from Araethyrea to Cynuria in the south, with Argos as his capital, and Proetus would rule from Tiryns to Troezen.

"Thus placated, at least for the time being, the brothers settled down to rule their respective kingdoms, but always seeking a means to best one another. For Acricius, the loss of half his kingdom was bad enough, but he listened to the stories of Sthenaboea's fertility – how she bore her husband a fine son and three daughters. Acricius, for his part, only had Danae. While this young woman was a beauty to rival some who will remain unnamed..." Perseus implied, looking skyward with a sly smile, but not impugning any of the goddesses that might be listening.

"Very wise," Argus said appreciatively.

"...she was nevertheless a woman. Acricius desperately desired an heir to secure his lands from the greed of his brother. Each year, he worried about Eurydice's inability to produce a boy. After a few years, Acrisius undertook a pilgrimage to Delphi, to ask the oracle if he would have the son he so desired, from his wife or another woman. The answer he got sealed my mother's fate, as well as mine, my friends!"

Pausing for dramatic effect, Perseus was pleased to find the audience was entranced enough by the tragedy unfolding to start calling for answer: what was the oracle's prophecy? Even better, Polydectes was realizing that the young boy had managed to win the minds of his listeners. Instead of looking the fool, he had captured the imaginations of the sailors and island folk.

"Not only would Acricius die without an heir, it was fated by the gods themselves, that he would die at the hand of his grandson." Gasps from the crowd as they understood the divine mission that Perseus had been tasked with. "Acricius rushed home in a panic that his daughter, who had been seduced once before, might have taken the opportunity to conceive an heir. She was still without husband or lover and Acricius sought to keep it that way. In the courtyard of his palace, much like the one inside these walls," Perseus smiled. He had just equated Polydectes with his own unjust grandfather. "Acricius built a bronze-walled prison and locked his own daughter away from the world.

"In this attempt to thwart the will of Fate failed, my friends, as I am here to attest." Arms thrown wide, Perseus pressed on, "My mother's cell – and while it was a comfortable a cell as it could be made it was still a cell – was guarded by a eunuch and the only key to open the cage was held by her father. There were small windows to provide light and air, and it was through these, one night, that my father came to my mother. Taking the form of golden rain, the Lord of the Skies, fell on my mother, and like a spring rain fertilizes the fields, they made me."

Gasps of astonishment; this young man before him was the son of Zeus!?! Impossible! Only a demi-god could have such a figure! Where's that damned boy with the wine?

"That did not end my mother's suffering, nor the perfidy of my grandfather, no... While convinced that somehow his brother might have been behind the pregnancy, Acricius could find no other explanation that this -- yes, far-fetched one -- Danae had presented him with. Impregnated by a shower of gold? Impossible. Yet there was the proof, growing in her belly at a rate that was impossible, were this a child of Man.

"As the moment of my birth approached, Acricius thought to kill his daughter and her unborn child, but he was visited in his fields by a seer, Melampus. Some of you may have heard of him."

"I have," said Argus. "He is locked away by King Phylacus for stealing his cattle, although it is said that he took the blame for the actual thief, his brother Bias. He has the sight, the ability of prophesy given him by Apollo, they say. But do go on..."

"There he told my grandfather that to take the actions he sought would go against the wishes of the Fates and the Gods, and would bring down the wrath of Zeus himself upon the man. He did not believe this wise man until he turned into an eagle and flew away. He had been speaking to Zeus himself! Terrified by the prospect, he did the next best thing. Hoping to avoid being directly responsible for our deaths, and wishing that nature might take its course, he placed my mother and me into a small ark, just large enough to carry us, and set us out on the ocean!"

The sailors were beside themselves. The sea was a dangerous master, they knew; Poseidon was a fickle and tempestuous soul that could be gentle and giving, and in a flash angry and deadly. The sea was no place to throw a babe and woman. Better to expose the child on a hillside and be done with the girl! one man cried. Perseus quieted them with a wave of his arms. "At this, Zeus asked his brother to make our passage safe and soft, taking us across a flat calm to this very island...where we were discovered by a fisherman..."

He ended the story with a turn to his surrogate father and raised the bowl with a smile to him. "Dictys took us in. He asked nothing of my mother, and raised me to be an honest, good man."

"Dictys!" yelled the symposium in toast. Polydectes' triumph had been snatched from him. Again, this whelp had stopped him from getting what he wanted, just as his very existence had kept Danae from his bed. For despite her earlier troubles with her uncle, Danae was a wiser, thoughtful woman who refused his advances, so long as her son was in the house.

Now, all eyes were on the monarch. Summoning up a grunt and a nod, Polydectes responded, "A fine tale and well told, I think we all agree." The festivities resumed, and Perseus returned to his seat. There was some discussion about Polydectes' choice for a wife, for he was looking to marry.

Argus leaned in close to Perseus, "A fine tale, indeed. Even a true one, as you said, young master. Although I don't believe it was in the guise of Melampus that Zeus came to Acricius."

"No?" Perseus chuckled.

"No. Melampus had not yet been given the sight by that time."

Perseus studied the old man for a moment, "And you would know this how?"

"I know of him."

"Ah... It worked for the story."

"That it did."

The wine bearer came around again and Perseus shook his head at the image of Medusa. "You do not like the *krater*?" asked Argus.

"Hardly scary enough to protect the wine, is it?"

"That is a sad tale, the story of Medusa."

"How so? She defiled the temple of Athena. Dictys has taught me that you should honor the gods, if not out of love, then out of respect for their power and their capricious nature."

"Exactly. The gods do sometimes show cruelty. They have their reasons, of course, but they are, for all their power, remarkably like us. Given to their passions, which, like everything else about them, are more grandiose, harder to control." Argus sighed, " Medusa, like your mother, was foolish and young, and she was vain to the point of stupid. She caught the eye of Poseidon and he persuaded her to sleep with him. She hadn't counted on it being a ploy by the sea god to insult Athena, by taking her in the temple of the goddess. On the offerings dias, if you can believe it?" he chuckled.

"Do you know Medusa as well as Melampus, old

man?"

The smile on the ancient slipped and for a moment there was something about him that he could not place, a strangeness that seemed larger and more powerful than the old man's frame could contain. "Dictys did teach you to respect your elders, yes?"

Perseus was surprised, "Yes. I did not mean offense."

"It is, as we have been discussing, the foolishness of youth?"

"Precisely."

Argus said cooly, "You will need to shed that quickly. The future before you is much more dangerous that you would believe."

"What say you, Perseus?" came a call, disturbing their talk. He looked over to find Polydectes looking at him inquiringly, along with half the symposium. "I said...the most likely candidate seems to be Hippodamia, the daughter of Oenomaus. She is said to be beautiful and intelligent, but her father has a challenge for her suitors. To win her hand, they must best her father in a chariot race. The other men of the village have offered me horses, gifts to weaken the sovereign's will. What will you give for your adoptive country?"

"My lord, I would gladly give you a gift for Oenomaus," said Perseus, "but as you know, I have no inheritance. My mother and I, like orphans, have lived on the good graces of your brother. I have done my best to repay him by working his boat...but I have nothing of value to give."

"It is a shame the son of Zeus has been reduced to the status of simple sailor, isn't it?" The symposium burst into laughter, and Perseus could feel his face flushing in anger.

"Keep your head, boy," whispered Argus. "The moment is nearly here."

Polydectes was holding out his bowl for more wine. "Perhaps you could render me a service..."

"Maybe he could drive the chariot," suggested one villager.

"He does not know how to drive a chariot," Dictys reminded him.

"Oenomaus certainly doesn't need a load of fish,"

Polydectes chided him. He glanced at the serving boy and his eyes narrowed. "You could," he said, setting aside the bowl. He took the krater from the server and turned the snarling face of the Gorgon toward him. "You could bring me a priceless gift. One no one else would provide him. One which would guarantee my marriage to Hippodamia..." Perseus understood the implied promise: *and shift my interest from your mother.* "Bring me the head of Medusa."

This reduced the company to peals of laughter. The very notion was ridiculous. Only Argus, who was watching him intently, was not laughing. Quietly, he said, "The head of Medusa is a dangerous thing, young Perseus. It would bring great credit to he who would end her reign of terror. Taken from her it would be a potent weapon a hero could use to avenge himself on those who have wronged him."

"How would I even know where to look for her?"

Argus smiled, "Silly boy, I will direct you."

"You? But..."

The eyes had changed. Instead of brown they were gray, almost the same color as his eyes. Over the noise he heard Polydectes ask, "What say you, Perseus?"

He stood quickly and faced the symposium. "My lord, I will bring you Medusa's head."

The room was shocked to silence. Polydectes leaned forward on his couch, "You will not be allowed to return without it. This is a vow for a hero, Perseus. If you do this, it is a vow before the gods. You will not set foot on this island until you have the Gorgon's head...or she has yours."

"Truly," said Argus, softly.

"I will do as you ask."

The island's nobles and the sailors burst into animated conversation and some of the men were slapping Perseus' back, impressed with his courage. One wished him a swift crossing over the Styx when he got there, which he assumed would be moments after he found Medusa. Dictys was talking with his brother quietly, intensely.

When he sat, Argus was smiling at him. Perseus said, "I don't even know where to start..."

"I do." The voice had changed. Instead of a gravely

hoarse wheeze, Argus was speaking in a light, musical female voice. Perseus looked to the old man, and found what leaned toward him was a woman – easily his height and tan. She was, like him, a bronze color that few men and women could achieve. Her green-gray eyes were filled with humor and intelligence, and the smirk on her face gave her a playful, pleased look. Her dress was finer than any he'd seen. She was feminine in build, but he could see the play of her muscles under the skin in the lamplight. He started to speak, but she laid a hand on his arm. The skin was cool to the touch and Perseus felt his heart start and his loins stir.

"They see Argus, my would-be hero. But you know me, don't you?"

He gasped, "Athena..."

"This is a great opportunity for you, my mortal brother. With a bit of luck, and a bit of help, you should prevail. There are great things expected of you, and as you said, you have a destiny."

"My grandfather?"

She laughed, "You want to jump to the end of the tale this early? Where would the fun be in that?" She leaned close, "You will need a few days to prepare for your trip. Tomorrow, you will make your sacrifices to the gods. Do diligence to the sea god and your father, so that they may give you calm seas and strong winds to set you on your way. Say your goodbyes to your family. Then board Telephemus' ship – he will be happy to have you for a few days – and he will carry you to Samos. Once there, we will meet again."

"What will I do there?" he asked.

"I will show you the face of your enemy, so that you will know her from her sisters. There you will also have to glean Medusa's whereabouts from the Stygian witches, daughters of Phorcys and sisters of the Gorgon. They are appropriately named: Deino, Enyo, and Pemphredo.[2] They are ancient things, and can be quite cunning."

"How do I get them to tell me where Medusa is?"

Athena smiled, "I won't do all of this for you, little

---

[2] **Dread, Horror, and Alarm**

brother. Now let's pave your way..."

She stood smoothly and moved to the rack where the visitors had deposited their spears and other equipment. Athena took hold of Argus' walking stick and Perseus watched it transform in her hand to a spear. The weapon's tip gleamed gold, but the sheen was not that of bronze. The length of the shaft was translucent, like quartz. Some of the guests were inquiring if the old man was retiring for the night.

"Polydectes!" she called. "I thank you for your hospitality, and for the entertainment." With that, there was a flash of light, and they all saw a white owl flap its way out of the room.

The assembly leapt to the their feet, and some dropped to a knee in shock and supplication. Dictys stood, mouth agape. "A god! A god at our symposium!" shouted Polydectes. He was standing beside his brother, looking from the doorway to Perseus. It would have been quite the boon to Polydectes for people to know he had hosted a god, but as the guests were crowding around Perseus, he felt a wave of anger and jealousy.

"You spoke with it?" Polydectes said.

Perseus corrected him, "Her. Our guest was the third born of immortal Zeus, the wise and brave Athena."

The king looked wary, but said little else. His guests were beside themselves and plied Perseus with questions to which he could only shrug at answering. While the others interrogated him, he was able to ask Telephemus about his course and found he was headed east. Perseus inquired if Telephemus might carry him to Samos on the business of their recently departed guest, and the captain was only too happy to oblige. A passenger favored by the gods could only bring good luck to his vessel, Telephemus opined. From that point on, the symposium degenerated into speculation into the nature and motives of the gods, and whether or not a sacrifice needed to be made for her visit. Perseus was in a daze for a while, before finally staggering, half-drunk, home.

When Perseus woke the next morning, he was headachy and tired. Dragging himself off of his raised mattress, he relieved himself into the jug the servants had left in his quarters and staggered through the house to the courtyard. There, Dictys was gathering his meal and gear for the day's work, and Danae was sat at the reflection pool. Both turned their attention to Perseus as he wandered in.

"Wine," laughed Dictys, "a sweet mistress at night, and a nagging wife the following morning."

Danae reached out with her leg and kicked the older man lightly in the calf. "Dictys tells me it was an eventful night."

"No more so than usual, mother." Perseus ruffled his hair and squinted against the morning light coming from above. Through the opening he could see clouds were gathering. "What, you don't have visits from Olympians regularly?"

"Just the once," she said bluntly.

Wincing, Perseus sat on the edge of the pool. "Sorry..."

"Don't be. Athena is the guardian of great heroes. Still, what were you thinking? Hunting the Gorgon...for Polydectes."

"Your lord," Dictys reminded them, "if only for the time being."

Danae bowed her head slightly. "I spoke out of turn, my lord."

"Don't do that," Dictys said. "You do not have to show submission to me. This is your house as much it is mine. This is your country now, but that also means Polydectes is your ruler, and while I love my brother, he can be a vindictive fool. He's been denied wooing you thanks to Perseus, and he delighted in an opportunity to goad the boy into this foolish quest."

"Right here," Perseus reminded them.

"But the Gorgon? What was he thinking?" she asked Dictys.

"Still right here," Perseus repeated.

"He was thinking to prove himself in a company of men. And he was quite drunk."

Perseus glared at the captain, who suppressed a laugh. "Even in that state, he wove one of the best tales I've heard in a symposium in some time. And his boast about Medusa! That brought the approval of a goddess."

Danae insisted, worriedly, "It's still dangerous."

"I know it's dangerous, mother. Give me my portion, would you, Dictys? I think I'm going for a walk this morning to clear my head and plan my trip."

Dictys shrugged, "I was going to talk about that with you while we waited on the day's catch."

"Tonight. Yes?" Perseus said. "I have to make the appropriate sacrifices before I set off."

"Set off?" Danae asked, "When are you planning to set off?"

"Telephemus ships tomorrow," Perseus told her.

"Tomorrow!?!" she cried.

Perseus nodded. "The first part of this journey is already laid out for me, mother. I don't have a choice in this."

"He's right," Dictys interceded. "Athena, herself, has set him on his way."

Danae looked unhappy, but said nothing. Perseus gathered a small pouch of dried fish and fruit, and threw a water skin over his shoulder. Naked save for his sandals and the skin, he left the house and walked up into the hills east of the town. The daytime heat was starting to build, but the clouds that had been puffy and bright white were now being overrun by a stretch of gray, higher clouds. The incline was steep enough to be challenging on the loose soil, and at one point he stopped to look out of his home. He could see the fishing boats out to sea and wondered which was Dictys'. He passed a shepherd and his flock at one point and waved, but continued up through the scrub grass and juniper to the top of hill. The effort was enough to have him sweating, but not winded. On the crest of the hill, he stopped under an olive tree to scan the sky. To the west, he thought he could see rain streaming under the clouds. In a few hours, they would feel it here on the island. To the north, he could see Kithnos, to the east on the horizon was Pelagos. Over the horizon, four hundred stadia distant, was Argos, the land of his birth.

A few minutes' walk brought him to an old temple, one dedicated to Zeus. While most of the people of Serifos were adherents to Poseidon, being a seafaring people, this temple still brought the thousand or so residents of the island at least annually to leave votive offerings to the lord of the gods. It was a smallish building, square and simple. There were none of the columns and friezes that he heard adorned the grand temples in Athens. *Pinax*, stones with carvings of the gods, were placed on either side of the entrance. These showed Zeus seated on his throne on the one tablet, the other showed him in mid-throw, lightning poised to fall to earth and smite some unseen foe.

Perseus steeled himself and entered the place. It was dark inside, and the high roof was blackened from years of burnt offerings. A crude statue of Zeus, recognizable as such for his thunderbolt in his right hand and the enormous beard, stared in wide-eyed, almost crazed, expression. The god had been painted in the past, and the colors had faded over time, save for the cold blue-gray eyes. Eyes the same color as Perseus' own. The room for the priest was separated from the main chamber by a length of cloth.

An oil lamp burned near the dias where the offerings were left. He set out a portion of the food he had brought, poured olive oil over it and used a small bit of straw to catch flame from the lamp and light the offering. "Father..." he nearly choked on the word, "help me to bring honor to my family by succeeding in the tasks set before me. To Athena, your favored child, give me the wisdom and cunning to see this through. Take this meager meal from a humble boy and may it please you."

He wasn't sure what he was expecting. Maybe for the statue to talk to him, or for his father to show himself and give him some kind of support, or to feel filled with some kind of inspiration...no matter what it was, there was nothing. The statue continued to glare past him toward the entrance. The flames turned his votive into a greasy sludge in the bronze bowl on the dias. Perseus waited for a few minutes, then nodded to himself and rose. Outside, the heat was oppressive, but there was now a pleasant sea breeze blowing in from the northwest. The rain was closer now.

He made his way back into town, taking the path to

the temple of Poseidon, positioned near one of the wells for the city. It was noon by the time he arrived, and out to sea the fishing fleet looked to be turning toward home. A few of the boats had already deployed their sails and were moving toward the shore. The rain was only an hour or two behind them, at most, and the breeze had grown to a gusting wind. The air was still warm, but the moving air was quickly bringing relief from the heat of the last few days.

Poseidon's temple was newer, with simple Doric columns without fluting. The building was perhaps three to four men high, and the interior was large enough to accommodate a sizeable portion of the town. Inside there were two rooms, the main chamber had a statue of the sea god, bearded, glowering, and resting his weight on his trident. His skin was painted a faint greenish tinge, and the hair and beard were black. Blue eyes looked through the window toward the sea. There was a wide table below him, with bowls of offerings. There were two windows on either side to augment the light from the braziers burning near the god. A smaller room behind this chamber was the apartment for the priest. He was on hand, along with a few of the women of the town who were finishing their entreaties to Poseidon. They were dressed in simple chiton, with a length of cloth over their heads to preserve their dignity and propriety.

At the sight of Perseus, the women quickly cleared a spot for him at the offering table, and the priest smiled warily. Word of his visitor had already spread through the town. Perseus laid out the rest of his repast on the table and the priest quickly intoned the prayers to Poseidon. Perseus threw in his request for a safe and swift passage to Samos.

On his way home, he passed through the city. The people were packing up their wares in the marketplace ahead of the impending deluge. Servants were bustling about in pursuit of their respective errands, and as he passed the palace of Polydectes, he could see a few of the guests from the other night, including Argus. The old seer had apparently slept through the night of the symposium aboard the vessel, unaware that he was been impersonated by a goddess. He stopped to chat with them, and learned that Telephemus was down at the shore, preparing his boat for its trip.

Perseus walked down to the sea's edge, and found Telephemus' vessel grounded and anchored. The captain and his crew were quickly covering their cargo, and stepping down their mast in advance of the rain. Some of the fishing fleet were pulling their craft onto the shore and he could make out *Okeia* on her way in. The rain was visible a few stadia behind, dark streamers falling from the clouds to the water below. The sea was beginning to froth and throw itself on to the beach. Perseus could already tell by the break of the water that this was a mild rainstorm, nothing to worry about.

He arranged with the captain to be on hand the following morning at dawn to aid in resetting the mast prior to sailing. If all went well, they would raise Samos within a few days, a week at most. Perseus thanked him and walked along the beach to where *Okeia* was approaching. He could see his shipmates furling the sail, while a few men were bent to the oars to bring the ship in the last few hundred yards. Dictys and four others were stationed on the bow, waiting to jump off and help haul her onto the beach.

Dictys and Perseus exchanged waves and the young man waded into the water to catch the first line tossed out by the crew. A few moments later, he was aiding the crew, who were tumbling from the ship to haul on the mooring lines, and together they pulled *Okeia* ashore and staked her down. As they were finishing, the first drops were beginning to hit. They divvied up a portion of the catch between the men, then Perseus and Dictys made their deals with the merchants over the gunwale. Once the catch was away and the drachmas counted, Dictys and Perseus made their way home under a cloudy sky, soaked from the rain.

2. FAMILY MATTERS

The gateway to the home of the gods was situated on the top of Mount Olympus. This home was no terrestrial construct; it was one of the mind. To its inhabitants, it was as actual, as real, as the earth of the mountain named for it, but Olympus was an idea -- one that paralleled the physical world. It was laid out with the forum of the gods, a massive, round, temple-like building with a large dome capping the edifice, central to the city. Wide boulevards paved with fine white stones stretched radially from the forum grounds, like the spokes of a wheel, with a series of small roads circling a regular intervals according to simple mathematical principals. Viewed from above, it was a model of orderly construction.

Juniper and cypress lined the roads in orderly procession, trimmed to an ideal. The apartments of the gods and their attendants -- be they god, nymph, satyr, or mortal – stretched from the forum and were designed and built with Platonic perfection of shape. Although she lived here and was jaded with the place, Athena thought it beautiful. Despite this, she had found little in Olympus to please her of late. Fine music echoing through the city was pleasing to the ear, but lacked a certain energy and passion. The residents were busy at tasks, but there was none of the bustle and energy of a human city. Save when Dionysus was here, the city was a model of order. It had been since the last invasion by the enemies of the Olympians, the giants.

Athena's home was a grand one, with a view of the forum of the gods. It was an idealized replica of the Parthenon, her grand temple in Athens. Instead of limestone, the house was constructed of marble. Tall, with the more fanciful Ionic columns rising from a triple-stepped stylobate, her home was gleaming white with red and gold accents in the scrolls capping the slim columns. Steps rose through the stylobate at the front to the portico and the large red-painted doors that fronted the home. A massive space was the first room one encountered, and it was here that she could entertain. She rarely did. Rather, she would work her crafts, weaving or inventing her musical instruments, devising newer, more effective weapons of war, and these devices and her tools littered the place. Behind that were her apartments, a bedroom for her and a washroom; and those of her retinue, comprised of the goddess Nike, and her adopted son, Erichthonius. Now grown, Erichthonius rarely visited Olympus, and his rule in Athens had seen her cult grow. He and his son had overseen the construction of the Parthenon and every four years the Panathenic Festival and games were dedicated to her. It was her displacement of Poseidon as patroness of the city that had started the feud between her and the sea god. The rule of her adopted son had cemented her in the heart of the Athenians, and sealed the rivalry with Poseidon.

The goddess was currently in residence. She lounged at the large table that was covered with drawing and sketches of various fanciful implements of destruction, designs for improvements to the flute and trumpet, mathematical explorations. Her armor and weapons were hung on a nearby rack, gleaming in light coming from the large windows in the ceiling. Nearby, Nike was amusing herself by working Athena's loom. The dark-haired goddess was her near-constant companion. Her form was similar to Athena's tall, slim, yet powerful-looking. Her face was more beautiful than Athena's more matronly, handsome visage. Nike's wings rustled slightly as she worked.

"You've been quiet since your return," Nike observed. Her intense blue eyes regarded her mistress with interest. Nike was the only one of the minor goddesses that Athena would reveal her mind to.

"Yes."

"All is well with Perseus?"

"At present. He will be in Samos in a few days, and I will nudge him onto the proper course," the goddess said.

Nike observed, "You seem...unhappy."

"I am not," Athena lied. She was not fooling Nike, and both of them knew it.

Athena was bored. Something she could look forward to: ennui for eternity. In some ways, she thought residents of the underworld, where her uncle Hades ruled from his onyx palace, had more to look forward to than a god. She could feel the adoration of the people on the earth waning and could see a time in the future when they no longer believed or respected her kind. Their power would be sorely diminished and they would spend the rest of time, alive and irrelevant. She had brought up her concerns to Zeus and the others, but no one would give her a real hearing. Save Dionysus, who simply smiled and told her that entropy in a system was inevitable. He also darkly said, "...and most of us deserve to be rendered powerless and forgotten."

She agreed. Instead of staying involved in the lives of Man, the gods had increasingly retreated into internecine squabbling; now, all of their interactions with people were exploitative. Even the matter of Perseus...if she played this right, he would be a great hero, and several lines of destiny could be brought to fruition, and she would settle a score or two, while most likely creating a few more. He was her plaything, and while she loved him (as a man would a favorite dog, she supposed), he was simply a means to keep her life interesting enough to be lived. The goddess of wisdom did not indulge in self-delusion: she was as bad as the others.

"I am, perhaps, distracted," she smiled. Nike nodded in agreement, not fooled. "I think I will go for a walk."

"Do you need me?"

"No, dear. Continue," Athena indicated the weaving, "you've found nuances in the design I missed."

Athena did not bother to take her weapons or armor, instead drifting out in her chiton and himation thrown around her shoulders. She was in a strange mood, and her red himation, chased in gold, mirrored her sanguine mood and auburn hair. As she walked through the gardens around the forum, she was observed by nymphs and favored mortals. Few would risk to approach her. Despite her beneficial attitude toward the human race, she was a prickly creature – often cool and aloof to her fellow Olympians and other beings, sometimes openly aggressive and vindictive, but rarely openly emotional. She was a frightening thing, and knew it. She cultivated it, and used it as a shield to protect herself from the outside world. Even her chastity was an attempt to maintain control over her body and mind, and the passions lurking underneath her staid facade. Her sense of humor was playful and well-developed, and mirth was one of the few things she allowed herself to feel. With her need to control her surrounds, she was sensitive to insult and slights, and the anger could flare strongly enough to escape her grasp. When it did she made mistakes of judgment.

As with Medusa. She and Poseidon had been in competition for centuries, ever since her cult swept out of Libya and seduced the island worshipers of Poseidon. Her follows were stealing the love and honor from the sea god and it made her more powerful than she already was. He was, understandably, upset with this turn of events. Athena did not care about this. She did not care about the proud mortal girl who thought she could seduce a god without consequences. Athena cared that she had lost her temper and overreacted. Denied her vengeance on Poseidon, she had cursed the girl for all time, and in so doing, had created a monster that was killing innocents and spreading terror through the land near her lair. Now she was using another mortal to try to undo some of the damage, while keeping herself from accepting her liability for the reign of terror the Gorgon was creating.

The interior of the forum was cool and sound carried well throughout the building. The central hall was circular, with a reflecting pool in the center to allow them to see the goings on below on earth. The dome above had windows that caught and enhanced light, and the interior of the Hall of the gods was always brightly lit and airy. Twelve thrones ruled the room, spaced even around the room, save for those of Zeus and Hera, positioned side by side at the far end of the space. Athena's sat to the right of Zeus, closer to him than Poseidon, his own (elder) brother. Of the Olympians, only one did not possess a place here: Hades. He was represented most of the year by Persephone, and she would be with her mother, right now. Each throne had the symbols of their purview woven into them. Zeus' was dominated by lightning and eagles, Hera's by peacocks and lions, with small planters on either side that held poppies. Athena's was emblazoned with a large owl head on the seat back. Weapons of war were worked into the base and the sides, including a small lightning bolt. Besides her father, only Athena could command the force as a weapon.

Hera was not going to like her favoring Perseus. She was the patroness of the Argives, the people of Argos and Tiryns. She might acquiesce because the fate of Acricius was already ordained by the Fates, but she would see Athena's aid to Perseus as meddling. From another Olympian, Hera might be more receptive, but Athena was an affront to the Queen of the Gods, due to her birth. Zeus had philandered with Metis, and their child was fated to be greater than all the Olympians. To protect his reign, Zeus had eaten Metis, but his attempt had only partially succeeded...Athena was born out of Zeus head, taking with her (she mused) much of the wisdom and intellect that the Lord of the Gods had. Later, Zeus had opined that he had created the most perfect of gods -- a synthesis of male and female strengths.

Hera, angered by his hubris, sought to create her own child without her husband's seed. She created her own child and did it badly. Ugly and lame, Hephaestus survived his mother's attempt to be rid of him by tossing him from Olympus. Athena glanced to his throne, adorned with images of fire and machines. It must rankle the Queen of the Gods that her son and Athena were close allies.

Hera, while undeniably beautiful, was foolish, somewhat stupid, and petty even by the standards of the rest of her race. It was no wonder that Athena's father wandered the world, looking for mortal women to couple with. Their fruit was bad, as well. Ares, the fool god of war, whose main force was the charisma with which he lured men into slaughtering each other. Worse was his sister Eris, strife incarnate. All the other deities here were the spawn of the Titans, or Zeus and Titans.

"That's a very serious face, sister," said Apollo. She had sensed his arrival at her back. She turned and nodded slightly. "What wears on you?" he asked.

Apollo's preferred form was one to shake the restraint of any goddess or woman. He was tall for a man, but realistically sized – not like Ares' massive, overly compensatory frame. As always, he had his bow and quiver with him, with arrows that could strike a mortal cold dead, or infect them with disease. Dark curly hair and bright blue eyes, bronzed body, and sympathetic smile, Apollo was attractive even to her. His capricious nature had cooled somewhat recently, but he could be intolerably cruel at times, then by turns amazingly compassionate. Next to Dionysus, he was the most unpredictable of her siblings, and the most curious for that reason.

"Nothing important," she shrugged. "I am..."

"Bored?" She was, she realized. Deeply so. "You've been away a while. It's unlike you to not monitor the goings on between us."

"I had heard you had returned," she told him. "I was most distressed when you were sent to Troy." Apollo looked unconvinced. She added, "I asked to share your burden."

He observed, "Funny, then, that you did not."

"You've been speaking to Poseidon..."

"Imagine his surprise to find that many of his worshipers had replaced him in their hearts with...you," Apollo said. "You wasted little time enriching yourself while we labored on the walls of Troy."

"He returned some years ago. Where were you?"

Apollo shrugged, "Walking. Observing. Thinking. Our master, the king, was a wise creature for a man...Laomedon. He reminded me of you, in many ways."

"We could learn from them," Athena agreed.

"Father would dispute that, but then again, that was part of our problems, wasn't it?" he said, coolly. Athena looked away for a moment, ashamed.

"I should have been punished like the rest," she admitted.

Apollo snorted, petulantly, "Daddy wouldn't do that to his favored child. He had to know your part in the rebellion, but couldn't bear to punish his darling third born."

Athena could feel herself color up and she quickly tamped down on the anger she felt.

Since conquering his own father and taking control of heaven, Zeus had ruled with an iron hand. Most of the time, he ruled wisely. However, with his rule firmly established, he began to extend his control over Olympus and the world. There was some opinion by Hades and Poseidon that their lottery to establish their kingdoms had been rigged in favor of Zeus. His courtship of Hera was considered in bad taste by his siblings. His creation of Athena by swallowing her mother, Metis, raised hackles. For her, the last straw was the punishment of Prometheus, one of the few Titans that Zeus had not imprisoned in the bowels of Tartarus. Wise, kind, and the creator of mankind, Prometheus was increasingly worried about Zeus and the other Olympians, especially their predatory actions toward his favored creation. To help his beloved people, Prometheus revealed "fire" -- really all manner of knowledge -- to wise men across the Earth.

The Titans had been powerful, yes, but they had something this younger generation of gods did not seem to have: compassion. Prometheus found this quality particularly lacking in Zeus, something that Hera and Poseidon gladly agreed with. Athena had not been so certain, but her father's selfishness won her over to the Titan's way of thinking. When Prometheus stole fire for Man, against the wishes of Zeus, he was chained up and subjected to unending torture, his liver being eaten by birds every day, with the organ regrowing each night. Athena had conspired with Poseidon, in one of their few alliances, and with Hera to punish Zeus for his ways. They had carefully enlisted the aid of most of the Olympians. For Athena, it had been easy to convince Dionysus, who owed his life to her for rescuing his heart from the Titans that, on orders from Hera, had torn him apart in an attempt kill him. Dionysus, no matter how removed from his senses he might be – and he never really had been right again – would respond to her. With him aboard, she was dispatched to gain the aid of Hephaestus, who willing agreed. His love for her was an easy lever to use.

The Olympians trapped Zeus napping after a gigantic feast. Chained with hundreds of Hephaestus' best restraints, the Lord of the Gods railed and threatened and raved. The conspiracy, as they are wont to do, began to fall apart almost immediately. Hera's main desire was to punish Zeus for his philandering. She had never wanted to be his wife, but he had shamed her into marriage after raping her. Poseidon simply wanted a shot at ruling the Olympians himself, but Hades – hoping to escape his rule of the Underworld – argued the point. As the oldest brother, Hades had claim, and some of the gods began to pick sides over which of the two should rule. Athena sought to reason with her father, to make him see the wrongness in his rule, and pleaded with him to change his ways.

In the end, they were undone by a rival conspiracy. Hestia and the nymph Thetis had convinced the Hecatonchires, siblings to the Giants and the Titans and creatures of such strangeness that their own father cast them down out of disgust into Tartarus, to aid them in rescuing Zeus. These enormous things, possesses of a hundred hands and fifty heads -- terrifying even to the Olympians – readily agreed. Zeus had set them free to aid him in his overthrow of Cronus, and they felt compelled to assist. They surprised the gods, and while Gyges and Aigaion held off the Olympians, Briareus quickly undid the myriad chains.

Released, Zeus made the ringleaders paid the price for their rebellion. At least, two did. Hera was chained by the wrists and weighted at the ankles for her leading the revolt. Poseidon was sent (along with Apollo, who had openly mocked Zeus and taken his thunderbolt out of reach) to do service with King Leomedon, building Troy. The rest of the conspiracy were pardoned, including Athena. Terrified as she had been of what he might do to her, she asked that he pardon the others and allow herself to take the brunt of the punishment. Zeus refused. She should join Apollo and Poseidon in their labor, Athena argued. Zeus refused. She would be penalized in a more subtle way, Zeus had told her, by knowing that she should have suffered from her infidelity, but did not.

It proved a well-thought out punishment. Hera and Poseidon never forgave her escape from suffering for her actions. The other Olympians assumed she had been let go due to her position as Zeus' favorite child. Guilt and loneliness were her punishments. It had worked.

"I fear we've turned too much on ourselves," she

said. Apollo nodded. He moved to his throne and sat lightly. "We cannot be sick in body...but in spirit..? We fight among ourselves, instead of doing our duty to those other creatures whose lives we affect. We are petty, callous. Prometheus was right about us."

"Dangerous talk, that," Apollo reminded her. "But, you're right. We have need for some kind of drama to entertain and engage ourselves. Since the Titans were locked away, we have been stagnant. Perhaps it's something in our nature?"

Athena considered this and sank into the chair beside Apollo's, that of his twin sister Artemis. "Perhaps. We hold an exulted position, powerful and privileged. Yet all we seek to do is pursue petty self-interests. I've noticed the same quality in the rulers down on the earth. Small potentates that seek only their own venal pursuits. Maybe it is a quality of power itself, that once had, the use and maintenance of the same become the sole purpose of those who have it."

Apollo looked shaken. Here in this hall, Zeus could see and hear all. Athena knew this as well as he did. "Dangerous talk, sister, especially for one so wise."

"He knows my mind on the matter," she said firmly. Out of the corner of her eye, the air seemed to shimmer. Apollo's expression grew wary. Athena slipped out of Artemis' throne to stand as Zeus joined them.

"Indeed I do," Zeus intoned. Dressed in glowing white, his beard and hair curly black, Zeus was a sight to see. He regarded the two with cool gray eyes, the same color as Athena's. "Apollo, I would speak with my daughter."

The god tossed her a sympathetic look and removed himself in a flash. Athena crossed her arms and waited for Zeus to berate her. Instead, he moved to his throne and sat heavily. He gestured to her own seat. She sat, leaned on the left arm, her look defiant. Zeus held up a hand to calm her. "What is it?" he asked.

"I don't know what you mean, father."

He sighed, "You have been different these past years. Sad, distracted...annoying. You've been spending much time wandering the earth. I would know why the dearest of my children is unhappy."

"You were listening to my conversation. So you know."

He shook his head. "That is not why. However, your concerns are well-founded. We have been less than what we were. You were even right about me, to an extent." He gave her a threatening look, "Although, you will not repeat that."

"I wouldn't dream of it," she responded. After a pause, "I created a monster in a fit of...pique."

"Medusa," he said.

"She is a burden to Man. She kills with no remorse; indeed it may be one of the only ways that she can alleviate some of her suffering." Athena laid a hand on her breast. "I caused that."

"She was living with your priestesses and was studying to be one herself," Zeus said. "As the daughter of a sea god, Poseidon was jealous of her following your cult. He seduced her to get to you. And he succeeded marvelously! It is something other gods would have loved to have seen...or caused."

Athena was more direct, "She was a pawn in our feud."

Zeus nodded, "However, she still defiled your temple. It was your right."

"Yes, but it was unnecessary and unjust. The real insult was from Poseidon."

He grumbled, "I thought we'd settled that."

"No. You settled it. For you. For him. I was denied my justice."

"Medusa was dear to him. You destroyed her face and her mind," explained Zeus. "He was punished by proxy."

"That only works if you care about the proxy," Athena snapped, "I think none of us truly care about those creatures on the ground and in the sea we so callously toy with."

"You do, or you would not be so upset," Zeus smiled.

"No!" she leaned forward. "I *should* care. I *want* to care... and I do not."

"I don't believe that," Zeus told her. He stood and

approached her throne, laid a hand on her shoulder. "Why did you decide to aid Perseus? Not because he is your brother, I think."

"No."

Her father took her chin in hand and raised her face. He was shocked by the mournful look she had. "Because, through him, you can right a wrong that you caused in a moment of righteous, I would say, anger."

"I can't undo the curse," she explained.

"So, you will end it the only way you can."

"Not directly, though," she stated flatly.

"That would imply you were wrong," he smiled. The King of the Gods looked on his daughter kindly, an expression rarely seen by those he was not attempting to seduce. "Shepherd your brother through his labors. Help him be who he is supposed to be. Then put this behind you, Athena. After that, do better. If you do this, I will promise to try...to attend to some of my character defects you once pointed out to me."

*****

The volcano rose out of the eastern side of Sicily, dominating the countryside and smoking ominously. The mountain was deadly dangerous, but it was also the source of the rich soil that allowed for the productive fields and towns that spread around its base. Aetna was named for the nymph that inhabited the forests on the foothills. Aetna was also remarkable for what lay under the surface, woven through the empty lava tubes...the Forge of Hephaestus. This was Athena's destination.

She manifested just inside the forge, carrying with her a wrapped object Hermes had collected from Argos for her. After her talk with Zeus, Athena had enlisted Hermes' aid in preparing Perseus for his labor. The messenger god was only too happy to help; the theft would stir up the court of Acrisius, and he intended to be on hand for the fireworks when the monarch discovered the object missing.

She did not have to wait long for one of the

attendants to arrive. Moving with unnatural grace, more godlike than woman, the attendant was gleaming with reflected light from the hanging lanterns that lit the antechamber, itself crafted from the obsidian rock of a lava tube. The lights used no fire and never extinguished. Hephaestus had only told Zeus how he did it, but Athena had a few ideas as to the *techne* behind the creation.

The attendant was golden in color, her skin some unknown metallic composition that moved like skin and hid her complex mechanical nature. Her hair was spun gold strands, her eyes glowed faintly with inner fire. She was staggeringly beautiful, obviously crafted on the smith god's spouse, the cuckolding Aphrodite. It spoke with the voice of a flute (an invention of Athena's) -- high and musical, almost chime-like. "Welcome, my lady. Our master awaits you in the main workroom."

The attendant led her through the forge, past other attendants. All were unique, but all managed to look like Aphrodite. They were working diligently with other mechanical people, the false men were made of silvery metal that replicated skin. There were creatures working here, as well -- satyrs, men, other things -- but the mechanical men were the mainstay of the forge. Athena found it interesting that, despite her having embarrassed him and having broken his heart, Hephaestus chose Aphrodite as the model for the attendants and not his consort, Aetna.

The forge was a warren of workshops, unidentifiable machines, and storage rooms. All were busy with activity. The forge never slept, even when the god did. The air here was blisteringly hot. No mortals worked this area, only the mechanical women, who seemed unaffected by the stifling atmosphere. In the main workshop, she found him.

Hephaesuts was a massive man, build much like their father, Zeus. He towered over the attendants, his body powerfully built except for the ruined legs -- the product of Hera having thrown the infant god from Olympus in a fit of pique over Zeus' various indiscretions, but capped off by Athena's birth. He might have been handsome, but the heat of the forge had turned him a strange reddish-black color, and his hair and beard grew long and unruly. Muscular to the point of near grotesqueness, Hephaestus was a humbling, harrowing sight. The ruined legs were supported by braces that bore all of his weight. As a result, his legs muscles were withered over warped bones.

As she entered, the attendant motioned for her to wait. Fires fueled by the magma below lit the forge in bright, reddish light. The scene she was witnessing was terrifying even to a god. Attendants were working at removing the braces from the god's legs, following his instructions while he hung from a cradle that suspended him above the floor. "That will do," he told them. "Now the saws…"

"What are you doing?" Athena asked loudly.

Hephaestus saw her and after a moment's embarrassed look, he beamed. "Experimenting! I think I've got it, Athena!"

She walked toward him, shooing one of the attendants seeking to stop her out of the way. "I'm afraid to even ask."

"Actually, I could use your help," he told her, "I could use your steady hand and strength…" To the attendants, he quickly explained, "Not that I don't trust you, darlings! Such fine creations -- better than women!"

"Thank you," Athena said huffily.

Hephaestus quickly backtracked, "Present company, of course, excluded."

"What are you doing?"

"Fixing myself," he grinned excitedly.

"Fixing..?"

Hephaestus motioned to one of the golden women, "Show her. Be amazed, sister!" The attendant handed her a leg. Diamond-like bone was surrounded by a complex web of gray material, connected with metal tendons and ligaments. "I left the skin off so I could see the inner workings. It's better that way, don't you think?"

"Fascinating," she confirmed.

Hephaestus beamed, "They'll look mean, intimidating." Softer, to himself, "I can't wait to see Ares' face…"

"You're putting these on yourself?"

"Absolutely. These old legs are near useless, anyway, so why not improve on the design. The bones are a diamondoid lattice -- as strong as Olympian bones, if not more so -- and the muscle accurately mimics the workings of the real flesh. It will even respond to my thoughts like the real thing."

Athena was astounded and repulsed at the same time. This was her usual reaction to Hephaestus. She was about to ask him if it was a wise thing, but his moods were quickly changeable, and the excitement and joy of invention that she saw in him was rare. If she hoped for him to do the work she was going to ask for, she would have to handle him delicately.

"How long will it take for these...legs...to start working properly?"

"It should be instantaneously."

"Should be?"

Hephaestus caught her tone and gave her a look, "I've tested them."

"On an amputee?" she inquired.

"Yes," Hephaestus looked impatient. Then he saw the parcel leaning against her leg. "What is that?"

Athena patted it, and said absently, as if it was a passing thought, "I was hoping you could modify it a bit. I need it rather quickly, but if you're intent on having your legs hewn off..."

"What is it?" Hephaestus shifted in the harness he was hanging from to have a better look. She unwrapped the bronze shield, the face covered in a spiral of pictograms detailing the life of a warrior.

"The Shield of Abas," she told him. "I need it readied for a special trial. One of our mortal relatives is going after the Medusa."

"Ah..." he muttered knowingly, "Your personal monster. Another hero to the slaughter?"

"Not if we make certain he can succeed," she said reproachfully. The cocky smile evaporated from the smith god's face. "It can wait."

Hephaestus stroked at his unkempt beard and gave her a longing, thoughtful look. With a sigh, he told his attendants to replace the braces on his legs. "Time enough to get this done, I suppose. So what did you have in mind?" he asked.

3. THE JOURNEY BEGINS

The servants were busy with dinner, and Danae was in her rooms with a few of the other local women when Dictys and Perseus arrived. They were soaked by the rain, and they stumbled out of the weather. They could see the courtyard of the house was beginning to see standing water from the rain. The men retreated to the common room, where one of the house slaves provided them with cloth to dry off, and wine and bread to fortify themselves.

"I saw you speaking with Telephemus. Everything is in order?" asked Dictys.

Perseus replied, "It is. I leave tomorrow morning at dawn."

"You have no weapons, no armor...do you even have a plan?"

"Athena does," Perseus said. "I was going to ask to borrow your old sword."

"It's yours," Dictys told him, immediately.

"I am to go to Samos, there to see the face of the enemy. Athena is to show me how to tell Medusa from her sisters. There's also the matter of finding her, but I have a line of inquiry already."

Dictys nodded. "I will admit that I have some trouble accepting this."

"We both knew this day would come, and I would have to leave. If only to make good on the prophecy Acricius set in motion." Perseus shrugged, "I'm just on my way early."

They were silent for a while, simply relaxing on the room's couches and letting the wine take its effect. Danae entered the room tentatively. Perseus sat up and acknowledged her, "Mother..."

She crossed to sit with him. "So you are going to do this?"

"Of course. I made an oath. As much to myself as to Polydectes."

She snorted, "Polydectes just wants you away from the island. He thinks that if you are not around I would be more likely to submit to him," She caught Dictys look of concern. "and he'd be wrong. I do not wish to be any man's property. I've been used enough, I think..."

"It is a concern for all of us," said Dictys.

"I'm more worried about you," she told Perseus. "You are a piece in an enormous game, my son. Forces well beyond our mortal strengths are at play, and you can never fully know what their intent is."

Perseus shrugged, "It is their wish. You and Dictys always told me to honor the gods. Once I find her, and when I am done with her, I will return and set some other things to right." Danae was surprised by the firm, calm manner of her son. He had always been a playful, lighthearted child and not a little bit impulsive. Even now, she could see him bubbling with excitement for his quest, but there was a thoughtful, cautious look in his eye. Of late there was a much more thoughtful and adult version of her son beginning to show, despite his youth. Both she and Dictys had noted that the man Perseus would be was starting to form before their eyes. She was both scared and proud. As if reading her thoughts, Perseus said, "Don't worry, mother, I intend to be careful. This," he tapped his temple, "always wins over this," he finished, slapping his bicep.

The servants had dinner prepared and in the lingering daylight, Persues and Danae, and the captain ate their meal of fish and rice in a tomato sauce. He could see that Danae was desperately trying to hide her concerns, but Perseus' enthusiasm was evident, and growing more powerful over the course of the evening. Dictys was just as concerned for the boy's safety – he was, in nearly every way, his son, too – but there was a strength and confidence in Perseus that made the captain believe that great things were on the horizon. There was a good head on his shoulders, and if his parentage was what Danae said it was...Dictys could be looking at a legend in the making.

After dinner, the three set up an offering to the gods for Perseus' safe and successful journey. A shank of lamb, some rice, fruit, and a few other tidbits were burned on the offering plate below the house gods, fairly crude figurines that were identifiable by their symbols of power, and they all made their prayers. Dictys called on Athena to watch over the boy and provide him with guidance and wisdom, after a short synopsis of her great deeds. (The gods, he thought, were nothing if not a vain lot.) Danae entreated her once-lover, Zeus, to protect his boy and speed him home safely. Perseus' was succinct: let him do their bidding successfully, and bring honor to his house.

Danae quietly retired to her apartments. Perseus wandered outside and stood near the house, looking up into the cloudy sky. The rain had finally broken, and the clouds were breaking in the west. The sun had just set, but the underbelly of the cloud mass was lit from below in a strange gold-green color. The air smelled damp and fresh, the heat of the day had been beaten back somewhat, and the would-be hero could feel his impatience to be away and into his adventure threatening to take over. Dictys joined him and followed his gaze. "A fine evening."

"As you say," Perseus agreed.

"Be cautious," the captain advised.

"I intend to. Don't worry, Dictys; you've taught me well."

The older man smiled, "I have at that. I'll still worry for you."

"How long before Polydectes needs to produce his gifts?" asked Perseus.

Dictys shrugged, "I am to head a delegation to Oenomeus to sound him out regarding my brother's suit."

"I would have thought that was already settled if he was planning to send gifts."

"Not necessarily," Dictys repsonded, "It's a short haul by sail, and if the king agrees to allow him to pursue Hippodamia, we'll need to be ready to provide the bride price with little notice."

Perseus glanced at Dcitys, "You don't sound fully convinced of that."

"I'm not. All is not as it seems, young Perseus."

"I've been hearing that a lot today," said the boy.

"I'm away to symposium, son," said the captain, clapping him on the shoulder. That he was not inviting

Perseus told the youth all he needed to know about the nature of this 'symposium.' "I will be home in the morning to see you off."

Perseus watched him walk toward the other buildings of the town, feet crunching on wet gravel. He turned his attention to the darkening clouds. There were breaks in them to the west and the north, and stars were peeping out at him. Taking in a breath, he told the sky, "I'm ready, father."

He had trouble sleeping that night. His heart was going quickly, he felt alert and anxious – but in a good way. Until now, his life had been so mundane, with only the incredible story of his birth to provide some kind of mystery, some sense of importance to it. Now the promise of the fantastic was in front of him. His feelings were indescribable: he was frightened and elated, confident but with the knowledge that mortals bound up in the machinations of the gods rarely came away unscathed. His thoughts oscillated between visions of glory and a name immortal, and the terror of failure and ignoble death.

When Eos stretched her rosy fingers over the sky from the east, presaging Helios' rise into the sky, he was out of bed, gathering a few things for his trip. Unusually, he dressed in a simple wrap of cloth around his waist and sandals. He gathered a leather belt he rarely used to hang the old sword on, and fashioned a carry bag from a stretch of canvas and rope. He went out and hunted up a few things to eat – some figs and dates, dried fish, and some bread – and dropped those into the sack. He collected the old bronze sword from Dictys stores and a small collection of drachmas he had managed to save and those went into a scabard and coin purse, respectively.

Perseus slung the bag over his shoulder. He looked around the humble room, the low bed, and the few other possessions that he had: a few toys gathered over the years, a few other bits of clothing, the bow and arrows that he was never particularly adept at. A few small number of things for a very small, if until now satisfying, life. Perseus took it in quietly, deep in thought, and sighed. Adjusting the load over his shoulder, he backed out of the room. The reverie ended abruptly when he smacked his head into the edge of the doorway. Chuckling, he pulled closed the rickety wood door and quickly tread out into the still damp courtyard. The open roof showed some clouds glowing golden with the first light of morning, against a rose colored sky. The stars were going out quickly.

The remains of the offerings burnt last night were an oily sludge around a bone. Perseus poured a bit of olive oil on the remains, lit it with a bit of flame from one of the oil lamps still burning in the courtyard, and stood back. "Father, help me honor you in this quest. Divine sister, lend me your wisdom so I can succeed. Hermes, help me to be cunning." He could not think of anything else to say.

"You're champing at the bit, aren't you?" his adoptive father chuckled. He was beaming and seemed at ease. Dictys clapped his hands on the young man's shoulders and gave him the once over. Nodded, looking pleased. "I'm very proud of you, Perseus."

They embraced quickly. "I will be back soon enough. You may not have sired me, Dictys, but you're my father." Perseus patted his own breast.

"You mother will be up shortly," Dictys told him. "Will you breakfast with us?"

"No time. Telephemus is putting to sea shortly. I promised to help step the mast." He smiled at the captain, "Besides, I have gods waiting on me, Dictys. It wouldn't do to keep them waiting, would it? We said our goodbyes last night. I don't know that she could bear another parting, do you?"

Dictys nodded and walked him out of the house. The morning was cool and damp, and the two men tromped down to the beach. Some of the locals were preparing their vessels, and Telephemus' crew were already on hand, securing the cargo, settling their gear and getting set to restep the mast. Dictys and Perseus shared a short embrace, then the young man climbed into the ship to help with the work. He watched his adopted son and felt himself torn between pride and concern. He retreated to *Okeia* to start the morning's work on the ship.

The sky lightened and the sun cracked the top of the hills as Telephemus' crew pushed the ship out into the water,

Perseus among them. Once floated, the ship was ready to set off. From the stern of *Okeia*, Dictys waved to Perseus, who he could see settling his gear in the waist of the ship. The former boy waved back. The patched sail expanded in the breeze, showing a green trident painted on the canvas as a prayer to Poseidon. Dictys watched the vessel slowly crawl away across the water. He continued to follow the progress as members of his own crew arrived for the morning's work. Eventually, Perseus' ship rounded the point to the south and was gone.

Dictys was determined not to cry.

*****

The passage to Samos was surprisingly smooth. The wind was light, but steady and pushed Telephemus craft across the Aegean at a steady five knots or so. They passed Paros to the south, then Naxos the next day. The sea was calm and the crew credited their fortune to Perseus' divine sponsor. He did not remind them that Athena and Poseidon were rivals for the affections of many seaside cities. His very mission spawned from their enmity. His silence was more to avoid reminding the sea god of this than his current shipmates. Five days passed checking lines, bailing from a small leak that required them to put into a small, apparently uninhabited island to patch the caulking. Stories were told and Perseus learned about the goings on back in Telephemus' home of Boeotia, the relations with the Thespians and the ever-present Athenians. He heard of the Athenian navy, with its spectacular triremes that put even this well-sized craft to shame. Then on the afternoon of the sixth day, having seen Icaria to their portside, they raised Samos, a relatively large island only a fifty stadia from the Lydian coastline.

Deicterion pressed against the shoreline, bounded by a high wall of rock. The city was tightly built, with the homes clutching to the side of the sheer mountain. The jumble of buildings came together in a fashion that was pleasing to look at – whitewashed walls terra cotta and cobalt trim climbing the cliff-face. Perseus could make out the trails that wound back and forth across the steep incline. Instead of a beach to pull up onto, Deicterion was fronted by a long, low seawall and there were fishing boats tied up to wood pylons along the length.

Perseus held furl the sail while other men leapt to the oars to guide the ship in the last few hundred yards. On the shore, people were forming up, drawn by curiosity and caution. There were a few dozen men, only a few armed. Women were watching from their windows. The crew brought the vessel alongside the quay and a few of the townspeople called for the mooring lines. They caught the ropes tossed to them and tied the ship to the pylons, while Telephemus and his mates pulled the ship to the wall and secured her.

"We will be here for a few days, young Perseus," the captain told him.

"My business here could take me some time," the youth told him. "I may not travel again with you, Telephemus."

"Where will you go next?"

Perseus shrugged, "That I am hoping to find out."

Perseus gathered his few possessions while Telephemus conversed with the men ashore. Satisfied that the sailors were no danger, the townspeople welcomed them to Samos and proved eager to trade with Telephemus for his cargo of wine. Perseus slipped ashore while the sailors and merchants were talking. He stood for a few minutes, taking in his surroundings. Atop one of the shops, watching the events was a white and gray owl. It met his eye, cocked its head, and took to the air. Instead of winging away, it did slow turns over one of the alleys. Perseus squared his shoulders and walked that way.

The owl flew up the alley, alighting on a building. When Perseus reached it, the owl flew off again, leading him through town to the goat path that wound up the side of the cliff-like hill. It was preening itself, standing on top of a *herma*, a pile of rocks that was a dedication to Hermes, the god of boundaries and those who travel past them. Perseus watched the bird for a moment. It paused in its preening, eyed him suspiciously, and then turned its head to gaze up the hill.

"Up there?" he asked it, feeling foolish. The owl's

head wheeled back around and it blinked, one eye first, then the other. In a flurry of wings, the bird climbed into the air, four hundred feet along the cliff face, and disappeared over the hill.

Perseus nodded to himself, bent to pick up a stone, and set it carefully on the top of the *herma*. Hermes, Perseus remembered, was also the escort for the dead traveling to the afterlife. For the next hour, Perseus walked the bends of the road, climbing to the top of the hill. It was staggeringly warm that day, and half way up, he stripped down, and shoved his few clothes into the knapsack, leaving only the belt and scabbard, and sandals on. At the top, he had a fantastic view of the town below, and Perseus could see Telephemus' ship alongside the quay. Deep blue ocean, speckled with aquamarine and wine color stretched away to the south and west. To the east, he could see the Lydian coast, just visible as a shadow on the edge of the world.

The path took him along a ridge, and he could see a flock of goats in a slight valley to his right. Their master was laid out under a fig tree, eating his afternoon repast. Perseus found the owl on a marker at a crossroads, where the path split, heading along the ridgeline, or climbing the next hill. He didn't need the owl to lead him. There was a temple, shaded by an olive tree, on the ridge. Perseus walked to the temple, a simple square of rock with a pair of pinax on either side of the doorway. The relief on the two stones showed a figure in a low girdled chiton, armored breastplate and helmet. It held a spear and a shield rested against her hip. The other showed the same figure, helmet pushed back on her head, playing a flute.

Perseus realized he had not brought an offering. He hesitated, then entered the temple. The roof was soot-blackened from years of offerings being burned. The statue of Athena was a simple stone affair, with just enough detail to make her identity known. The paint had long since flaked off. Perseus stepped back outside and looked around. The sun was hovering above the sea to the west, swollen and hot.

The wind shifted, and Perseus heard birds taking to the air. When he turned to look for them, two figures were standing on the porch of the temple, watching him. Athena was dressed in a fine, sheer gown, her thick auburn hair loose around her shoulders. With her, in a simple cloak, a winged, round brimmed hat to defeat the rain, and a fine set of golden sandals with small wings on the heels was a tall, bronzed man with a swimmer's build and a friendly face. He carried a *kerykeion* – a short staff with two snakes intertwined along its shaft and topped with a pair of wings, and he had a large sack slung over his shoulder and when he carelessly dropped it the sound of metal rang out. Perseus recognized him immediately not just from the stories he had heard over his lifetime, he just knew, in his bones, this was the herald of Olympus: Hermes.

Perseus was suddenly aware of his nakedness, and for the first time in his life was somewhat embarrassed. "None the worse for wear," Athena said. She motioned him out of the temple.

"He's definitely his father's son," Hermes added. The messenger strode up to Perseus, looming over him. He gave Perseus the once over. "Are you ready for this, little man?"

"I am," Perseus told him. He hoped he sounded confident.

"You have a long journey ahead of you," Hermes informed him, "and several stops on your way to finding the Gorgon. When you get there, you will need a few things to be successful."

Athena hefted the bag and brought it over to Perseus, setting it down between them. Perseus found himself glancing over the goddess, admiring the figure he could almost see through the cloth. A natural, adolescent reaction began to happen, and Hermes gave him a light smack on the back of the head. "Focus."

Athena gave him a (literally) withering look. "Listen to me carefully. Medusa is a dangerous foe. More so than you will expect. She has spent years avoiding heroes like you who would kill her for the glory. She hides well, strikes by surprise, and her very image turns men to stone out of fright. Hundreds of men have died looking into that face I gave her and it has driven her mad."

Hermes needled, "Wasn't that the idea, sister?"

She held Hermes' gaze for a moment and there was a slight rumble of thunder in the west. The messenger grinned casually. She continued, "Her madness has not clouded her intelligence. She is adept at seducing men, and her voice can be hypnotic. One quick glance can immobilize you with fear, and you will be turned to stone. Do you understand?"

Perseus affirmed, "I do."

"So, lesson one: Do. Not. Look. At. The. Gorgon." Athena stressed.

"Don't look at the Gorgon," Perseus repeated. "So how do I fight her?"

Athena cocked her head to side. "I would think that obvious."

"Either I have to fight her in the dark or go by the sound..."

"No."

"...or...a mirror? Reflection?"

"Maybe the kid's not a total loss," Hermes said. He was casually swinging the kerykeion back and forth. "Look in the bag."

Perseus quickly opened the sack. The largest object was immediately familiar to him. "The shield of Abas! Where did you get this?"

"I accidentally dropped it into my bag the last time I was in Argos," said the god. He shrugged and chuckled, "It happens."

Hermes was also the god of thieves, Perseus remembered. He was still a day old when he stole a herd of cattle from his brother, Apollo. Right now, he was grinning like a naughty child who, caught, was still proud of his indiscretion. Athena snorted, derisively. Perseus removed the shield and gasped. "What happened to it?"

The shield was bronze and circular, large enough to guard the user's torso and some of the extremities, if held right. It was almost three feet around. A sunburst in the center was surrounded by a spiral relief of the history of his family from the events of Danaus through to Abas. Now, however, the shield was polished to an impossible shine, like a mirror, on both sides and the paint on the figures, which was constantly needing reapplication, was completely gone. The leather straps were new and more supple than he would have expected, and the rivets holding them on were seamless with the main body.

"Hephaestus," Hermes explained.

"The smith god owed me a favor," Athena added.

"Did he ever…" Hermes chuckled.

Athena cocked an eyebrow at the god, "You. Stop."

She took the shield from him. The heavy disc seemed weightless to her as she quickly slipped it onto her arm and adopted an aggressive stance. The metal gleamed brightly, and Perseus could easily see himself. Hermes appeared as a human-shaped flare of light, as if a sun were standing next to him. The temple and the olive tree next to it were curved and distended across the edge of the shield. Athena moved slickly, keeping the shield ahead of her, and tilting in slightly. He could see where her face should be in the reflection, and the metal flared like it was on fire. "You can see quite nicely, even at this angle. The convex angle of the shield gives you a widened field of vision."

She indicated the arc of vision she was talking about, then in a movement so fluid and fast Perseus could barely follow it, she spun on a heel and was next to him, shield held in front of both of them at high port, as if to defend their heads. In the metal back of the shield, he could see the temple plainly, although the glare from Athena's reflection was nearly bright enough to drown out the rest of the view. Her breath on his neck was like a hot desert wind.

"Both sides will give you the ability to see," she told him. Athena shifted the shield showing how just the right angle would allow him to see in front and behind him with very little movement of the eyes.

"I understand," Perseus told her. Athena slipped off the shield and handed it to him. Hermes took up the sack and reached in.

"You will need these," he told Perseus, and tossed a pair of sandals to the ground at his feet. They were copies of the shoes the Olympian was wearing. The golden wings stirred, like an animal shifting in its sleep. "If you took a ship, it would take you weeks to find your way to your next destination. If you were successful in navigating there."

"Where am I going?"

Athena told him, "To find Medusa you need the Graeae. They are sisters to the Gorgon, and servants of the Lord of the Underworld. They know where the Gorgon is hiding, right now."

"They will also be able to direct you to the Stygian Nymphs," Hermes offered.

"I am looking for the Stygian Nymphs?" Peresus asked.

"Why would he do that?" Athena added.

"They have a few things he will need to make this quest successful," said Hermes.

"They will?" she inquired. Then with a harder note to her voice, "What have you done?"

"Nothing, dear sister, nothing," the god cried, mock defensively. She looked unconvinced. "They have a *kibisis*....essentially a special leather bag, to carry the Gorgon's head safely. Her blood falling to the ground could have...interesting...effects."

Athena nodded, as if she hadn't considered that. "That's all..?"

"You are so cynical, my sister!" Hermes laid his hand on his breast, feigning hurt. "The *kibisis* is from the kingdom of my uncle, the God of the Underworld. The nymphs have it, but cannot leave the banks of the Styx."

"The crones you are after always know where the Styx and the entrance to the Underworld is," Athena added, "but they are stubborn and hard to pry the information out of."

"You simply need to use a bit of charm, my dear sister," Hermes taunted.

"The Styx moves?" asked Perseus.

"Doesn't a river always move? Not just the water, but the path of the flow itself. The Styx is like any other river, save it is also a river of the mind..."

Perseus told her, "I don't understand."

"They have the power of sight. They can see things

outside the realm of Man's reality. You will figure out how when you get there," Hermes told him. "They live in a cave near Tartessus, the Graeae. It is a city near the gates to Oceanus, far in the west. It could take you a matter of hours to get there with those," he indicated the sandals, "but at that speed, you would not be able to breathe. With a few stops for rest, you should make it in two or three days."

"The trick is to navigate wisely," advised Athena. "You could fly straight there, but if your path is off the slightest over these distances, you could find yourself quite lost."

Hermes added, "And I don't feel like finding you."

Athena ordered, "Straight west until you reach the far side of Sicily, then south to the Libyan coast. Follow the coast to the strait, then northwest along the cast to Tartessus. There you will be able to find the Graeae's lair. It will take a bit longer, but it is guaranteed to bring you to your destination."

Athena indicated the bag again, "The last piece..." Perseus obediently retrieved a short scythe – the wicked-looking curved blade was polished to a high shine. Like the shield, he could easily see his surroundings reflected in the bronze-like, but not bronze, metal. Athena reflected as a blazing star near the hilt. "It would take something truly impressive to break the blade. Like the shield, it is the workmanship of the divine smith."

"I don't know what to say..." Perseus stammered.

"Your success in this matter is of great interest to me, little hero. When you are through with this endeavor, you will return the sandals to Hermes, and you will bring me the head of the Gorgon. That is all the thanks I will need." Perseus nodded. There was an emotional chord to her responses that he couldn't quite identify. Dictys has always said women could be mysterious. Perseus assumed that goddesses were suitably more enigmatic.

She motioned for him to follow and led him into her temple. Hermes followed to the doorway, but did not enter, instead leaning against the doorframe and toying with his staff, absently. "The shield, aim the inside at that wall," she ordered. Perseus turned the shield around, catching the light the goddess emitted and focusing it on the far wall, behind her statue. The relief work in the wall was painted and he could see the dancing figures of three woman-things. Two of them possessed serpent bodies that turned into female forms from the waist up. The middle one was a woman in shape, but all their faces were terrible: eyes wide with madness, heads haloed by serpents. Their hands were a peculiar color and their sharp claws gripped the air. Around them were ossified men and animals. The faces were incredibly well crafted, much more lifelike than he was used to seeing.

Athena touched each image in turn. "Stheno," the Gorgon was harsh-faced and intelligent-looking. "Medusa," she indicated the middle figure. Perseus could see the beauty that Medusa once possessed, submerged under the greenish-tinged, scaled skin and fear-inspiring, fanged grimace. "Euryale," tapped the figure to the left.

"She and her sisters are the daughters of Phorcys, a lesser sea god; and Ceto, a creature of the deep. The first two have always had this aspect, and resided under Mount Olympus. Medusa..." the goddess ran her hand over the image and Perseus felt himself shudder involuntarily. "...is the only mortal of the three. The others, as you can see, are serpent-like in the body. This is how you will know them from Medusa."

Athena asked, "What do you see in the shield when you look at me?"

"Light."

"You will see the true Medusa in the shield, my mortal brother," Athena said quietly. "Not this." She tapped the image of the Gorgon. "You will see Medusa as the beautiful young woman she was. This has been the downfall of others that would have destroyed her. One used reflection to protect him, but was so taken with her image that he dared to look at her. Another was distracted and torn apart by Stheno."

"She is seductive, her reflection alluring, and she is fast." Athena told him. "You cannot allow yourself to be swayed by her words or looks. I cannot stress enough how dangerous this adversary can be."

Hermes waved her off from the doorway, "Medusa's dangerous, but she's hardly the worst of the three sisters. Stheno is quick, powerful, and vicious. She has easily killed more men than her two sisters combined. Euryale has a roar that has felled men."

"They live together?" Perseus asked.

"They do," Athena told him. "Compared to them, Medusa is easy prey."

"Are you trying to scare the boy out of this?" Hermes finished.

She snapped, "I am trying to prepare him."

Hermes waved her off, "You're quick footed, quick witted, and you've got the all-father's blood running through your veins, Perseus. You have the advantage. Just don't let it go to your head, you being mortal..."

"They often work in tandem," Athena frowned at Hermes. "Caution and planning are what will save you and end her. Just remember, this..." she tapped the boy's temple with a fingertip. "Always wins out over this," and she squeezed his arm. Hard. Perseus caught his breath at the strength in her slender fingers.

Hermes clapped his hands. "Now, for the fun part! Come outside!"

Perseus glanced at Athena, who nodded. The two exited the temple and walked to where Hermes was waiting. He kicked the sandals toward Perseus. "Put them on."

"Now?"

"Trust me...you need practice," said the god. Athena's mood lightened at this and she retreated to the olive tree to enjoy the shade and watch the proceedings. The white and gray owl fluttered out of the branches to land on her shoulder, cooing to her. Hermes waited patiently while Perseus changed sandals.

"I should have worn clothes," he muttered to the god.

"Oh, she may not have known the touch of a man, but she appreciates the aesthetic, young Perseus." Hermes suppressed and smile and leaned close, "I don't think she's shown this kind of favoritism before..."

"I can hear you," Athena said, not looking up from petting the owl's head.

Man and god looked appropriately chastened. The sandals were on and came alive with a clattering of wings on gravel. Perseus was instantly turned on his ass and the sandals began to pull him upward, dragging him along the ground. Hermes snapped his fingers and pointed to the earth. The sandals hesitated, then settled to the ground, wings rustling restlessly. The god's footwear, sensing their companions' mood, were shifting their wings sympathetically.

Perseus picked himself up off of the ground, but he could feel the sandals stirring, threatening to throw him again. He regained his balance and glanced querulously at Hermes. The god was grinning, chuckling. "That's perfectly normal."

"They are not intelligent, the shoes. About the same as a raven or a dog. They will respond to your posture. They will sense your intent. Most of all, they will sense if you are not completely in control." The god straightened, looked to his left and up. The sandals on his feet burst into furious action, sounding like a hummingbird, and he rose up and to the left. A few feet higher than Perseus' head, they stopped climbing. Hermes crossed his arms and looked down at Perseus. "They will learn your kinesics over time, and will simply "know" what you want of them." His stance changed ever so subtly and he sank to the ground. Once down, the sandals were still. "Your turn."

Perseus steeled himself, then looked into the sky, willing himself to rise. And he did. The sandals raced into the blue, and he could feel his weight bearing down painfully on his knees and ankles. The ground fell away like a stone dropped from a cliff. "Whoa! Too fast!" he shouted. He bent forward to get a look at the footwear and suddenly he was racing east over the hills of Samos toward the water. The mainland coastline was ahead of him and approaching at staggering speed. The air was forcing itself into his nose and lungs. Perseus rocked backward and he came to a sudden stop, then began falling backward, but not downward, toward the island. He flailed his arms trying to gain his balance and control of the sandals. Up, down, sideways, he was out of control, breathless, and dazed.

Strong hands gripped his shoulders and stood him up. Behind him, Hermes was laughing. "Absolutely awful!" He turned Perseus to face him. "You have to be in charge of the sandals, not the other way around. They are like any animal. They have to respect you and know who the master is."

Perseus was looking down, past his feet. A thousand feet or more of empty air separated him from the wine dark sea below. Hermes shook him sharply. "You have to be in charge. Confidence. Trust me on this, confidence is often half the battle. If you convince yourself the world works how you want, the world will often bend to your whim, god or mortal." Hermes smiled broadly, "We're just much better at it."

He pushed off and Perseus nearly went into a tumble. He corrected his stance and shot toward Hermes, who easily dodged the boy missile. The god fell in alongside. "Lean in to go faster," boomed the god. The two raced over Samos in a flash and Perseus found he could barely breathe. "Less aggressive to slow down," Hermes instructed. Perseus couldn't hear his own response to this, but the god's voice cut through the roar of the air with ease. Perseus eased back, adopting a stance less a sprint and more of a walk. He slowed rapidly as the island of Icaria loomed ahead.

"Much better. You're getting the hang of it, young man." Perseus nodded proudly, shifted his weight to turn and respond to Hermes...and dropped like a rock. With a yelp, he tried to assume control over the sandals. They jerked him side to side, spun him, then acquiesced just before he hit the water. Hovering over the ocean waves, he watched Hermes descend to join him.

"No, I was wrong. You still are awful," he said, amused. "You think you can get by to Samos without running into something solid?"

"No promises," Perseus gasped.

"Well, then...follow me!" Hermes dashed off to the east, staff held in front of him as if indicating the way. Perseus, with a deep breath, leaned in and concentrated on following the god. The ocean sped by below his feet, and he could feel the occasional spray on his legs. Perseus tried to direct himself upward, and he rose quickly, Hermes always just ahead of him, jinking from side to side playfully.

They were close enough to the hill to make out Athena and her olive tree when Hermes brought himself to a hover. Perseus clumsily stopped, did a slow circuit back to him, and held station. Hermes said quietly, "Take this how you will, but right now, your life is not yours. You are simply a tool in things bigger than you."

"Why are you telling me this?" Perseus asked.

Hermes glanced toward the waiting goddess, "Because it amuses me to stir the waters. We are old, Perseus. More than you can imagine. Our lives are strange to you, but there is one constant in the universe: hubris. All things wrong come from self-love, Perseus: jealousy, fear, hatred, greed... Hubris destroys *everyone*, gods included. We just can't be rid of the pain by dying, like you can. This leads us to do things we regret, and cannot undo.

"I would have you understand this and retain your humility and wits. Do not fully trust us. Any of us..." Hermes said. "It would be a welcome change if one of those favored by us did not come to a bad end."

"You're saying Athena has an ulterior motive?"

"Isn't that obvious, hero?"

"And so do you..." Perseus acknowledged.

"Absolutely." Hermes tapped Perseus' chest with his staff and flew off, down toward Samos and Perseus followed him unsteadily, but with more confidence. They landed, Hermes with a light step, Perseus at a near run and tumble. Athena laughed, a beautiful sound to Perseus' ear. She walked to them, owl perched on her shoulder.

Hermes aimed his staff at Perseus, "Awful."

"Not bad," she corrected.

"Terrible, in fact."

Athena asked, "You think he can fly to the Atlas' domain safely?"

"I think he can get there. The safely part?" Hermes shrugged. "I have other things to attend to. Try not to kill yourself with those things. I'll see you tomorrow when you leave."

Perseus inquired, "You will?"

"What? Miss the chance that you'll fly into a tree? Of course, I'll be there." Hermes lifted from the ground on hummingbird wings. "And remember what we talked about..."

He was gone, streaking into the sky like a meteor in reverse.

"What you talked about..?" Athena hinted.

"Just...how to control the sandals, mistress."

"You have to learn to lie better, my young hero, especially to one such as me. You don't have my brother's skill in subterfuge." The goddess regarded him with cool, intelligent eyes. "We will meet again."

In a flash, she was gone. The owl was left flapping in the air, shocked to find his perch gone.

4. THE THREE CRONES

Perseus arrived back in Deicterion late in the afternoon, having spent the day practicing with Hermes' sandals. With the shield slung over his shoulder and the sickle on his belt, he quickly learned that the weapon needed to be secured well. The swinging blade had cut his thigh with the lightest of sweeps, caught by the air as he was flying. He would have to sling his makeshift knapsack and cloak under the shield during flight, otherwise they would be caught by the wind and lost.

When he was finished, he took off the sandals and placed them in the knapsack, put his old shoes on, and with the sickle he wore openly on his belt, and his great-grandfather's shield carried openly and proudly, he walked down into the city. With little money, Perseus could hardly afford to feed himself, much less lodgings. Telephemus took pity on him. The captain provided a few days of provisions for the great quest and gave him leave to sleep in the ship that evening. Perseus kept his gear close that night; some of his shipmates were casting too fond gazes toward the shield and sickle.

The night passed slowly, with Perseus drifting in and out of sleep. Each time he woke, he would check to make sure the divine gifts were still with him. Each time sleep came harder and his anticipation for his journey grew. The sky was rose-colored in the east and the stars were winking out slowly across the bowl of the sky, but the sun was still under the horizon. Perseus sat up, damp from the sea air, and glanced about at the sleeping men in the ship. Carefully, he replaced his sandals. The little wings stirred fitfully, picking up on his desire to be away. He packed his gear into the knapsack and tied it off, then fed the cord through the arm straps of the shield and slung the kit over his shoulder. He settled the scythe on his belt, settling the weapon behind his right hip, where it appeared to not catch the airflow as much. Quietly, he slipped over the side of the ship and walked toward the end of the quay.

The town was still quiet and he walked unseen to the end of the wharf. "Ready?" asked a voice behind him.

Perseus turned to face Hermes, who was squatting on the edge of a roof, watching him with a sly smile.

"Athena is not with you?"

Hermes shrugged, "She's around. Watching. She likes to work in the background."

"She said due west," Perseus relayed.

"She did at that." The god stood slowly. "No point in wasting time, then!" he boomed. Hermes shot into the sky, his staff pointed in the direction of his travel. Perseus turned to follow and the sandals hurled him into the air. He nearly lost his balance, dipped toward the sea, then rocketed into the lightening sky, chasing the quickly dwindling figure of the god.

Samos fell away and the Aegean curved out below him. Icaria was on his right, Paros and the other islands in front and moving steadily toward him. Hermes has slowed some, and was flying backward, turning to watch Perseus' progress. The young hero leaned into the air, like he was sprinting, and the vibration from the sandals changed. The air ripped past him and shook his shield and scythe. Hermes shifted to the right and spun, falling in alongside Perseus. Islands were visibly moving below them, slowly but noticeably. "Better," the god observed. "Still slow, however."

Perseus tried to respond but his words seemed to be ripped from his lips and obliterated in the roar of the air. Hermes, however, he could hear clearly. "I could cross this sea in a few minutes without discomfort," he answered Perseus. "For you, that would mostly likely flay the skin off of you. We will go as fast as you are comfortable with."

Perseus asked into the wind, "How long will you travel with me?"

"For a little longer. Then I have things to attend to. Travelers to take to the Great Beyond..."

"If I may..? What is your interest in this?"

Hermes laughed, the sound cutting through the wind. "A fair question, but one I am not disposed to answer. I will tell you this. My kind are forces of nature, Perseus, and we can be capricious. Ultimately, we are servants to Fate and Justice – but not justice as you would know it. Our actions are limited by our purpose: to see fate unfold as it should. It can be a crushing burden. It can also make for a wonderful diversion."

"You're doing this for fun?" Perseus inquired.

Hermes grinned, "We are, like you men, also creatures of passions. Except we do not have to govern ours. Our immortality and our abilities allow us to do as we please, so long as we do not interfere with the course of Fate, and with little thought to consequence. However, occasionally, the results of our actions, the damage done, become too obvious for us to ignore. Being passionate creatures, a few of us are given to compassion. When that happens, we intercede to try to put things right. Often with disastrous effects to those we interfere with."

"Medusa," Perseus said. Already, he could see the coastline of Serifos rising the horizon off to his right, in the west. "Athena is looking to put her error to rights."

"I would not call it an error, young hero. I doubt she is able to hear what we are saying; we are moving quickly enough that she most likely cannot keep her attention on us, but I would not count on that. She is one of the strongest of us, and easily the most crafty." Hermes warned. "She punished Medusa because she could not do so to Poseidon. Being a creature of rare conscience among us, she seeks to stop the murder and fear that Medusa and her sisters have spread."

"To put things right," Perseus stated.

"As for me...it amuses me to be involved in your quest for reasons of my own." Hermes leaned more aggressively into the wind and Perseus followed suit. The rush of the air past him was making it difficult to breathe. The two flew on over islands of the Aegean, close to his adopted home of Serifos, and over the Peloponnese. To the north, the lands of his grandfather were visible. The hills and mountains of Sparta flashed by underneath them, and they raced out into the air over the Ionian Sea. The sun rose behind them, racing them to the western edge of the world.

Perseus' initial fear and exhilaration of flying was being to leave him, and he was feeling the first touch of boredom and they ripped through the cloudless sky, over a uniform expanse of ocean. The horizon curved slightly below him, as if the world was a shield and the water and land were painted on its surface. Just as he was starting to have his mind wander, the god spoke up.

"You can get to your first stop from here." Hermes pointed ahead, where the first hint of land was rising out of the ocean. "That is the land of the Locrians, allies of the Spartans. It is a land favored by Persephone and Aphrodite, a land of law and peace. Continue to follow the sun and it will lead to Sicily. When there is no more land and the Mediterranean is before you, stop and rest. You will cross the sea to the south, into Numidia, then following the coast of Mauritania to the Pillars of Atlas. If you travel straight west over the Mediterranean there is a good chance you will veer off course.

"On the north side of the strait is Hispania. Tartessus is on the coast, the second major city you will see. It will take another day to get to Tartessus if you keep a good pace." Hermes told him.

Perseus made to thank him, but Hermes flashed away to the north, leaving him suspended high above the sea, moving faster than he thought possible. Still, he was not fast enough to beat the sun to its zenith. He could feel the bite of hunger and thirst, but pressed on over the rugged mountains and hills of Locria to the strait between Italia and Sicily. He followed the northern coastline of the island, the sun steadily gaining a lead on him in their race toward the western edge of the world.

It was late afternoon when Perseus landed clumsily beside a river flowing into the sea. There Perseus tasted the water and found it sweet, and drank until he was nearly sick. He settled his gear and made to eat a humble, meager meal. To Hermes he offered the ripe figs and dried fish and thanked him for his council. Then he placed a bit of lamb in some bread, and threw a date on top. Then he set it aside and said a quick thanks to Athena, before eating himself. Perseus napped for an hour or so, waking as the orange sun was touching the indigo edge of the sea. Too excited to remain and rest, he gathered his equipment and with a last glance at the offering to the goddess, launched himself into the sky, heading south for Africa.

When he was gone, a lone figure strode out of the stand of trees that had been near to his camp. Armed with spear, armored with greaves and breastplate over a short tunic and skirt, her helmet concealing her face and red hair, Athena walked down to where the offering sat on a grape leaf, the whole votive resting on a rock by where Perseus had slept. The goddess jammed her spear into the ground and laid her helmet on top of it. She bent down and took the food, quickly devouring it, while looking into the sky for a sign of the man. Although hundreds of stadia away, her keen eyesight made out the speck that was Perseus zipping away toward the continent that was the birthplace of her cult.

She could feel Poseidon's attention on her. The sea had been a nearly flat calm, was now beginning to grow agitated. Athena regarded it with cold gray eyes, then replaced the helmet on her head and took her spear out of the ground. She waited, challengingly, for a few moments, but Poseidon's spirit had moved off and the sea was settling.

*****

Even at altitude and cooled by the air rushing past him, Perseus could feel the heat of the sun. He had spent most of the second day flying just off the coast of Africa, where the ocean pulled some of the punch out of the sweltering air. The shore was a line of desert backed by a mountain range in the south that some said was where Atlas stood, holding up the sky. Green groves and farmland dotted the coastline, and small cities passed occasionally. As Hermes predicted, navigation was terribly easy this way, keeping the line of the coast to his left. As the second day wore on, and the sun was beginning to drop out of the sky, Perseus followed the curve of the land to the north and the Pillars. A line of clouds over the strait was dropping refreshing rain and he had to slow to take the sting out of the drops hitting him. A strange wedge of white limestone jutted out of the water on the north side of the ocean and he could see some small boats clustering around the western edge.

He was over Hispania now. Turning west, he followed

the coast until just before the sun went down. Tartessus was hunkered down on a wide river surrounded by marshlands, and Perseus set down expertly just outside of town among reeds and grasses by the river. There he changed out of the winged sandals and rearranged his load so that he could draw his scythe or use his shield quickly. Bone tired, hungry despite stops for lunch and dinner, and badly dehydrated, he squelched into the river to refill his water skin and drink his headache away. His skin was deeply bronzed, burned from the wind and sun during his flight., Flies and gnats had been loosed into the air by his wading in the riverside mud, pestering him. A lone boat was tacking up the river.

      In the growing twilight, Perseus wandered along the river to the city. Built on the river rather than the sea, Tartessus was much larger than Serifos or Deicterion, but paled in comparison to the great cities of Troy or Athens. Or so he'd heard, having never been to either. The buildings were low and simple in design, their plaster-covered walls whitewashed or painted with votive images, and topped with peaked roofs, rather than flat ones, and tiled in terra cotta. Near the outskirts, cheaper dwellings were wood or piled stone, and thatch-roofed. The streets were packed dirt, often with mud in the puddles here and there, or gravel and paving stones near the wharf on the river.. Naturally, Perseus gravitated to the port, finding a space alongside a building that was mostly shielded from view while affording him a look down the length of the river front, and settled to eat the last of his provisions. He could hear strange music, on an odd scale he'd not heard before, and could tell there were a few establishments along the wharf that might be some kind of public house. Sailors and other townspeople seemed to be attending a couple of these places, and Perseus assumed that they were some kind of open symposium.

      He jolted awake a few times, having drifted off to sleep, at changes in the ambient noise, but he had not been accosted in any way. The last time, Perseus snapped awake to find himself feeling weary and cold. It was quiet, the city asleep, and the rhythmic creaking of the ship and boats tied up set up a counterpoint to the cicadas chirping. The shield was cold against his back, and Perseus pulled his cloak from his bundle and wrapped himself. The stars above were bright and the spill of the Milky Way drew his eye.

"A humble resting place for a hero," a soft voice observed. Perseus gripped the scythe and rolled to a knee. Standing quietly, observing the docked boats and the massive river beyond, was an older man, dressed simply and holding a cup. Nearby, a spear with a helmet resting on the point, and shield rested against the wall of the building. He had an open, pleasant face, and though it was dark tonight, with no moon, yet he could make the figure out with ease. He was sipping something from a cup and looked relaxed, and chuckled at Perseus' surprise.

"I doubt most heroes are impoverished, like me."

"You would be surprised." He gestured to the nearby, now quiet, tavern. "You could have gotten word of the Graeae's lair from the sailors earlier..."

Perseus stood, returning the scythe to his belt. "I will do so tomorrow morning. Who am I addressing?"

"I am known as Zanthius, a simple river sailor from these parts...but that is not who I am, is it?" Perseus could hear the man's voice melting from a raspy tenor to a musical, and decidedly not-male, mezzo-soprano that was becoming all-too familiar. "As for the direction in which to go: The cave lies that way," he indicated the far bank of the river. "Any of the herders or farmers will be able to tell you where your quarry are. They avoid the place, of course.

"I will be watching over you tomorrow. I can most likely not interfere in any way, but be careful. These creatures are crafty," the man warned. "Also, I expect that Hermes has a little trick to play with his nymphs. If there's anything else that comes with this sack they have for you, I expect you'll inform me."

"Absolutely, my goddess" Perseus said. "You suspect he means me ill?"

"Strangely, no," Athena-as-Zanthius replied. "There's mischief here, no doubt, but it is directed at one or more of my kind. I want to know what to expect." Zanthius finished his drink and with a flick of his wrist, sent the cup spinning far out over the river. "Get some sleep and stay sharp tomorrow."

He dropped the helmet on his head, picked up her spear and shield and in a flash was gone. The afterimage Perseus had was that of the goddess, resplendent in armor.

*****

The cave was surprisingly easy to find. Perseus had managed to explain his quest, that he was looking for the Graeae, to some of the sailors in the city, where he could find some people who spoke Greek. The response to his claims to be searching for the crones elicited sympathy and respect from some, skepticism and laughter from others. All thought he was at the very least a bit mad, if not suicidal. All thought, if he were successful in finding them, he would be dead within a day.

Outside of town, communicating with the locals was more difficult. The local farmers and shepherds distrusted him and they spoke Tartessian. Perseus did not. None knew the tongues that Perseus had been exposed to in the Aegean. Still, he was able to mime his intentions to a shepherd who sent him in the right direction. When Perseus looked back, the man was making some sort of gesture, shaking his fist with his fingers up like horns.

The land around the city was mostly flat and marshy, but a solitary hill swelled out of the ground a half day's walk from Tartessus. The ground was craggy, the earth dark and pumice-laden. The trees were misshapen and sickly looking. The heat that had been with him throughout the day was more concentrated here. The ground was cooking the soles of his feet right through his sandals, and the shield was nearly burning him where it touched flesh. The dampness of the marshland had made the heat oppressive, and the humidity seemed even more evident here. Near the crest of the hill, he could hear a strange buzzing sound, then realized he was hearing the chanting of multiple voices. The voices were similar in register, feminine but with a strange, metallic sound to them. Perseus could smell a strange scent descending the hill, and he could taste copper and char.

The cave wasn't hidden, and around the entrance, he

could see strange markings on the rocks. Skeletons of animals and half-rotted corpses of others were staked around the ground in front of the cave as a warning. The sounds of the day, of cicadas and birds, even the wind, had died away and the air was dead still. From the cave, the drone of women made his teeth vibrate. Perseus stopped to put the shield on his arm and draw his scythe. The noise of the Graeae was causing the flying sandals to rustle and jump nervously. He had a sudden hunch that he might need the footwear. Quickly, he replaced his sandals. Ready, the shield in front of him and scythe held low, Perseus entered the cave.

The heat did not abate with the darkness, and he hesitated a few steps inside to let his eyes adjust. The sandals were restless, but were grudgingly behaving themselves. There was a dull, reddish-orange glow deeper in, and his shield looked like it was on fire as he crept along the rough gullet of the cave. The floor was worn smooth in the center from long use. He turned right at a fork in the cave, toward the voices and light. The corridor widened and he found himself high above a large cavern. Steps were carved into the rock and led to a bowl-like portion of the cavern. The area was littered with crude furnishings and was lit by a few torches around the periphery of the bowl. In the middle and deepest part of this stone basin, he could see a strange cauldron-like object. The interior of the cauldron glowed orange, like liquid fire or molten bronze. From his vantage, he could see images flitting across the surface of the fire, but it was unfocused and confusing.

Shuffling slowly around the cauldron were three bent figures, wrapped in gray muslin. Their words were unintelligible and rhythmic. Perseus could feel some of his energy being sapped by their undulating voices. One of the figures had moved to where he could see the face. Devoid of healthy color, wrinkled, the woman had empty eye sockets. Her mumbling mouth was toothless. Behind her in the circle, the next woman was similarly hideous, but Perseus could see the single tooth glinting like a knife in her mouth. She was holding a struggling bird, and with a single, swift move, she used the tooth to slit it open. The tooth cut out the innards and scooped them into the crone's waiting mouth. She smacked her lips with delight, breaking the hum of the other's oration.

"What is it?" cried the first, "What have you got?"

"Delicious!" the second declared.

"It is a seagull," the third exclaimed. "Give us it, my love!"

"Do you have the tooth?" asked the first.

"I have it," the second said. "You can have the bird and the tooth, if I can have the eye."

"I have the eye," said the last. Perseus could see the right socket held a bloodshot eye, the left was empty. A blue iris floated in a sea of blood red. "I will trade you, sister."

"Unfair!" shouted the first. "I have had neither for such a long time!"

"You had the eye this morning," the third admonished her.

"...but not the tooth! We are so hungry, sister," whined the first.

"Blah blah blah... You had the tooth nearly all day, yesterday!" moaned the second, tooth flashing in the light. She made a halfhearted attempt to slap at the first, and missed egregiously. The third, with the eye, cackled.

The last of the witches stopped suddenly, and slowly turned toward the entrance of the cave, squinting. Perseus stole back into the shadows and turned the shield toward the wall to prevent the gleam of the metal from giving him away. In the dank light, he realized, the shield and scythe were a danger, their highly polished surfaces a beacon for the creature with the eye.

"We are not alone, my sister," hissed the third. All of the Graeae stopped circling the cauldron. The two without the eye were moving slowly, their heads twisting from side to side, snakelike. The sighted one was peering up toward him. "I saw...a reflection where none should be."

"Where?" cried the first.

"What would it matter?" teased the second, "You can't see or eat, my dear."

"Foul Enyo!" snapped the first.

"Dread Deino," continued the first, singsong, "So dreadfully useless!"

"Shhh!" the third – Pemphredo, Perseus remembered – shuffled away from the cauldron, closer to the steps. "Who are you, honored visitor? Why do you hide?"

The other two chuckled, the sound like dry leaves. Deino said, "I can smell him! It is a man...a young one, too! Oh, is it handsome, sister?"

"He is too frightened to come out!" said Pemphredo.

Perseus felt his way back from the entrance of the cavern and found a space in the rock where he could stash the shield. He set the scythe down with it, as well, and covered them with his cloak. He slipped back to the edge of the cavern, where he could see two of the crones moving to join their sister. The sisters knew their home well enough to move with some confidence, not halting or cautiously. The three women were gathered at the base of the steps, Pemphredo glaring up at him.

Perseus could see their faces and under the aged, corrupted skin there was something sadly beautiful about them. He could see the resemblance between them, and the elegant curve of their cheekbones, how the absence of teeth had reworked the set of their jaw and created slack in their lower faces that made them so wizened. Steeling himself, Perseus stepped out onto the top of the stairway.

Pemphredo gasped. "It is handsome! Such lovely features, such a healthy glow! He is not fully human, my sisters; that is sure!"

"I am Perseus, son of Zeus and Danae," he told them.

"A demigod!" Enyo enthused. "Oh, let me see him!" She clutched at Pemphredo, trying to find the eye in her sister's face. Deino countered, "It's my turn!"

"I am here to find the whereabouts of the Gorgon, Medusa." The three of them, stopped scrabbling at each other and turned to look at him, coldly. He persisted, "I am here at the command of my father's favorite child, Athena..."

All three hissed at him, "You will not have her!" shouted Deino.

Pemphredo dashed up the steps at him with preternatural speed. Perseus had been ready for an attack, but had not expected the swiftness of his opponent. The crone raced up the stairs, clearing half the distance between them before he could react. Before she could reach him, however, he leapt from the top of the steps. The sandals burst into frenzied action and he clumsily crossed to the far side of the bowl that the Graeae lived in. Pemphredo stopped, and all three followed his progress. Perseus assumed they could hear the hummingbird thrum of his shoes. He landed, but already the other two crones were closing on him. He quickly backed out of the light from the cauldron and torches into the rough maze of the cavern.

"Careful, my sisters!" shouted Pemphredo. The other two hesitated, casting about for his scent or sound. Perseus tried to breathe shallow and quiet through his mouth. He stepped slowly and careful, stealthily. In the shadows of the cavern, he could see Pemphredo descend the stairs and join her sisters.

"I would have had him by now," Enyo complained. "Give me the eye."

"It's my turn," whined Deino. "You have never caught a man..."

"So tasty!" Enyo crowed. "Come here, little hero, so we can taste you."

"Sister, please!" Deino whimpered. Pemphredo reluctantly reached up and peeled the eye out of her socket. Perseus felt his stomach lurch. Deino found her hand, and transferred the orb into her face. Blinking, she looked around the cave.

"He's up there, in the back somewhere," Pemphredo told her. Deino stared into the darkness Perseus was hiding in.

"I can hear the wings," said Enyo. She pointed toward him. Perseus glanced down at his sandals and glared, willing them to be still.

Deino scrambled up the incline from their home into the craggy shadows of the cavern. Enyo followed, less gracefully. Pemphredo moved to where the rock allowed her to climb more easily. They were separated from each other.

Deino, turned toward Enyo, "Give me the tooth, Enyo, so I may finish this one."

"Come for Medusa," said Pemphredo. "We will tell you nothing!"

"Especially for the third born," Enyo added. "She is unjust! She wronged our cousin."

"The tooth," Deino said, "hurry!"

Enyo looked uncertain, then she pulled the tooth from her mouth with a sickly wet sound. As she moved toward Deino, uncertainly, Perseus saw his chance. He dashed out of his hiding place. Deino, hearing him, turned, but he had charged across the distance between them quickly. Shoulder down, he hit her square in the chest and knocked her over. Before she could react, Perseus snatched the tooth out of Enyo's outstretched hand and threw himself down the slope into their lair.

The tooth was warm and slick, and appeared to be made out of a silvery metal. He held it out in front of him as the three wailed. "You will go hungry, crones, without this! I will ask you again: where can I find Medusa?"

The three of them were converging on him at speed. Enyo and Pemphredo knew the area well enough to move swiftly, but only Deino could see him. She charged into the lair, shrieking murderously. Perseus' ears burned at the sound and he could feel the impact of the sound in his limbs and chest. He launched himself over the cauldron and Deino. She wheeled to track his flight, staggered. Enyo plowed into her and the two went two in a screaming tangle of limbs and gray, decaying clothing. Pemphredo knelt by them, crying for the eye.

Perseus stopped near a bloodstained table. Three plates and knives were on the table, three cups, as well. Nearby was a single bronze lamp. He lashed out and hooked the support with his foot, kicking the lamp over and spilling oil across the ground. Fire spread out from the lamp and began to peter out. He raced to the next lamp, keeping an eye on the crones. They had pulled themselves to their feet and were racing toward him, spreading out. Enyo was behind him, Pemphredo moving ahead, with Deino headed right at him.

He smacked over the next lamp, spraying burning oil across her path. Deino retreated as flames nearly lit her clothing on fire, covering her face as burning oil rained down around her.

"Sisters!" she called. Perseus jumped up on the steps to the entrance, dodging Pemphredo and landing behind her. The flames from the two fallen lamps were going out, plunging more of the cavern into darkness. The Graeae were confused, Deino still recovering from the fire burning her face and bits of her clothing. He paused as Pemphredo was bending down, hand out. Deino was reaching for her face, plucking the eye from its socket...

Perseus pounced. The sandals flew him over the cauldron, and he dipped low to reach for the eye. He lost his balance as he snatched the eye, tumbled across the floor, and picked himself up in time to see Enyo bearing down on him. She grappled him, her claws digging into flesh and drawing blood. He twisted away and threw her to the ground, stunned at her strength. She began to rise, but he slashed her cheek with the tooth. She screamed and collapsed, clutching her cheek. Perseus shot into the air, nearly hitting the ceiling of the cave, and dropped in the shadows of the cavern.

Deino and Enyo were holding each other and sobbing, while Pemphredo was thrashing, clawing at the air around her. "Give it back! Give it back!"

"I will," he shouted, "but only if you do as I say."

"He lies!" Enyo moaned. "He lies!"

"I do not! You will tell me where I can find Medusa. When you have done that, I will give you back the tooth." The three cried piteously, "You get the eye when you tell me how to find the Stygian Nymphs."

The Graeae fell silent and looked confused. "The Stygians?"

"Hermes commands it," he told them.

"We cannot tell you where they are, Perseus," said Deino. She pointed to the cauldron. "We can only show you."

He warned them, "I am not a fool."

"No, great mortal son of Zeus," Pemphredo added. "We are not lying. Scrying!"

"What?"

"We scrye," she said. "We can see! But we need the eye."

"No." They wailed again. "Can you show me or not?"

The three conferred quietly. "We can," said Pemphredo.

He crept out of the darkness, moving softly and keeping the cauldron between him and the three. He brandished the tooth like a knife, careful of attack. The crones were moaning and chanting again, and the red shimmering surface of the cauldron became agitated, frothing and shifting. The surface might be moving, but he could see the Pillars of Atlas flash by and he could almost feel the spray of the ocean, smell the salt of the sea as the vision raced southwest. Then there was an island a craggy chunk of land dominated with the black slope of a dormant volcano, rich with vegetation in the hills, but drier and hot near the ocean. There he could see empty villages and then, near a cliffside, a large ramshackle temple complex. Scattered through the place were stone figures – men, animals, a centaur – frozen in different positions, but all their faces bearing a look of abject terror. Inside the large, impoverished temple was a beautiful woman with long thick blonde hair. Perseus was stunned by her beauty and the look of anguish on her face. He could see despair and madness in her blue eyes.

"Medusa," intoned Pemphredo. "She lives near the shore on Cerna, away from man and beast."

"It is an island in the vast realm of Oceanus beyond the land," Enyo informed him, still cupping her bleeding cheek. Her blood was a thick, clotted fluid that reeked.

"We have done as you asked!" shouted Deino. "Give us our tooth!"

Perseus considered the landscape he was seeing. He would be able to find his way there, he was sure of it. He tapped the tooth on the ground, the sound ringing through the cavern. "Here," he told them, backing away. The three rushed the area and after a short fight, Deino came away with the tooth in her mouth and looking pleased with herself.

"Now...the Stygian nymphs. Where are they?"

"We can take you to them," offered Pemphredo.

"Show me where they are," he ordered.

Enyo explained, "The Styx is a place of mind, young hero, clever hero... It can be reached from here," she indicated the cauldron.

"I don't believe you," said Perseus.

The witches moaned, then chanted. The images in the cauldron changed, smearing and resolving into a long, bland plain devoid of life. There was a river, and beyond it a field of movement that he couldn't make out. He could hear voices, running together into a featureless high-pitched buzzing, like the twittering of bats. "The Fields of Asphodel..." The scene shifted, moving away from the river and the shades toward a garden. The trees, the earth, everything in the picture was deeply colored, over-saturated, and while there was light to see, the sky was dark and strangely featureless. Shadows flowed in the image, things moving just out of sight. Deino expounded, "The Garden of the Hesperides."

"Where is it?" he asked.

Deino crowed and the others followed suit. "It is here," she indicated the cauldron, then pointed to her head, "and here."

They laughed again, and Perseus felt his jaw muscles cramping in anger. "How do I get there?"

"That's the easy part, young Perseus," said Enyo. "Just touch the surface.."

He glanced at the moving surface and the view of the Garden underneath. It was a trick, a trap, he knew. "How do I know you tell the truth?"

"You have our eye," shouted Pemphredo. "We will not hurt you, little man."

"Know this," he told them, "I have hidden the eye in this cavern. If you harm me, you will never find it."

The three wailed and he was glad they hadn't realized the eye was still in his hand. Steeling himself, he reached out, just shy of the surface. "Well..?"

"We will not act," the crone promised. "But beware, foul man, the nymphs may offer you fruit from the trees.

Golden apples that will entice you. Do not take them," Pemphredo warned.

"Why not?"

Enyo clucked, "Stupid man, they are Hera's. They are not for such as you."

"...and Hera would be most distressed that a bastard of her husband's would take from her." Deino added.

"She would strike you down," Pemphredo said.

Enyo finished, wailing, "...and we would not gain back our sight!"

He touched the luminous surface of the cauldron's contents.

The Garden unfolded around him, stretching in all directions. He was surrounded by impossibly lush trees, bushes, grass. He knew some of the plants, others were new to him. The heavy earthy scent was not that of his native isles, but something more ancient and deep. The sky was dark and without stars, yet there was an ambient light coming from...he couldn't say. Birds chirped unseen, cidadas thrummed, and something moved, sliding and rustling. The air was still and thick, cool but not uncomfortable on his naked skin. Something snorted behind him, and hot breath gushed across his back. Without his shield or weapons, Perseus felt a flash of fear and jumped away from the breath, turning to face it.

The head peeled out of the dirt, wing-like folds shaking clean on either side of the serpent's face. Gold, emotionless eyes regarded him maliciously, and the fanged mouth opened slowly. He stepped back from the thing and could feel its body moving under the earth. Another hiss sounded to his right, and another serpent head emerged from the canopy of leaves over head, the body curling around the trunk of the tree. Golden apples hung from the branches reflecting the monster's head. Another burst out of the bushes behind him with a snarl that shook him to his bones.

"You should not be here, pretty thing," sang a light, beautiful voice. The side of the tree nearest him warped and from it emerged a woman. Her skin changed color, the deep brown of the tree trunk fading to a light brown and green striping. Deep green eyes smiled at him, as the small, slim figure peeled loose of the tree. She was slight, girl-like, and her thick brown hair moved like there was a breeze in the still air. "We so rarely see the living here..."

Around him, the serpent heads moved warily, forked tongues tasting the air. Their bodies disappearing into the ground, and Perseus could see their forms moving under the earth and spotted where two of the bodies joined. She indicated the serpents, "Ladon does not tolerate interlopers, beautiful man. Thieves are not welcome here."

Ladon's multiple heads shifted, circling him, and rumbling ominously. He braced himself to move, feeling the shuffle of the wings on his sandals.

"I am not a thief," Perseus bristled. In the back of his mind, he could hear Deino disputing this, as his continued possession of their eye showed. "I was sent here by the herald of the gods, himself. I am Perseus, son of Zeus and Danae."

The nymph moved closer to him and purred. The sound was duplicated from several of the trees, and he watched as more nymphs emerged from the trees, all of them similar in look to the first. Their colorations were subtly different, one more green and brown, one with reddish highlights to her skin. "Our mistress would be much distressed to know you are here!" said another. The three nymphs crept toward him, threateningly. In front of him, Ladon opened his mouth wide, teeth dripping poison.

He could hear Enyo as an echo, *Quick, my dears, find the Eye before Hera strikes him down...*

"My father would be distressed to find out something had happened to me," he retorted. *Would he really?* Perseus wondered.

"The lord of gods has many children, little thing," said the reddish-skinned nymph. Her smile was open and inviting, her voice coaxing, but he could hear a bite behind it. "One bastard either way...who would notice?"

"I would," boomed a familiar voice. Ladon's heads snapped about and the nymphs shrunk back slightly as Hermes descended through the tree canopy. "I warned you Perseus would be coming, did I not, Erytheia?"

The red skinned nymph looked chastised, "You did."

"Where are the items I left with you?" Hermes asked.

Erytheia motioned to the first nymph, who scampered back to her tree. Her arms disappeared inside the trunk, merging with the bulk of the plant. Perseus could see more of Ladon's heads lurking, watching the proceedings with ill-disguised hostility.

It is not here, he heard Enyo's voice in his head.

He must have it, Pemphredo responded.

The nymph turned from the tree and a large leather sack emerged from the meat of the trunk. There was something inside the kibisis, large and round bowing out the material. Hermes motioned for Perseus to take the bag. "Hurry, Perseus, the Graeae know you've fooled them."

He is over here! Quickly, my sisters! said Pemphredo. *Who has the Tooth?*

I have it, answered Deino. Her voice, though faraway, was like a hammer strike on his head.

Perseus took the bag with his left hand from the nymph. He could feel ghostly hands on his arm, incredibly strong. "Go," said Hermes, "Now."

Perseus withdrew his arm from the cauldron and the Garden collapsed in his vision, falling away like rain into the surface of the vat. In his left hand was the kibisis, his right hand was outstretched over the surface of the liquid. Pemphredo had him by the right arm, and Enyo was advancing on him rapidly, her arms questing for him. Deino was coming around the cauldron on the right.

He swung the heavy leather bag at Enyo. It hit her on the side of the head, staggering her. Pemphredo shrieked and clawed at his face, but he twisted in her grasp and swung the bag into the back of her head. She fell away, more from surprise than injury, and stumbled into Deino's path. The two sisters recovered quickly, but he had already sidestepped them, and away from the cauldron. Next to it, he could see their eye, glaring up at him from the dirt.

"You want the eye?" he growled "or shall I stomp on it?"

The three stopped and screamed in unison. He willed himself into the air, flying up to the entrance of the cavern. "You cheat! You thief!" they cried.

"I am neither," he told them. "The eye lies where I was standing."

Swiftly, Enyo and Pemphredo were on their hands and knees, patting the ground. Enyo found it first and popped it into her face. She spun to snarl at him. "As good as my word," he told them. He shook the kibisis, waved to them, and stepped away. He quickly snagged his bundle with his gear and threw it over his shoulder, jamming the new kibisis into it clumsily. He could hear the arguing between the sisters over who would have the eye and tooth, who would kill him. He grabbed his scythe and shield and retreated from the cave to the outside world.

He emerged into blinding sunlight and heat, trying to keep the shield angled for behind him to protect from the crones, should they attack him. He could see the bruising on his arm from where Pemphredo had grabbed him. The scythe and shield gleamed bright and he ran down the hillside until he was out of the area of twisted dying trees. The wind was blowing here, and the sounds of birds resumed.

"That was clumsy." Athena waited for him, resting her weight on her spear, her helmet perched on the point of the spear. Not far away, another gloriously-faced, raven-haired goddess with bronzed skin and magnificent wings watched the exchange with a smile.

"I found out where Medusa is, didn't I?" he said defensively. "I got out of the Garden of the Hesperides, didn't I?"

"You did at that," she acknowledged. "And you went in with no idea of what you were going to do. You left your weapons behind and might have needed them against Ladon."

"Would it have helped?" he asked.

"Not a bit," she conceded. "That's not the point. You cannot simply rush into a fight and improvise. That's a sure way to lose. A good plan can, and often must, be modified in the face of changing situations. You retain the initiative. A bad plan, or no plan, leaves you on the defensive and gives your opponent the advantage."

"Understood," he nodded.

She sighed, "Let's see it."

Perseus hesitated, then hooked the scythe to his belt, and dug out the kibisis. Both goddesses reacted to the object. Nike observed, "This is from the underworld."

"Yes," Athena took the leather bag and opened the top. Her facial expression froze and she took a deep breath. "I have a sibling to batter insensate."

"What is it?" Perseus asked.

Athena pulled a simple-looking helmet from the sack. It was black, chased with red, and made of formed leather and some kind of scales. "This is not good," the goddess observed.

"How did he get that?" a shocked Nike asked Athena.

"I borrowed it," came a voice from above. Hermes flashed into view next to Perseus.

"Borrowed?" Athena repeated.

"Yes."

"Not 'stole'?" she added.

"Don't worry, dear sister," Hermes laughed.

"Not 'stole'?" she said again

Hermes looked hurt, "No, I did not steal it."

"So if I ask Hades about the Helm of Darkness, he will confirm that you asked to borrow it." Athena asked.

"That might be...inconvenient," the god admitted. She started to respond, but the god snagged the helm from her grasp and showed it to Perseus.

"It makes you invisible. And anything connected to you – your shield, for instance," he grinned. "Medusa, you could probably fight without this and win.,,but against her *and* her sisters?

"It would be difficult," Athena admitted.

Hermes snorted, "It would be impossible. With the Helm, you have a real chance at surviving this."

"Should I?" Perseus started to ask Athena.

"Yes," affirmed Hermes. "No," growled Athena.

"It's alright," Hermes told the goddess. "Really."

She sighed, exasperated, "You stole an object of power..."

"Not 'stole', borrowed," he corrected her.

Perseus asked, "What's an object of power?"

Nike answered, "It is an object that represents the power and authority of a god. Zeus has the lightning bolt, Poseidon the trident, Hera the golden apples...and the Lord of the Underworld has the Helm of Darkness."

"...now in your possession," Hermes pointed out.

Perseus nearly dropped the helm. "Not good..."

"No," Athena confirmed.

Hermes fended off the enraged goddess, "I told you, it's not a problem."

Athena slapped her helmet on her head, and gripped her spear angrily. Hermes took a cautionary step back. With a nod to Nike, the two disappeared in a burst of light. The kibisis lay on the ground. Hermes chuckled, "She's on her way to see him," Hermes told Perseus, nodding his head toward the ground. "We have to get moving on this."

Perseus asked, meekly, "Did you steal it?"

"Where would be the fun in asking for it?" The god handed him the helmet. "Where are you off to?"

"Cerna. It seems to be an island beyond the Pillars."

"A tough journey to navigate. You must fly a careful course southwest into the realm of Oceanus," Hermes said. Perseus was surprised to find he almost could sense the direction he would need to go, glanced past the hills to his west. The god continued, "Wear that when you meet Medusa. Otherwise, keep it out of sight. Best the owner not know who has it."

Perseus recovered the kibisis and jammed the helmet back into it. As he did, Hermes flipped him a salute with his staff and shot up into the air. Perseus watched the god describe a parabola eastward, curving back toward the ground, then disappearing in a flash, like a meteor. He adjusted his load, and once ready, launched himself into the air and headed southwest.

5. THE LORD OF THE UNDERWORLD

Dark, dank, and cool, the underworld stretched away in all directions from the massive castle that was the seat of Hades. Mist drifted over the Lethe and the Cocytus rivers, and the smell of death permeated the air. A strip of fire marked the boundaries of the River Phlegethon. Beyond that would be the Styx, the boundary of the Underworld, served by the Acheron. Dull whisperings of the dead twittered like bats, and created a quiet, sad noise. What light there was came from a wide plain of green fields, and that was unnaturally bright and golden, and made the rest of the land here seem that much more desolate. This was Elysium, the home to those dead who had done good in their lives, and near it the Gardens of the Hesperides. Pale shades shuffled aimlessly across the Plains of Asphodel, ghostly and only half-seen. The fires of Tartarus were barely visible in the opposing direction to that of Elysium.

It was a terrible place.

It was not a place for the living, nor the immortal, and Athena could feel the tug of the dead all around her. She had manifested outside of Hades palace in a flash. The spirits around her drew back in surprise and fear, then crowded in close around her, drawn by the unending light and warmth that her form contained. She used her shield to fend a few ghosts off, and clear her path to the palace. The dead were lined up, waiting for the opportunity to enter the citadel and be judged by its master. As she walked toward the forecourt of the vast complex, she could see Cerberus with his three heads and gleaming silver eyes, growling with nervous energy in reaction to her presence there. A trivium of former men sat in judgment of the dead, just as much specters as those around them. The goddess recognized the former rulers of Crete, Rhadamanthus, and his brother and successor, Minos; and the last was Acacus, the once king of Aegina.

The judges, like the other dead around them, gaped in awe at her. Athena knew that they were not seeing her womanly form, but the raw energy and fire that was her actual form. They could, in death, finally see the glory of the

Olympian true form, and those that had not been wailing in terror and loss were moved to spectral tears by her beauty. To the living, her true form would immolate in an instant; to the dead, she was a source of warmth and comfort. She had been told, once, that Persephone would sometimes walk through Asphodel to bring a moment of loveliness to their eternal rambling.

Cerberus fell back from the approaching goddess, triple heads vying with each other to watch her, and licking his triple set of lips. She lifted a single finger, and the massive dog squatted on its haunches and looked forlorn. Behind the judges' panel was the entrance to the massive main hall of Hades' home, where his two guards were regarding her with open hostility. One had the lower body of a goat, satyr-like. His massive body rippled with muscle, and he towered over the goddess. He stood to one side of the doors into the hall, his brother on the other. Each regarded her with a single eye, hatefully.

"Pallas," she addressed the goat-legged Cyclops, "I have come to see your master."

"Are you lost, bright one?" Enceladus asked insolently. Athena eyed him under the brim of her helmet. Of late the Cyclops and their brothers, the Giants, had been increasingly aggressive and ill-mannered.

"You would do well to remember to whom you are speaking," she reminded the monster. "I will see your master, now."

Chastised, the Cyclops grunted and led her through the towering hall to the god's audience chamber. The entire palace was carved from obsidian and onyx, the surfaces shining with the light of the torches and braziers. The walls were covered in gold and silver filigree from a time when Hades had attempted to make his lot as master of the dead more palatable, to draw visitors. Yet none of the Olympians came to visit, only the condemned. Over time, he simply stopped trying to make his home anything more than livable. The size of the place was staggering, even by Olympian standards, as if Hades hoped to overcome the dark and the closeness of his realm.

Athena considered this as she strode through the hall behind Enceladus. The grand architecture was meant, she thought, to lessen the claustrophobic quality of the Underworld. She was sympathetic. Many of her fellow Olympians were, although they would never admit it, claustrophobic. Their infancies had been terrifying and painful. Hades, and with him Poseidon, Demeter, Hera, and Hestia had all been consumed by their Titan father, Cronus, who sought to protect himself from Fate and the prophecy of his downfall at the hands of his son. For ages, they survived the crush of his belly, the vile acids inside. They were immortal and could not die...but they could suffer through the pain and injury of their captivity, doomed (it seemed) to spend eternity being consumed repeatedly. It was a horrible beginning to a life, and explained much about her kind.

Her siblings had never experienced this kind of hell, nor had her father, but she had. Her mother was the Titan Metis, the personification of craft and wisdom, and it was fated that she would bear children more powerful than their sire. Zeus took her as consort and when she became pregnant, he followed Cronus' example. He tricked her mother into changing into a form he could devour. Trapped inside Zeus, Metis worked tirelessly, in agony, until she had produced a set of armor and a spear for her daughter, crafted from Zeus himself. Her father had been tortured by Metis' work as she crafted Athena's weapons from his innards. Then when her daughter was born, Metis dressed her in her armor and drew herself to the largest size she could manage inside Zeus. This gave Athena enough room to mature somewhat.

Whereas her uncles and aunts had not the strength to escape the prison of their father's stomach, Athena had clawed and fought her way out of Zeus' belly, doing the sort of damage that even immortals have trouble repairing. Eventually, Prometheus had aided the tortured Zeus, splitting his skull and releasing Athena, gore-covered, armed, and ready for a fight. Her "birth" had shocked and frightened her fellow gods. They knew the prophesy of Metis, and were now confronted with a creature that seemed bent on their destruction. Zeus, in no condition for a fight, immediately acquiesced to her demand to regurgitate her mother. Then in a move that shocked the rest of the Olympians, she denied herself revenge, instead gaining concessions from her father that included the use of his thunderbolt.

The experience of being born in darkness and pain had crafted a tough, determined creature, and her mother's ordeal convinced her to never allow herself to be used by others: chastity and cool reason would be her only real companions. Hades and the other Olympians that had been devoured had not had the protection of their mother's body, as Athena had. She had only had to survive the toxic internal environment of her father for a short time, but she could easily envision the hopelessness, desperation, and pain of their ordeal.

She was convinced that most of the first generation of Olympians were at least half mad. Hades was the worst of the bunch. On top of the hell of his childhood, Hades was the oldest of the male children and the heir to Cronus' throne, and to his mind was cheated of his rightful position by his more charismatic and crafty little brother, Zeus. He not only did not rule the heavens, but had been given the most odious of the kingdoms of the gods, a dark, oppressive, and hopeless place that could only remind Hades of his stay in Cronus' stomach. Hades' mind was warped in ways that Athena could barely comprehend; with his history, she doubted he could have turned out any other way.

He was a figure to be pitied, as much as feared.

The audience hall was impressive. It was much like the forum of the gods, but where Olympus was airy, with white columns, the thrones of the gods placed around the periphery of the vast space, and open to the sky, Hades' hall was circular, ringed with black columns chased with silver and red highlights, and capped with a domed ceiling. Two thrones occupied the far side of the room, and there was no scrying pool in the center of the room. Behind the columns and following the wall was a trough of fire to light the interior, and the flickering wall of flame around the walls made the entire chamber feel alive with restless energy.

Hades was dressed, as always, for a fight. Leather

greaves on arms and legs, a leather breastplate and pleated skirt. A wide belt held a short sword, which was thrown over his lap. The lord of the dead was slumped in his throne, contemplating his cup resting on the arm of his seat. A large pitcher sat on the ground between the thrones. As Enceladus stepped out of the way, and Athena entered, Hades raised his bloodshot silvery eyes. His face was a weary, careworn reflection of her father's: the black beard and hair was shot through with gray, the powerful jaw and cheekbones were sallow and lined. Her kind did not age, did not look old…save for Hades. The expression of boredom mixed with deep thought broke when he saw her, turning excited and childlike for a moment.

"Athena! My darling niece!" he gushed, jumping out of his seat. This creature that was so frightening that men dared not say his name and often turned their faces away when they propitiated him in temples, rushed up to her and took her hands in his, leading her to the throne that Persephone occupied half of the year. His touch was cold and dry, unlike the usual warmth of her kind. "It is so good to see you. None the worse for wear, I suspect. What are you doing here? It's so good to have a visitor. Things here are so…but never mind that! How are things on Olympus? I haven't seen you in how long? How is my wife? Wonderful!" The words spilled out quickly, almost melting together.

"I've come on a serious matter, uncle," she told him. "Regarding Hermes."

Hades face fell as she spoke, and she immediately felt guilty for breaking his mood. His lot obviously weighed heavily on him, and he only wanted a moment's levity and kindness. Athena, however, felt the crawling, chilling quality of the Underworld working into her and she was anxious to be out of the place. Relenting, she told him, "Persephone is well. She's with Demeter, of course."

Demeter, like Hades, had been one of the original Olympians eaten by Cronus to protect his rule. Her particular quirk was her inability to be away from her daughter, Persephone. When Hades had stolen the young goddess away to be his wife, it had nearly destroyed all life on Earth when she refused to allow the plants to bloom. Only after strenuous mediation by the other gods, and the eventual intervention of Hecate, an ancient creature that is said to predate the Titans and so mysterious and powerful -- chthonic -- that she struck terror in both the Titans and Olympians so that they were loathe to talk about her, were Demeter and Hades able to come to an agreement. Persephone would spend six months of the year with her husband in the Underworld, the rest with her mother. Demeter and Hades were locked into an irreconcilable hatred, as a result.

"No doubt filling her head full of lies about me," he fumed. Moments ago, Hades had been a figure of cheer and need, desperate for companionship. Now he sulked in his throne and glowered about him like a madman. "Every time she returns home, I have to spend half our time together trying to undo the damage that frigid whore does."

Demeter, Athena mused, would say much the same thing about Hades. Just with different vocabulary...

"I could try to intercede," Athena suggested, although she was loathe to.

"No no no," Hades grumbled, "It wouldn't do any good, anyway."

"I suspect not."

Hades sighed softly. "So why have you come to me? I know it wasn't to brighten my hall."

"That's not true," she stopped when Hades glared at her from under beetled brows. "Mostly not true. I've been about on Earth for a time. I've barely even graced my own house, much less anyone else's." Hades seemed to perk up slightly. "It's about Hermes..."

"Yes, and what does the divine thief have to say?"

"Rather, what he has done. He hasn't visited of late?"

Hades said, "Of course. He's here often, bringing me my...subjects." His eyes narrowed. "What has he done this time?"

"He claims to have borrowed something."

"From me? Not that I would know of." Resignation shifted to a slow, boiling anger. "He's taken something from me, hasn't he? One of the dead, perhaps?"

"No. Your subjects are here and can only leave at your whim; we all honor that," she reminded him. "It's an object...he's lent it to a mortal. A nephew of yours."

"Outrageous!" Hades boomed. The flames guttered in the troughs around the room and the wailing of the dead increased outside the hall. "I will have him thrown into Tartarus for this!"

"Uncle..."

"I will personally take from him all of that which he has! All he cares for!" thundered the God of Death. The dome was sounding a bit unstable under the sonic onslaught.

"Uncle..."

"I will..!"

"*UNCLE!*" Athena said, calmly, but her voice matched his for volume. Hades paused and looked at her in surprise. "It is for a nephew of yours. This would go a long way to smoothing relations with your brothers, and it would also be a personal favor to me, were you to ignore the insult. I will personally make sure that the Messenger brings the object back." She dropped her voice, menacingly, "And you know how persuasive I can be."

Hades faces cycled through various emotions, from rage to thoughtfulness to understanding, then to a cunning smile. "I will ignore the insult if you assist me in punishing Hermes in some way."

"A practical joke, of sorts? I won't start a war between us, unless it is to avenge myself on the Sea, himself."

"Zeus wouldn't allow it."

"No, he wouldn't," she agreed firmly. "But Hermes could do with an appropriately embarrassing moment, and yes...I will assist."

"What did he steal?"

"What do you think?" she responded.

Hades blinked once, unbelieving, "He would not!"

"It's Hermes we are discussing. He would, if only for the sport of the thing," she said, "and in this case, it also could mean the difference between life and death for one of father's mortal sons."

"What is life or death to me? For me, is there any

difference?" Athena could see his point. She would die, if only inside, if she were to have to remain in the Underworld. Hades pointed a gnarled finger at her. "I want it back."

She said, proudly, "You will have it. I swear it."

"Go, then," Hades waved her away. When she sat in Persephone's throne instead, he looked on in disbelief and hope.

"I thought that I might stay a while and tell you of the goings-on in Olympus and on Earth. Unless you had other plans..."

She thought he might burst into tears in gratitude, and Athena was ashamed that her father has cheated his eldest brother, relegating him to darkness and solitude.

6. THE GORGONS
Perseus landed in Cerna a day later, on a spit of land that stuck out to the north, only ten stadia from the temple complex that was his destination. The air was thick, hot, and dry, despite the breeze from the vast ocean. No matter the direction he looked, Perseus could see no other sign of land, and he was in awe of the scale of the water. During his voyage, he could feel Cerna pulling him toward it, as if the scrying cauldron hadn't just showed him the place, but somehow linked him to it; he had been terrified, worried that he had strayed off course, certain he hadn't, but increasingly unsure as the sea ate all of the land he could see on the horizon, leaving him alone, sunburned, and hungry as he raced over green-gray water.

He was close now, a few minutes by air or foot. Turning from the vastness of the sea, he walked a short while through the tangled woods to a small town. Upon arriving, Perseus quickly ascertained that it was abandoned, and had been for some time. The buildings had been knocked about by the seasonal storms of the place, and the thatched roofs -- something new to the boy-hero -- collapsed under the strain and neglect.

He investigated for a time, poking his head into the mostly single-roomed constructions, the only sounds being the crash of waves on the nearby cliff face. There was a jetty at the bottom of the sheer rock face, the sea only a few yards below the town, the dock dilapidated and sagging into the sea. No boats were visible. Furnishings were left, often buried under collapsed thatch, but most had taken their clothing and valuables with them. He found a bracelet of silver, intricately worked to resemble rope, with a knot at each end. He slid the heirloom into his bundle. There was no food, and his stomach rumbled with hunger. It would be unwise to go into a fight weakened, so he fashioned a few snares from rope he found in the wreckage of a building and tramped into the forest to set traps. Warblers and swifts chirped and called in the boughs. Along the way, he found a small brook of clean water and filled his water skin, then returned to the town to rest. He set himself up in one of the half-collapsed buildings that would provide shelter if it should rain, and would conceal him behind thatch that had collapsed from the roof. One of the walls had crumbled at some point, giving him a wide area to escape, should he have to. A quick hard run and he could throw himself into the sea to escape.

Perseus dozed for a while, then as the sun was dropping behind the treeshe walked back to check his snares, and rabbit ensnared in one. He quickly killed, gutted, and skinned the animal -- it was fat and healthy. Once back in his shelter, he worked for nearly an hour to get the tinder to catch for a fire, but by sundown he was warm, and soon after,well-fed. At some point after that, he slept...

...and woke to the sound of movement. A strange sound, like something being dragged, woke him suddenly. The fire was out, the embers still crackling and smoke still curling up through the air. Slowly, he retrieved the Shield of Abas, edging toward the opening between the fallen wall and the thatch that sagged from the roof.

There it was again: dragging, rhythmic. He could hear something else...something hissing faintly. Snakes? Perseus felt his blood run cold. If a Gorgon was here, he could be facing not the mortal Medusa, but one of her more dangerous sisters. He retreated to his bundle and carefully, slowly unwrapped it to find the Helm of Darkness, a simple black war helmet with red accents. As he did, he heard the sound of something tossed aside. He adjusted the scythe so that he could get to it quickly, then planted the helm on his head. He could still see his body and arms...was it working? He picked up the shield and looked at his reflection. All he saw was the darkness of the ruined house.

He slipped back to the edge of the thatch and using the shield, looked around the corner, out into the single path through town. Under a sky resplendent with stars, the Gorgon was slowly moving among the buildings, and he knew he was facing one of the deadlier of the three. The long serpent's tail writhed on the ground, propelling her along. She was naked, her upper body human but green-gray in color, and her face was not hideous as he expected, but beautiful in a terrible sort of way: her eyes were black pools, the lips likewise. A mass of asps swayed in a halo around her heard, their heads questing this way and that for a scent or sight of prey. The creature moved smoothly, gracefully, and without hurry. The images he had been shown portrayed Stheno[3] as powerful-looking, Euryale[4] had looked more svelte, like the apparition now moving slowly, purposefully through the ruins.

Perseus caught a whiff of himself, sweaty from the heat of the day, with a slight metallic tang of spilled blood from the rabbit. He readied himself to bolt, but realized that the wind had picked up after dark and was cutting across the spit of land, the air would mask his scent, but not well. As he watched, the Gorgon stopped, her head turned to the seafront, the snakes turned to face that way as well, looking like hair blowing in the breeze. She quickly slithered to the set of steps that had been hewn in the rock that led to the jetty, disappearing.

After a moment, Perseus followed to the edge of the cliff, risking a look over the side using the shield. The Gorgon was on the jetty and the water in front of her was spinning slowly like a whirlpool, but the water was rising up from the surface, forming into a powerfully built dark shape with thick, curly black hair and beard. The boy froze at the sight of Poseidon, the Sea God, but neither he nor Euryale seemed to see him. The wind was carrying their conversation away toward Africa. What was the Sea God doing here? Did he know about Perseus' mission? Was he here to stop him?

Perseus was not waiting to find out. He carefully moved back from the edge, but Poseidon did not notice. The helm, it seemed, hid the user even from an Olympian. If Poseidon was here to warn Medusa, he had little time. He had turned the vision he had seen of the temple complex over and over in his mind during his flight, trying to work out the best ways in and out, and the most strategic places to find and fight the Gorgon...he had hoped for a few days to reconnoiter the area and plan, like the goddess had suggested, but now it was time to act. If the Gorgons hunted the area for victims, the

---

[3] **Stheno: "mighty" in Greek.**

[4] **Euryale: "long springing" or "far jumping" in Greek.**

likelihood he would be found would be higher if he waited. If he rushed into the fight unprepared, he would wind up a decoration for the monster's garden like so many other would-be heroes. He dashed back to the house, grabbed up the leather satchel the nymphs of the underworld had provided and launched himself into the sky, sandals carrying him toward Medusa's lair.

The moon had yet to rise, but the brightness of the stars and spill of the Milky Way gave him enough illumination to make out the temple complex. The ground around it was desolate and sandy; the life sucked out of the ground as it had been from the creatures now posed throughout. The temple was not just a place of refuge from the world for Medusa, it was a place to escape life itself. The complex was situated on an abutment of stone, raised above the surrounding sands, and the walls that surrounded it were weather worn, parts collapsed on the weight of sadness as much as the mudbrick they were fashioned from. In the central courtyard, terraces rose from the entrance gates to the main temple, which was closest to the cliff by the sea. Perseus could see other small buildings set apart from the main edifice. These would have been places for the acolytes, one was a smaller temple to a lesser, local god no longer worshiped. Everywhere he saw petrified animals, a satyr here, a centaur there, and everywhere men in armor, men with weapons, men all with the same look of disbelief, terror, and resignation.

Perseus landed near the temple, next to a pool that had once sported a fountain. Brackish water filled the pool, insects playing on the surface. He cast no reflection in either the shield or the surface of the water. Other than the pounding of the sea against the cliffs behind the temple, he could only hear his heart pounding. For a moment, he wished he was back on *Okeia*, hauling lines, pulling up full nets, rowing...anything but standing in a strange, faraway island, in the lair of incredible beasts, waiting to kill or be killed. He was the son of a god, yes. He was not, however, immortal. He was scared.

Also, he stank. He remembered noting that when he saw Euryale winding her way through the abandoned town...they couldn't see him, but they could most likely smell him. Some creatures could track him that way. Perseus stepped over the lip of the pool and submerged himself. When he surfaced, he cast about quickly -- still no sign of the enemy. He grabbed a handful of dirt and sand outside the pool and scrubbed quickly at his chest and armpits, and groin, then submerged himself again. Mosquitos had taken the opportunity to bite him. They seemed to have no problems finding him.

    Dripping wet, but much less pungent, Perseus moved away from the fountain and drew his scythe. He shook the blade and his shield, trying to rid them of water. The polish on the shield barely allowed the water to find a grip and it was nearly dry by the time he started moving toward the temple, using the victims of the Gorgon for concealment. Over the breeze and the ocean's rhythmic roar, he could hear the sound of a woman's voice singing, the song dirge-like. Light flickered at the doorway to the temple. Medusa was home.

    He slipped up the steps, shielding himself from view with the wood columns that supported the structure. The whitewash on the mudbrick walls was flaking and faded, making the building look dirty. Two columns supported the portico, which was bound on both sides by walls, and a large doorway led into the *cella* -- the central chamber where the plynth for offerings and the statue of the god would be present, as it would be this way at home, he reasoned. Perseus slipped up to the entrance and using the shield, looked inside. There were few bowl-like braziers around the room, oil in them burning fitfully enough to illuminate the *cella*. There were more statue-like figures around the room, one in the middle of a sword strike that would never fall, a centaur reared up with an arm thrown over his eyes to shield them, and a man in full armor lying on the ground, shield on his arm levering him up from the ground, sword poised to stab and a shocked look on his face. The votive plynth had trinkets from the men piled on it, as well as plates of food or other offerings. The statue had been painted and was the only thing in the room that was well-cared for -- tall, blue-green skinned, with black beard and hair and intense blue eyes, holding a trident: Poseidon! There were scribblings and painted daubs on the walls from near the ground to taller than a man, there was a loom with a half-worked cloth on it, and everywhere there were planters with flowers and small plants. The only other door in the temple led to the *adyton*, the priests' room where there was more light, duller. It was the source of the singing. This was the only way in or out of the building; there were no windows or doors.

It was a bad place for a fight. If one of Medusa's immortal sisters were to appear, he could be trapped in the building with little chance of escape. Worse, he would be killing inside Poseidon's temple. He knew the story of Medusa and did not think the sea god would be amenable to the slaughter of a former lover in his house. Had the goddess hoped he would insult Poseidon in that way? Heap insult on insult?

Perseus looked about him quickly, gauging distances, lines of escape, then steeled himself, putting the shield ahead of him, angled so he could see the room while looking down at the curve of metal. He called out, "Who is it that sings so mournfully?" He was glad his voice did not crack as it sometimes still did.

The singing stopped. "Who is that?" asked the voice. It was a light alto, beautifully pitched, infinitely feminine, and Perseus felt his heart catch for a moment. "It sounds like a man...but there have been no men here for so long!" Something was moving in the adyton, and he could see the shapely figure silhouetted on the far wall though the door. Around the head, a dozen serpents moved ceaselessly, restlessly. "Come, guest, tell me your name?"

Perseus quickly stepped behind the rearing centaur and shifted the shield to see the other doorway, scythe ready. Striking her head off, he realized, was going to be difficult, to use the shield best, he would need a good hard backswing, but that would expose his back to her. A forward strike and he would have to resist looking up from the shield, as they would be very close when he attacked. He replied, "I am Perseus, son of Danae of Argolis and the high lord Zeus, who rules the skies!"

"More than a man!" Medusa exclaimed, "And yet less than one. A boy, I think, but one close to manhood."

He could see Medusa come into view. In the shield, she was slightly foreshortened, but he could see her fine build -- muscular, slim, firm and full breasts, her skin pale and flawless, her face -- her face froze him for a moment, moved with love, lust, pity. Her hair was thick, flowing, and the color of honey, a reddish blonde. Perseus was struck dumb by her. Only her eyes, blue and wide, hinted at the madness and evil of the woman. She cast around, looking for him. Her movements were surprisingly quick and agile, and he could sense the raw power the curse had imbued her with. "I have not had a man in so long! Come to me my young demigod, and I will teach you the ways of love."

Perseus willed himself to look away for a moment and center himself. His body was reacting to her in a completely different way. He could feel his fear and arousal battling for control of his wits. In the shield, he saw she had stopped in the middle of the room, turning slowly. "Don't be afraid, my boy..."

"I am not afraid," he heard himself say, reflexively, defensively. In the shield, Medusa's head snapped around and she focused her attention toward him. She slipped to her left quickly and he lost sight of her in the shield. Perseus started to move right to keep her in view, thought better of it and shifted the shield to the left to see around the stone flank of the centaur. She was close! Moving nearly silently in her bare feet. Beyond Medusa, he could see the Gorgon reflected in a pile of trinkets, one of which was a smashed mirror. There he could see her true form -- the skin still taut and muscular, but green-tinged and with an almost scale-like pattern, the slender, youthful hands he'd seen in his shield warped into gray skinned talons. The perfect feet were similarly malformed. The face was the personification of madness: the snakes had bitten her many times over the years, the green-gray skin was scarred, the blue eyes crazed and bloodshot. Her golden hair had been replaced by a dozen or so asps which were questing about, looking for him.

"Have you come to kill me, *hero*?" she spat. Even angry, her voice was alluring. "No stomach for a fair fight?" Perseus slipped to his right, keeping the centaur in between him and the monster. He could her shadow as she stopped to throw aside her loom, screeching when she didn't find him, and wheeling toward where he was. He had slipped behind one of the braziers and dropped to a knee, watching her in the forward curve of his shield.

"Is that what happened to these poor souls?" he taunted. "One glance and they are petrified by your face?"

"I did not turn them to stone!" she cried, "I did not cause this face...*this face*...to kill! I am not the monster!" She advanced through the room, quickly, throwing anything that got in her way around wildly. "Where are you, you coward!?!"

She threw the offerings off of the plynth, making to strike behind it and not finding him. The noise was enough to cover his movement and he ran to the entrance, keeping her in sight in the back of the shield. As he made his way through the doorway, he smacked the scythe against the stone, alerting the Gorgon to his position and gouging a line in the doorway. Once he was out, he threw himself forward, the sandals taking him out into the night swiftly, and he turned sharply, circling back to the side of the temple. As he landed behind one of the columns along the base of the building, Medusa burst out into the night, looking about wildly for him.

"It's not fair!" she wailed. "It's not fair!" then angrily, "I will find you, little man, and you will join my works! I will have you placed specially, little hero, so that you will be a warning for anyone else who comes, Zeus' son!" The snakes whipped around, scenting him, and Medusa raced at him. Waiting until the last moment, he closed his eyes and hurled himself into her path. Medusa hit the shield hard, lost her footing and went off the temple base, falling the six feet to the sandy ground, while Perseus was knocked back into the wooden column, his breath driven out of him. The Helm of Darkness toppled from his head and rolled away. He staggered, his scythe scraping on the stone, then he picked himself up, setting the shield to find Medusa.

She had leapt onto the temple and cleared the distance to him on one go! He saw the gorgeous face, locked into a rictus of hatred, her delicate hands -- those clawed, powerful appendages, thrust out to find him. He raised the shield quickly and he was propelled back into the wall of the temple, her snakes trying to get around the shield to bite him. He slashed low with the scythe, striking her left foot and eliciting a scream from Medusa. She fell back and he launched himself past her, off the temple, the sandals slowing his fall. He hit the ground running, and could see Medusa in the reflection inside the shield giving chase, limping where he had cut down to her foot.

"There you are! There you are!" Medusa crowed. He was faster, but not by much, a quick turn by the statue of a shocked villager (he surmised), his basket of goods -- strangely empty -- lifted to protect him. He dashed into a series of trellises that had tomatoes and other food plants growing on them. Medusa was not behind him, but he could hear her ragged breathing on the other side of the trellis as she paced him. Ahead there was a drop off for this terrace, and he could see ocean spray flashing up from where it had hit the cliff. Without the Helm, Poseidon would see him, might aid Medusa. Just as they reached the edge of the trellises, Perseus jumped into the air, letting the sandals carry him up and back. Sharp claws snatched at him, cutting his ankle, and shaking his concentration. He hit the ground on the shield, rolled awkwardly and came an inch from cutting off his own nose with the scythe.

He was near the temple. He started to cast a glance backward to find Medusa, remembered the consequences and looked away. "Poseidon, my love! Here is my assassin! He will be my greatest gift to you, my love; the son of your brother that kept you from the sky!"

Perseus ran toward the temple, limping. Medusa was faster now. He could see the Helm of Darkness and raced to it. He switched hands with the scythe. It was trapped behind the shield now. Useless. He crouched low, snatching up the Helm. Medusa was close. He could hear her grating breath, the hissing of the snakes. He slammed the helmet onto his head and heard the Gorgon shriek in defiance. In the reflection, he saw her right behind him, hands outstretched, snakes as well. He grabbed the scythe in his good hand, sidestepped to his left, and planted his feet, stopping. As he did, he slashed out and back, keeping the Gorgon in his sight in the shield.

Medusa's body lurched past him, running a few steps and falling, skidding, into the sand. Her head disappeared from view and Perseus closed his eyes, feeling it bounce off of his shield. He heard it land on the ground. Blood was gushing out of the body and turning into snakes. Perseus pushed the scythe into the ground, took the kibisis that had been folded into his belt, and opened it. Eyes closed, he felt around until he grasped a flaccid snake and hefted Medusa's head into the bag, quickly tying it closed.

The ocean was slamming into the cliffs, shaking the island, and Perseus nearly lost his footing. Turning, he could see the spray of the waves arcing high into the air and showering the temple, him, the body with foam. The sea was rising, more agitated, with waves breaking over the cliff, washing across the ground. The snakes that were forming from Medusa's blood were scattering from the wetness. Medusa's body was foaming and writhing! He stepped back and could feel the cold grip of the sea on his ankles. The water felt like it was tightening around his feet and Perseus launched himself into the sky.

Hovering over the temple he could see a mammoth figure forming out of the ocean -- deep blue-green skin, dark explosion of hair and a thick beard, trident in hand. Perseus could see other shadowy figures moving in the darkness in the temple complex and quickly looked away, using the shield reflection to track the wailing Stheno and Euryale. Poseidon stomped onto the land and the roof of the temple collapsed explosively. The god strode to Medusa's corpse and stood looking down on it.

The body was convulsing in the wash of water that was sloughing off of the god and then suddenly she burst open! Impossibly, two figures launched themselves from her remains. The first was a man, only far, far too large to have been contained in Medusa's body, he was of gargantuan proportions -- twice as large as any man Perseus had seen and *growing!* The other figure almost seemed to have been made of sea foam as it exploded out of Medusa's corpse, but quickly solidified into a white horse with a resplendent set of wings.

The Gorgon sisters had reached their sister, only to be repulsed by these births.

"Chrysaor! Pegasus!" the Sea God cried. His voice split the air like a thunderclap and Perseus drove himself higher and farther from Poseidon. Chrysaor was now three times the height of a man, still shaken from his nativity, and startled by the god. The winged horse was flying circles around the head of Poseidon. "My sons...you are all that is left of your mother now. Her beauty," he looked to Pegasus, "and her strength..." this to Chysaor. "Now away, my boys, away from this unhappy place!"

Chysaor regarded his father for a moment, then looked to the Gorgons who had slithered near to him. To Perseus' surprise, their images did not turn the giant to stone. As he watched, they led the creature away from his father. Pegasus turned to the east and raced away into the night. Below, the boy-hero could see the body of Medusa had completely vanished with the birth of her sons. No gore, nothing was left. Poseidon stood in thought for a moment, then rumbled, "I know you are still here, my nephew, though I cannot see you. I know who sent you. It is only because of your divine birth and your utter ignorance of the way of us Gods that I will spare you my wrath...

"That I will save for the one who gave you this task," Poseidon threatened, "but you, young hero; you whom I saved from death in my waters not very long ago, you go forth with your victory and pray our paths do not cross again!"

*****

Perseus had watched Poseidon leave, his bulk turning to water and raining upward, as if to deluge the stars. The droplets of water glowed like diamonds, quickly lost among the glow of the Milky Way. He did slow turns over the complex, watching the other sisters lead the giant Chysaor into the woods to the south of the complex. Once he was sure it was safe, he dropped into the ruins of the Temple of Poseidon. The roof had caved in during the sea god's entrance, but Perseus was able to find some trinkets and coins not completely buried that he might use to trade for food on his way home to Serifos. Once he had the loot secured, he threw the shield over his back, sheathed the scythe, and winged north to his hiding spot in the destroyed village. There he collected the rest of his possessions, arranged them so that he would be comfortable, and not waiting for the dawn, headed straight east toward Africa and away from the cursed island of the Gorgons.

7. CONSEQUENCES

Poseidon raced to Olympus and he manifested in the forum to find his quarry immersed in a discussion with his brother, Zeus. As the personification of the oceans splashed into form, Zeus and Athena broke their discussion to turn toward him. "YOU!" boomed the Sea God, advancing swiftly toward the goddess, "You assassin! It wasn't enough to deface, to ensorcel Medusa, you have to kill her, as well!?!"

"You forget yourself, brother!" Zeus shouted.

"Do not! Do not protect her!" Poseidon raged, "Do you forget who it was that allowed Prometheus to steal fire for Man, who provided him the route in and out of Olympus, who covered for him while he did so?"

"I do not forget, Poseidon," Zeus began.

Poseidon jabbed a finger toward Athena, "She is a snake in the garden! *She* revolted against you and suffered *no* injunction, no punishment! Your own sister hung from chains, in agony for her part, I was made a servant, as was Apollo. What did she suffer?" He stalked toward Athena, who rose from her chair and set herself, ready for an attack. Zeus stood, made to intercede between them. "This creature you bore picks at us -- steals our worshippers' hearts, while she plots against us all. She must be stopped!"

Zeus had started to react, realizing the severity of Poseidon's anger, but Athena was like a lightning flash, snatching her spear up that had been resting against her throne and wheeling out of the way of Poseidon's attack. She struck him with the shaft, hard enough to shatter boulders, and send the Sea God tumbling, knocking over her perch, her helmet that had been on the arm of the chair rolling away. Poseidon slammed into one of the supports of the forum's dome hard enough to shake the building. He lashed out, his form turning into a geyser of water that struck her in the center of her breastplate, throwing her across the room and through Demeter's throne, shattering the stone.

The lightning bolt crashed from the skies above Olympus, passing harmlessly through the open ceiling and dissipating its force through the water-form of Poseidon. He convulsed back into his man-form, reeling from the force of the blast. Athena leapt to her feet, spear poised for the throw, and Zeus turned his attention and the sizzling lightning bolt in his hand toward her. There was a second's pause when Zeus was afraid that Athena might take the chance, might throw the spear. Zeus had never cast lightning at his daughter and she was the only one other than himself who had been allowed to wield the weapon. Zeus wasn't entirely certain that his bolts would stop her.

Athena glared at Poseidon, cast a similarly aggressive look to Zeus, then slowly lowered her spear. Her time in Hades' realm had left her tired, shaken, and distracted. Poseidon should never have been able to land his blow. "Again? Again he strikes at me and you stay my hand?"

"That is disingenuous, daughter," Zeus warned, "You did set my son on his path to kill Medusa, did you not? You did this knowing that it would offend the God of the Sea, did you not?"

"Did you think I wouldn't retaliate, my niece?" Poseidon scolded her.

"Enough!" Zeus commanded. He noted the arrival of several other Olympians, drawn by the commotion. Demeter and Persephone, peeking around one of the columns, fearfully; his sister-wife Hera at the doorway, a satisfied smirk on her face. It would please her, he knew, if he were to take his own daughter down. "I will have no more of this! Brother, can it not be a kindness that Medusa was spared a long life of torment..?"

"...at her hands!" Poseidon protested.

"...and her victims, innocent and hero, alike, their suffering has also come to an end," Zeus said, voice filling with compassion. "This is a good thing, brother, no matter the pain involved."

"It is unjust!" Poseidon told him.

"Medusa's actions, while impelled by her transformation, threatened beast and man alike. It needed to end, as I'm sure you can see...as did her suffering." Demeter and Persephone were standing in the open, now, watching the proceedings with interest. Hera stalked around the periphery of the forum, moving past Poseidon to sit carefully in her throne next to Zeus'. The whole time, she gazed at Athena in a combination of open hostility and mocking satisfaction. At that moment, Hermes swept into the forum and paused to watch the events.

"I will have a peace between you," Zeus demanded, "NOW!"

Athena set her spear and leaned on it, feigning indifference she did not feel. Poseidon flexed his hands rhythmically, openly seething and still numb from the lightning strike. Finally, he gave a curt nod.

Zeus thundered, "Swear it!"

"I swear to take no action against my uncle, the Sea," Athena said simply.

Poseidon grumbled, "I will make no assault on your daughter, the Third Born, brother."

Zeus sat heavily. "Athena and Hera may remain, the rest of you...out! Not you, Hermes!"

The messenger god had turned to leave and now froze in his tracks. Zeus gestured with his lightning bolt to the center of the forum, where the floor was marred by the strike earlier. Demeter and Persephone quickly hustled through the door, and Poseidon rumbled and shuffled out. No one present was under any illusions that the feud between he and Athena was at an end. Hermes advanced into the forum, looking about him for escape. Athena recovered her helmet, rested it on the crown of her spear, righted her throne, and sat.

"My daughter tells me that you made off with our brother's symbol of power," Zeus told him. Hera jumped at this and fixed Hermes with a look of reproach. "This is an unforgivable breech, Hermes. Apollo's cattle was bad enough, but the Helm? What were you thinking?"

"In my defense, lord, I was thinking only of the safety of your mortal son, Perseus," Hermes said this, looking back at Hera, knowing even the mention of Zeus' progeny from one of his dalliances would hurt her far more than any direct insult. "His chances of success with the Gorgons, when all three were present on Cerna, was in doubt. While I have complete faith in his abilities, which he received from you, but it would not have done for these creatures to have harmed so noble a boy-hero. As you said, the time for their carnage to end was at hand."

"It never occurred to you to pass this by me, or Hades, more importantly?"

"Has it ever?" Hera responded.

Hermes feigned hurt, "That is unkind. I did not take the helm for my own purposes, but to help another. I have every intention of returning the object, and would have done so without the Lord of the Underworld being the wiser, were it not for the tattling of Wisdom, here." Hermes nodded toward Athena.

"You know what this could have led to," Athena protested.

Zeus silenced them with a raised hand. "Hermes, you will find Perseus at once. You will retrieve the Helm of Darkness, and you will *return it* without hesitation. Do you understand me? If you do not do this, the repercussions will be extreme."

"I understand and obey, Greatest of Us," affirmed Hermes obsequiously.

"Away!" Zeus waved him off and Hermes exited, blurred out of the forum.

"This cannot continue," Hera said to Athena. "This squabble of yours is creating division amongst us."

"Our very natures are causing division among us," retorted Athena.

Zeus put up a placating hand, "Athena is guiding Perseus on the course the *Fates* decided for him. There are few things that bind us, my wife; fate is one of those. We are the forces that make those fates unfold as it should."

"Ideally," Athena quipped.

"The *Fates* did not decree that she and Poseidon should war on each other," Hera stated.

Zeus chuckled, "You know the mind of Fate, do you?" It was an unsubtle jab, Athena thought; Zeus was only Olympian that was privy to the design of those goddesses -- much older that even the Titans. They wove the fabric of the lives of many, their tapestry space and time itself. Fate, contrary to what Zeus would have them believe, was not absolute. Her father had once admitted that fate was not fixed, that the events around a person could bend the weave of destiny. The free will of the mortal or god could create patterns that would change the path of an individual, but in the end, probability and the predilections of the creatures caught in the Fates' web would lead to certain outcomes. One could improvise with the tune of one's life, but in the end, there was a theme that would not be deviated from.

Athena had some knowledge of her own destiny -- to be the greatest of her kind, more powerful, more wise, than her sire. Athena thought she had yet to rise to fill that destiny, was not certain what it could entail, what she was meant to do with that greatness.

Hera said petulantly, "You know I do not, husband."

"Perseus will be guided through his labors until he fulfills his part in the grand story," Zeus declared, "and you will avoid antagonizing Poseidon any further, Athena. You are my dearest child, but do not disobey me in this."

Athena nodded slightly.

"...and make certain that Hermes does as he was told."

Alone in the forum, Zeus turned his attention to his wife and sister. Hera was looking better after her punishment for aiding Athena's uprising. She would not meet his eyes, and fidgeted, eager to be away. Their marriage had always been a contentious one. Before he had even considered her as a wife, Zeus had a roaming eye. Rhea, his mother, had noted this after she had discovered he had slept with Demeter and had forbade him to marry. Zeus had disabused his mother that she could dictate to him in a way that he would admit he was not proud of. Then in an act of spite and lust, he married Hera, his oldest sister and a dear friend. Hera, he found out, was also petty, given to (rightfully so) jealousy, and was nearly humorless. Even the boring Demeter was a respite from time to time. Zeus had quickly found that immortals lacked a certain spark that came from their finite lives; he had learned his lust with the satyrs and nymphs, and with Prometheus' most beautiful creation, woman.

His philandering hurt her, and while Zeus tried to

hide his dalliances to spare her pain, he had not stopped. Because, as Athena had pointed out to him only days ago -- the Olympians were a damaged lot. Half were mad from their torturous childhoods in Cronus' belly, the other half were born to immortality and power, and were spoiled by their entitlement. Despite his infidelities, he still loved her, but he knew he would never be able to reign in his excesses.

No one had been able to make him, until Athena's rebellion. Even then, it had taken guile and the efforts of nearly all the Olympians to humiliate him. When he was free, he punished those he knew he could. Hera was the easiest of all. As the eldest daughter of Cronus, she was haughty, humorless, and on occasion, not a little stupid. Her punishment was that of public humiliation, hung naked for all to see above Olympus.

He said uneasily, "You know why I had to do what I did..."

"I do not. I am the eldest daughter of Cronus, and I am the queen of the gods. My dignity should not be sullied in such ways." Hera sniffed, "You say you love me, but you do not respect me!"

Following the script of many a husband before and to come, Zeus replied, "That's not true. I respect you. You are more than my wife, you are my friend. However, order must be maintained, or our natures would cause us to war on each other, and we could unmake all that has been made. Think of Demeter's fit of pique when Hades took Persephone. She would not allow plants to bloom; she would have *killed* everything on earth just to prove her point..."

Hera pounced, "That she wanted her daughter back? That you -- her brother and lover -- *gave her daughter* to your brother, Hades, as a bride? That she thought your love and respect might bend your arrogance for a moment?"

Zeus bristled and Hera's moment of mutiny quickly collapsed, "Careful. I did not give Persephone to Hades. He took her."

"And you did nothing."

"He was preventing the dead from moving on! What was I supposed to do?"

"Make him give her back."

"It's not that simple."

"Isn't it? Or is it because you know that our eldest brother should be rightfully sitting where you do?"

Thunder shook Olympus and Hera stopped talking. "If Hades thought he could take the sky from me, he would," Zeus told her. His words send tremors through the home of the gods. "*No one* can take that which is mine."

Hera said nothing, but believed differently. The abomination Zeus had created in swallowing Metis leapt to mind. Zeus should be punished for his actions, Hera thought, but she had neither the courage nor the will to make it happen, and while she wished at times that Athena would teach her father a lesson, her hatred and disgust at the Goddess of War's very existence, and her recent degradation at Zeus' hands meant that she would never again side with Athena.

Then an idea sprang to mind. One of such simplicity and subtlety that she knew she had to pursue it. She could avenge herself on Zeus and Athena, and never have her involvement known. "I am sorry, my lord," she said, taking his hand. She looked up into his face with her dark, sad eyes -- he could never refuse her when she played the demure damsel. It was working even now! "I am still distraught from my punishment. I will -- with your permission, of course! -- retire to collect myself. And tonight...come to me so that we may apologize to each other properly."

Zeus rumbled merrily in assent. *Strategy*, Hera though, *who needs strategy when you have sex?*

Perseus would be on his way home, by now, Hera knew. Athena and Zeus both were taking a great interest in this boy-hero, and were at great pains to keep him safe. He was important to them. Poseidon, her brother, was enraged at the cursing, then the murder, of Medusa. He would love to take his revenge, but dare not directly, or face his brother's wrath. Hera had a solution that would give both Poseidon and herself a bit of satisfaction at the expense of her husband and his warrior daughter, and that solution lay in Tyre.

8. THE NEXT LEG

Perseus flew east in the darkness, the sea below foaming and riotous below him the whole way. He could almost picture the Sea God below, striving to reach up and grab him, but the sky was the domain of his father, Zeus. Up here, he was safe from Poseidon's wrath. Now he understood the gift of the sandals. They were not just to carry him quickly to his destination, but to protect him on his way. As he flew on, he could feel the exertions of the fight and flight digging in. He was tired, intensely hungry, and thirsty. He tried drinking from his waterskin while flying and lost half the volume to the slipstream of air around him.

The sky above the horizon in front him presaged dawn, turned a leaden silver and dimming the stars, before returning to darkness, followed by the rosy glow of Eos. Under the brightening sky, he could see land approaching. He dropped over the sandy, wind-swept ground, looking for signs of habitation or vegetation. An oasis sprouted from the soil and he dropped, exhausted, next to the pool that was bubbling from the earth. He dropped his bundle and the kibisis, unbuckled the sword belt, and threw down the shield, collapsing to his knees by the water.

It smelled fresh enough and he quickly gulped down handfuls until he was refreshed. There was no reflection in the water, and Perseus took off the Helm of Darkness, putting it into his bundle. In the morning light, he could see the gore he was spattered with, dried to a deep brown. He used the water and sand to scrub Medusa off of him. The palm trees nearby yielded dates and another tree has oranges. Perseus gathered the fruit and ate heavily. Hunger satiated, he fell next to his equipment and was instantly asleep.

His dreams were filled with horrifying creatures, mostly snakes and snakelike monsters that sang with the voice of gods and attacked with shark's teeth. When he woke, he was still tired, sore, and teetered emotionally between pride and exultation at his success, and sadness and embarrassment for having killed the Gorgon. She had been made a monster, she had not been born one, but in the next thought, he considered all the innocent victims that had decorated her temple complex. In the end, Perseus reconciled himself to the rightness of his actions, divinely inspired as they were. He also felt different, in a way he couldn't explain: taller, stronger... There was a sense of confidence that he hadn't had when he entered the cave of the crones in Hispania.

Perseus resolved to rest here, then head along the shoreline to Hispania to meet up with the gods and return the Helm. It seemed a good idea to get it back to the Lord of the Underworld as soon as he could. While Hermes had not said as much, Perseus had gotten the impression he would take the Helm back near the Graeae's cavern.

He rested in the shade of the trees. A stray wind gust blasted through the oasis and Perseus sat upright, hand on the scythe. Hermes was crouched by the water, Caduceus balanced in his lap, hand stirring the pond at his feet. "You aren't where I thought you would be," the Messenger told him.

"It was easier to just head east for land than to try to figure my path to Hispania at night," explained Perseus.

Hermes shrugged it off. "Your success has caused quite the stir on Olympus. Our father, Zeus, is proud of you, brother. Poseidon, on the other hand, is beside himself...but he's often beside himself, so take that as you will."

Perseus set aside the scythe and retrieved the Helm of Darkness. "You've come for this?"

Hermes strode over to the boy-man and took the power object, hiding it away under the cloth thrown over his shoulder. "Your way home is simplest this way: head straight east and you will arrive as the northern shore of Africa, near Libya. Follow the coast past Aethiopia, then along the curve north to the lands of Troy. There you should be able to gain passage to Serifos, or fly there with some direction. It will take a few days, but you will have places to stop for food and water along the way. In Libya you will be safest; they are adherents of the third born, Athena. You will be safe until Troy."

"After that?" Perseus inquired.

Hermes cocked his head to the side, "You know the prophecy. You will go home and take your place in Argolis. How and when you do that is up to you, but when you bring that," the god nodded to the kibisis, "home to Serifos, soon everyone will know who you are and what you are."

"What is that?"

"A hero," Hermes intoned. "Do with that what you will."

"Will I see you again?" Perseus asked.

"You never really know," the Messenger chuckled. In a flash he was gone.

Perseus rested for a while longer, then launched himself northeast toward the Mediterranean. Where the kibisis had sat, a few drops of blood had fallen. The sands they mixed with wriggled and shifted, giving birth to poisonous snakes. All along his path, drops would fall from the sky and impregnate the ground, birthing serpents the whole way.

*****

Hermes arrived in the Underworld, but did not head straight to Hades gloomy palace. Instead, he dropped into existence in the Garden of the Hesperides, where he could make certain that the Helm would be returned to the God of the Dead. In the strangely lit, etherial forest, he could hear the rhythmic breathing of Ladon, the multi-headed serpent, saw dryads flitting between the trees, watching him. Waiting, glowing with inner energy, was his father's wife, Hera.

"Well?" she asked.

"I did as you asked. He'll fly round the bowl of the sea and eventually that will take him through the lands of the Phoenicians." Hermes responded, "The question is why?"

"You like a bit of drama, Hermes, and so do I," Hera said. "This should certainly be dramatic." She turned to retire, the dryads coming out of the woods to lead her away. Hermes sighed and trudged off toward Hades' stronghold.

9. A SLIP OF THE TONGUE
She certainly hadn't meant to offend a god. She hadn't even mentioned a god.

The symposium had been an enjoyable affair, celebrating the betrothal of her young daughter Andromeda to Phineas, the monarch in the faraway Bosphorous. Phineas was one of the brothers of her husband, Cepheus, returned from a long time away in the north. She could see the scene in her mind's eye, the gathering of the wealthy and influential of the town, and Phineas and his crew of sailors. Cassiopeia, herself, was looking resplendent in her purple *stola* -- the product of the murex that was fished up by the people of town. Andromeda had been present, as well, still in white to represent her virginity, with purple edging to her dress. There was wine, food, and laughter, and even Andromeda, who had been determined to ruin the evening with her protestations over her impending marriage got into the spirit of the event.

Her husband had inquired after his brothers still scattered, and Phineas had related, "As you know brother, but perhaps the rest do not, yourself, myself, and our brothers, Cadmus, Cilix, Phoenix, and Thasus were dispatched by our father, the ruler of Aethopia, the great Agenor..."

"May he reside with the heroes of Elysium!" cried Cepheus.

"Yes, truth!" Phineas responded, "Agenor sent us to find our sister Europa, who had been abducted. The stories of her kidnapping were wild affairs, hard to credit: some said she had been carried off by a gigantic white bull, others say she was swept away and rode a wave out to sea and away. No matter the story, however, it was obvious that the gods were involved.

"We set out in different directions, hoping to find our lost sister, but alas! None of us was to succeed. In accordance with our sire's proclamation that we should not return until she had been found, we remained in various places, establishing our kingdoms. We all have known the fate of the great Cepheus -- came to finally rule here in Tyre over the wide-sailing Phoenicians. For the rest of us, our brother Thasus stopped his search on an island in the Aegean that now carries his name. Cadmus -- as we all know -- wandered as far as the oracle at Delphi, then settled with Harmonia in Boeotia, building the great city of Thebes. Cilix and I wandered far to the north, where I created my kingdom on the straits of the Bosporus, and Cilix went further east. Phoenix, that unfortunate that so offended our father by seducing his concubine Clytia, he escaped punishment by fleeing to Thessaly and King Peleus. It is said he rules a city for Peleus, Dolopes."

"Europa was never found?" Andromeda had asked. Her voice was already turning a sultry mezzo-soprano, and her fine features were dominated by deep gray, almost black eyes, and thick, curly black hair with just a hint of red to it. When Phineas turned his attention to her, she colored up and looked away. In a few days, she would be his wife. She knew what would be expected of her.

"I have not seen her, but I understand that a woman much like her was taken by a great white bull to the isle of Crete, but we all known that Cretans are not to be trusted," Phineas said. "They say that the bull was Zeus, himself, and that she has married Asterius, the king there. It is rumored she has children."

"More likely," Cepheus said, "is that the Minoans of Crete stole her themselves, and this bull story is simply that -- storytelling -- to avoid the responsibility of their actions."

Phineas had responded, "Although, had you seen our beloved Europa, you too would have thought her fine enough to catch the eye of a god. Yet, she paled in comparison to your fine Andromeda, brother!"

Cassiopeia then committed the mistake that would doom her city. Flush with wine and mirth, she bragged, "Yes, but I would dare to say that our daughter takes much of her beauty from myself, Phineas!"

"Verily!" agreed Phineas.

"It has been said," (and it hadn't,) "that Andromeda and myself are the rivals of the nereids for our beauty."

Some at the party had heartily agreed, but a few of the guests had realized the gravity of her statement. Soon enough, so would all of Tyre.

The first hint of the sea god's anger was a short and violent earthquake early that morning which woke much of the town. Buildings shifted, streets buckled, and the animals were frenzied with fear. Cepheus and Phineas took some of the men out to look for injured, and in the dim light of pre-dawn they saw the next strike in the sea's arsenal. The tide flowed out, much further than they had seen, leaving fishing boats far inland, the water racing out leagues out from the town. Then it came, a solid wall of water swept ashore, dashing boats from the moorings and throwing them ashore. The stone surge wall was no match, and the ocean crashed over it without stopping. Whole buildings were dashed apart, washed inward, with their inhabitants still inside and none the wiser for the events. Stone buildings withstood the onslaught, but many drowned before they could run for higher ground or climb onto their roofs. Others were fetched up into trees and clung there, praying for mercy.

Cepheus was one of these. He and several of his soldiers saw the wash of gray coming their way and ran from it. The water picked them up and rushed them through the streets. Cepheus was run into an olive tree, and he climbed above the flow, holding on for dear life and quietly thanking Athena for the olive tree. The water then subsided, pulling back into the sea, leaving Tyre sodden, and much of it broken. With nowhere to turn for aid, the people began to turn up at the royal palace, seeking shelter and food.

Having escaped death, Cepheus and Phineas -- who related his escape by a wild jump to catch the hands of a sailor who was taking shelter on the roof of one of the sturdy old stone homes -- began to organize an effort to get people water and food, and find them some kind of shelter. Those without homes, he could do little for in the short term. Even homes that survived the wrath of the sea were damaged, water-logged, and unhealthy. Phineas suggested sending as many as could move out of town into the hills to find shelter, but Cepheus was determined to find a way to look empowered in the wake of the disaster. Cassiopeia and Andromeda leant aid to those they could. The ocean meanwhile had continued to froth and rage against the seawall, rattling the town over and over. *What had been done*, some wondered, *to anger Poseidon so?*

To find the answer, Cassiopeia had tramped through the cracked and muddy streets of her city to the Temple of Apollo, where lived the Oracle of that god. Only the Temple had been spared the battering of the ocean on its small hill overlooking the harbor. The oracle was a thin thing, her body eaten at by the strain of receiving messages from the Olympians. At the sight of the queen, her eyes grew wide and she pointed accusingly at Cassiopeia, "For the unwise, a word is as deadly as a dagger! The father of those you so brazenly compared yourself to is enraged, and he sends Poseidon to punish us all for your hubris!"

"What?" Cassiopeia said, looking surprised. Her mind's eye wandered back to the night before, the boast. "I meant no offense! I said nothing of offense!"

"Nereus prizes his daughters' beauty as you do," the oracle intoned, "and he will have a price for your insolence..."

Stunned, panic rising in her, Cassiopeia cried, "I have brought this to Tyre? What price? What price can I pay to placate the gods and save our city? Anything!"

The oracle's face twisted into a grimace of angry glee; she was channeling the words of the gods. "You will give that which you valued above the nereids..."

"No!" gasped Cassiopeia.

"...you will take your daughter, Andromeda -- that you judge fine enough to catch the eye of a god -- and you will put her out on the rock as contrition."

Cassiopeia had fled the temple, pushing past other townsfolk who were in the main audience chamber, begging Apollo to intercede on their behalf. "No!"

That evening, as Cassiopeia sequestered herself and Andromeda in the womens' quarters, refusing to meet with her husband or his brother, Poseidon's next penalty was rendered. Men that had been piecing through the wreckage of the proud Phoenician merchant fleet noted the ocean had risen dangerously close to the edge of the seawall. Before they could react, a massive fluke, prehensile and whip-quick lashed out of the water, snatching several into the sea. Silhouetted by the setting sun, the creature breeched the water, its breath launching brine into the air. The massive head and maw that evoked the fish or whale, the sinuous body that suggested a serpent, were of stunning proportion.

Every sailor knew what they were looking at. Many painted a maw and eyes to capture the strength of the beast, to let Poseidon know that their ship was not afraid of the sea. The monster was Cetus -- ancient, dangerous, and the mother of Ladon, the guardian of the Gardens of the Hesperides. The survivors fled from the shore to the palace, where once admitted, they related the incident to Cepheus. He was staggered by the implications. Like the town's sailors, he knew that Cetus was a cudgel that could only be wielded by Poseidon, one of their patrons and second only in their heart to Apollo.

Cepheus and members of the town raced to the Temple of Apollo, and there confronted the oracle. *What had been done to anger the Sea God?* they wailed, *And what could be done to assuage his anger?* Again the oracle related the offense to Nereus and his daughters, who had in turn complained to Poseidon (already in a foul disposition from the loss of Medusa, the abortive fight with Athena, and a host of other minor nuisances), who in turn lashed out at Tyre and sent Cetus to deliver sentence on the people for Cassiopeia's impertinent remark. The town would suffer from Cetus, their ships destroyed, their people devoured. For a nation built on the sea and trade with distant islands and lands, it was tantamount to death. There was only one solution the oracle offered: Andromeda was to be left on the rock in the harbor as a sacrifice. Nothing else would do.

Cepheus was horrified by the news and had shouted down the oracle. Phineas joined him in his abuse of prophecy, but the Phoenicians crowded the brothers, harassing and threatening them with violence. The king was dragged, along with Phineas, to the palace. Once there, they had spilled through the place, searching until they found Cassiopeia and Andromeda.

Cassiopeia set herself before her terrified daughter and glared at the simple men who had only yesterday been proud and happy to call Cepheus and Cassiopeia their rulers, and loudly declared that they would have to retire from their apartments.

"Cetus will destroy us!" they shouted. "She will kill our people and destroy our boats! She will keep us from the sea and the trade that feeds our children!"

"She will not!" Cassiopeia said tearfully. "For tomorrow, my daughter will save us all."

The crowd was stunned into silence. Andromeda quietly asked, "I'm going to what?"

Cepheus pushed through the sailors and merchants who now stood dumbfounded and embarrassed by the determination in the face of Cassiopeia, and the look of grief and fear in that of Andromeda. He knelt next to Andromeda and Cassiopeia. "For our people to survive, we must give propitiation... Poseidon has demanded your life."

"What!?! Why?" Andromeda cried.

Cepheus glared at his wife, "Your mother insulted the daughters of the god Nereus. Poseidon is punishing us for her hubris. As you were compared favorably..."

"This is not my fault!" Andromeda jumped to her feet, fists clenched. She turned on her mother, "Oh, you had to preen, didn't you, mother? Look how beautiful I am...look how much my daughter looks like me. Are you happy, now? Now that I'm to be food for some...creature!"

The people of Tyre gasped at the impertinence, and the anger their young princess was showing. Cassiopeia drew herself up. "I said nothing that was not the truth, daughter. I would gladly trade my life for yours," she lied, "but my punishment will be just as great, for my love of you."

Andromeda looked on her mother, shocked by her lack of comprehension. If she had heard right, hadn't Cassiopeia *yet again* made the statement that had caused this calamity to befall Tyre? The ground under the city seemed to agree, shifting fitfully, but not enough to drive them from their feet or damage the building. Her mother's pride, her vanity, would kill them all...unless Andromeda stood between the gods themselves and her town. "I hope your vanity will overcome your guilt and grief, for your sake, mother," Andromeda spat.

A collective gasp went up from the crowd, and Cassiopeia reacted by slapping her daughter, once, across the face. Cepheus interceded, instructing Phineas to take his daughter from the room. Cassiopeia had regretted her statements, her actions, almost immediately. Boastfulness had always been a flaw of Cassiopeia, but her normally sparkling personality and beauty worked to mitigate the consequences. Now, it would cost her Andromeda and the large bride price that Phineas was to pay.

Cepheus shot his wife a warning look, and announced, "Tomorrow, at dawn, we will satisfy the wishes of the gods!"

That morning, the parents found Andromeda dressed simply in a white stola, barefoot, her hair down. Her dark eyes were bloodshot from crying, but she stood proud and undaunted when the door was opened. "I'm ready," she told them. Cepheus nearly burst into tear with pride, and Cassiopeia hugged her reluctant daughter to her, weeping.

They paraded through the ruined town, Andromeda flanked by Cepheus and Phineas, Cassiopeia and other attendants following behind. The townspeople watched the procession solemnly, and the queen heard someone quip that it should be the mother going up on the rock, not the daughter. At the sea wall, a small boat was made ready. It had been salvaged from the wreckage of the port that had swept up into the town. In the boat was a hammer, the chains and manacles that would fix his daughter to the rock. At the site of them, he thought Andromeda would lose her will, but she rallied and stepped in without having to be forced. Cepheus rowed his daughter out, himself; no man was willing to risk death on route to the rock that rose out of the harbor like a jagged tooth.

There Cepheus hugged and kissed his daughter one last time, then took her stola, leaving her naked and trembling on the rock. He quickly locked the manacles and ran the chain from them to the rock, battering in the pin that would hold her fast. He could feel his heart breaking, and almost knocked the pin loose to release her and escape. He steadied himself, and jumping into the boat, rowing furiously for the shore and watching for signs of Cetus. Already, they could hear the strangely sweet high-pitched tones of the creature, could see it breaching the surface out to sea. Back ashore, the royal parents and the people of the town stood silently, watching for the sea to take the beautiful Andromeda.

Cassiopeia started to say something.

"You will not speak," Cepheus said through gritted teeth. "You will say nothing or I will put you out there, as well."

Cassiopeia lamented the violent and unfair nature of the gods silently.

Out to sea, Cetus' head broke the water and scanned the town, the rock, then arched back into the water, the incredible length of its body rolling along the surface. Vast, old, and hungry, Cetus was coming for Andromeda, and there was nothing that he could do to save his daughter.

Then their salvation dropped from the sky.

*****

Perseus had been traveling for days, stopping here and there. Ever since that first night in the oasis following his fight with Medusa -- if it could have been called a fight -- Perseus had felt an increasing sense of urgency and dread for his mother. It had been almost a fortnight he was gone on his quest, and he wondered what mischief King Polydectes might have gotten up to regarding his mother. He doubted that Dictys would break faith with his brother and challenge him over his advances. The only person on Serifos that would face Polydectes down was Perseus. Before this mission, Perseus thought, he would not have had the courage to confront the man. He flew as fast as his wind and sunburned skin could withstand, stopping only for food and rest.

His arrival shocked the residents of several towns. He would drop from the sky like a meteor, announcing himself and his lineage, the nature of his quest. Every time he told it, he elaborated here, cut there, and the story improved. Hermes would be proud of the tale, he hoped. In Chemmis, he so impressed the monarch there that they had offered to have him stay with the family for a time. It was also the first time he had been challenged to show Medusa's head. He had refused, citing the danger, but in the end, he rigged a series of mirrors so that the king could see the remains. When pulled from the kibisis, the head's jaw was slack, the eyes black and lifeless, but once the head was in the open, the eyes glared, the snakes topping her head moved sluggishly, fitfully. The malicious magic that kept her animate made his skin crawl.

After a day's hospitality, Perseus started the next leg of his trip, flying along the coastline of Phoenicia. He recognized Tyre from descriptions of merchants that passed through Serifos -- the sprawl of buildings, the temple on the hill, the jagged rock in the harbor. What he didn't see were the ships at port on staked on the shore. There was wreckage strewn through the town, boats barely identifiable as such mingled with the ruins of wooden structures. He dropped lower for a better view. People were massed on the along the seawall. Perseus followed their seaward gaze and spotted the thing under the water -- a gargantuan, sinuous thing with a whale's head, a serpent's body, long fins pushing it through the water toward the town.

On a jutting rock in the center of the bay that formed the harbor, he could see a tall girl, just turned a woman. She was beautiful and shapely with small, pert breasts; black curls catching the wind. She was standing proud and naked, afraid but undaunted. He could see the length of chain that held her to the rock. The monster was moments away, doing a slow circuit around the rock, its head now out of the water, the deep, lifeless eyes gazing on the sacrifice. Perseus felt a shock of emotion. More than lust (although there was plenty of that), more than pity, he looked at the girl and saw a kindred spirit -- strong and brave, and a pawn of forces larger than her. He dove down on the crowd.

No one had thought to look up. All eyes were fixed on Cetus and Andromeda. The first person to notice Perseus called out in surprise and he pointed up. All heads tilted skyward to see the young man, naked save for a shield, swordbelt, and bundle over his shoulder come out of the sky, winged sandals furiously beating the air. He landed on the stone seawall.

"What is going on here?" he demanded of the stunned crowd.

Phineas challenged him, "Who wants to know?"

"I am Perseus, grandson of Acricius of Argolis, son of Zeus, and slayer of Medusa!" Perseus shouted. "I was flying past," he smiled at that, "and saw a vision of such beauty as I have never encountered on that rock." *He was getting good at this*, he told himself.

"That is Andromeda, my daughter," Cepheus told him. "Poseidon has deemed that she must be sacrificed, or Cetus will kill our people, take our ships and crews. The lord of the sea has already struck us with earthquakes and a deadly wave of water. We have no choice."

"You do," Perseus said, "I will save your daughter and destroy Cetus, and that will be an end of it!" Perseus was not at all certain that Poseidon wouldn't simply cough up another monster from the deep to terrorize Tyre, but he already had a plan. "All I ask is for Andromeda in marriage."

"She is already betrothed and the price given," countered Cassiopeia.

"Betrothed to me," Phineas told him haughtily.

Perseus regarded the older man, then fixed his gaze on Cepheus. "Your daughter lives, Cetus dies, and your town is safe. My price is I leave here with her as my wife. But choose quickly..."

Cepheus and the rest of his party turned to look at the monster. It had finished its turn around the rock -- they could see its tail knock a massive gout of water over the rock, showering Andromeda with spray. Her shriek of terror could be plainly heard across the water. It was answered by the roar of Cetus. The creature's head, then a length of her body rose out of the water, rising as high as a mast over the girl, its scaly body catching the early morning light and gleaning iridescently.

"I agree!" Cepheus panicked, shouted.

In an instant, Perseus threw himself across the water, drawing the scythe and racing in at the monster. As he reached the rock, Perseus climbed, arcing over Andromeda and straight into Cetus' line of sight. The creature flinched to see the small man suddenly leap into view, flying straight at the monster's maw. Cetus lunged forward to bite him, but lost him in the sun, and Perseus turned hard, dodging the snapping teeth that were each as tall as he was. Cetus turned to follow, her body slithering a circle to in the water, her fluke slashing out to smash him into the water.

Only just was Perseus able to dip under the fluke, and he leaned back, the sandals snapping him to a stop them climbing backward. He pivoted hard and was facing Cetus. Her head blotted out the red-golden morning sun, and was coming around toward him, jaws opening. The fluke that had missed him was coming back up, exploding out of the water toward him. Perseus stopped cold, hovering and with both hands struck at the fluke. The gleaming blade slipped through the flesh of the creature like a knife filleting a fish. Blood rained into the sea.

Cetus bellowed, the blast of her cry knocking Perseus end over end and sending him toward the surface of the water. She pursued, her mouth rushing toward him. Perseus righted himself and dashed under the mouth, slashing up with the scythe and cutting along the tissue under the mouth. Cetus plowed into the sea, water exploding up and around Perseus. The creature's body slid past him, glistening rainbow colors with water, and plunging into the deep.

The crowd at the water's edge burst into cheers. Perseus, soaked and biting back terror, landed next to Andromeda. He dropped his bundle, shifted the shield to his arm, the sun shining blindingly off of the metal. Behind him, Cetus blasted out of the water, looking about for him, and fixed her attention on the rock. It was advancing quickly. "Get low and stay put. Whatever you do, do not try to swim for the town," Perseus told her. With a single stroke, he knocked the pin from the chains, releasing her from the rock's grasp. "Just stay on the lee of the rock from the beast."

She nodded and dove out of sight, hugging the rock, and Perseus wheeled to face the sea monster. Cetus was coming on fast, and Perseus waited until the last moment, then rocketed into the air as Cetus made to devour him. Jaws slammed down on rock, shattered stone and threw splinters of it into the air. Cetus rolled and lashed out with her fin, nearly disemboweling Perseus. He got the shield in the path of the next strike, absorbed the impact that knocked him out to sea. He hit the water hard, the breath knocked out of him, but the sandals pulled him up into the air.

Cetus was coming again.

Perseus set his shield in front of him, shifting it so that the spot of reflected light from its surface ran over the monster's eyes. It charged and bit down, but Perseus has slipped to the side, using the shield to bedazzle and confuse Cetus. He struck, thrusting the scythe into the beast's eye. Cetus reared up, and the force of her sudden movement sent Perseus high into the air, humors spraying across his shield and body. It was blinded to the right, and he kept moving to keep himself out of sight. Cetus howled in fury and pain, the cries -- Perseus could swear -- almost making words.

He had moved in toward the creature, above the flailing fins, in the angle of her sightlessness, closing for another strike. As if guessing his intent, Cetus suddenly dropped to the ocean, splashing through the surface and casting foaming spray everywhere. She had struck the bottom of the bay, and Perseus could see her stirring the muck up. Then he couldn't see her anymore. He slipped sideways, returning to the rock quickly. His scythe was injuring it, but unless he found a vulnerable spot, it would be like a single bee trying to sting a man to death. They would be at it all day and Perseus, panting heavily, doubted his endurance would hold much longer.

Landing on the rock, Perseus shouted, "Andromeda, whatever happens, whatever you hear, keep your eyes closed! Do you understand?"

"Who are you?" she demanded.

"Perseus, son of Zeus, Lord of the Skies, and Danae of Argolis, raised by the brother of the Dictys of Serifos, and slayer of the feared Medusa!" The water around the rock was thrashing, foaming and filled with silt from Cetus.

"Clever thing," Perseus said to himself.

"Why are you here?" she insisted.

"I am going to kill this thing, and then I'm going to

marry you."

Andromeda raised her head and stared at him, "What!?!"

"I asked your father to have you as my wife, and in exchange I would save you and your city." Perseus said, watching for Cetus' head. "That is, if I survive. The beast is proving a bit of a challenge."

Andromeda looked at him incredulously. "Do you just go around saving towns and maidens you don't know?"

"I do," he said, risking a moment's glance toward her. He hoped he looked confident and handsome.

Cetus surfaced fast, coming in low, like a dart. Her mouth was closed this time and she scuffed across the top of the rock, plowing into Perseus and carrying him off of the rock. The impact was mostly absorbed by the shield, but his left arm was completely numb from the shock and his right...was empty. Perseus slid over Cetus' head, and suddenly was punched in the chest by the exhalation through her blowhole. He sailed into the air, tumbling and dazed, the sandals temporarily useless as he nearly lost consciousness.

Andromeda ducked, clung to the rock as directly above her the beast slid past, endlessly, it seemed. Then Cetus was gone and when she looked over the crest of the stone, so was Perseus. Only his scythe remained, jammed in a small break in the rock. She scrambled up and snatched it from the stone, holding it clumsily in both hands and casting around for a sign of the boy or the monster. Around the rock, the sea was thrashed by the creature and the water was too murky to make out anything.

Perseus' head burst from the water, coughing. He was gasping for breath, spewing seawater, and then slowly rose out of the water. He looked dazed, and he held the shield low, like he was too tired to loft it. He was winging toward her and landed heavily on the rock, dropping to a knee. Gasping, he pulled the bulky leather bag from his side loose. "Get down," he said breathily, "and whatever you do, *keep your eyes closed* if you don't want to die."

Andromeda considered this quickly: He was flying about on winged sandals. He was fighting a thing vastly more powerful than he. He was going to be her husband. She ducked her head and closed her eyes. Perseus dropped the kibisis on the top of the rock and reached in, and was greeted with shifting snakes. He grasped one.

Cetus reared up in front of him, raining spray on the rock. She had her head cocked slightly to find him with her intact eye. Perseus shifted his head, using the shield as a mirror and lofted Medusa's head.

The monster paused. He could see the look of confusion on her face as her eye glazed over. Slowly, inexorably, the effect spread out from her eye. Her body was thrashing, but her jaw had locked half-open, the teeth and skin turned to stone, now her head. Quicker now, the body ossified, cracking here and there under its weight. Cetus toppled into the water, her tail smacking the ocean a few times before it, too, turned to stone.

Perseus, using his shield to see, put Medusa's head back in the kibisis. He could see in the reflection her beautiful face, slack in death, but the hateful blue eyes rolled in her head and fixed him with a look of utter contempt. The bag closed, Perseus sat heavily next to a soggy Andromeda. "You can look now."

She glanced about. "Cetus?"

"Dead," he sounded surprised, "I honestly didn't think that would work."

"What would work?"

"I scared it to death," he joked. He hefted the leather wallet. "I used Medusa to petrify the thing."

"Medusa? The Gorgon?" She sat upright and he examined the manacles, then used the scythe to carefully pry them open.

He acknowledged, "The same."

"Who are you again?"

"Perseus." He looked her in the eye, his light green-gray eyes lit up with pride. She was stunningly beautiful and Perseus found his spirits soaring.

"I think I love you," she told him. She knew it was just the gratitude speaking, but she was surprised at his reaction. He colored up like a boy, he became erect like a man.

She covered her mouth to hide her smile and looked away. The boat was coming out for them, she could see. Her father and one-time fiance were waving to her.

10. A HERO'S WEDDING

Once ashore, surrounded by revelers, Perseus turned Andromeda over to her father and told him that he would come to their palace momentarily. Then pushing through the throng of well-wishers, the boy-hero surprised Cepheus and the others yet again. He began using bits of the shattered boats, a bit of spar here, a bit of rope there, to build three simple, haphazard altars. Asking the townsfolk to provide elements for the offerings, he first burned a votive to Hermes -- thanking him for the gifts that had made him successful in his labors; the next was to "his divine sister" Athena for putting him on his heroic path and giving him the wisdom to succeed; the last and largest was to his father, Zeus, to whom he thanked for his birth, for those gods watching over him, and asked him for the courage, strength, and sagacity to do the right thing when he reached home in Serifos...and after that, when he returned to Argos.

    He meant every word of it, but with a relieved population of people around him, it was a brilliant bit of political theater, as well. Having sent Andromeda home with Cassiopeia, Cepheus watched the display from and distance, with a glowering Phineas by his side. "This upstart arrives from the sky," growled the brother, "and deprives me of my right!"

    "It is the will of the gods," Cepheus replied with typical Phoenician resignation. "We have already suffered from my wife's hubris at their hands. I cannot risk angering yet more of the Olympians."

    "It is not right! I paid the bride price!" asserted Phineas, "It is a breach of hospitality."

    It was a good thrust. Phoenician society, like the desert people inland, like his father's people of Aethiopia, revolved around notions of hospitality. A traveler was to be given support and respite. Like the desert nomads, sailors understood that a helping hand to another could mean that when misfortune struck, you could rely on a return of that generosity. "He saved my city," Cepheus spat back, keeping his voice down to avoid the people noting their argument. "He saved my daughter. What would you suggest? Renege on the deal made? Chase him from the city? Kill him? What kind of hospitality would that be, brother?"

They watched the last of the fires burst into the sky as Perseus gave thanks to Zeus. The townspeople...*his* townspeople, Cepheus thought, followed suit turned eyes and arms skyward to praise the lord of the skies for sending his son to rescue them. "He's dangerous," Phineas opined.

"He is, at that," agreed Cepheus. "But it is what it is..." The king moved off, heading for home, his brother and a few of his retinue in tow.

*****

Cassiopeia was beside herself. The marriage had been arranged to a king...not some boy with magic sandals and a monster's head in a bag. A real monarch, which between their families, would allow them to bracket the much larger and more powerful kingdom of Troy. It was a match that would lead to an alliance that could keep them safe against other, more hostile forces in the region. It would bring in -- had brought in -- riches to buy Andromeda for Phineas. A dowry that would enrich Cassiopeia's life. Now her husband would give all that back to marry their daughter off to this boy for the grand price of *nothing*. This hero, this...who was he, anyway!?! He claimed to be the son of a god, and despite seeing him fly, despite seeing him best the sea monster Cetus, despite all that, Cassiopeia doubted Perseus' lineage. A god's son would surely be rich, wouldn't he? Could pay a bride price, couldn't he?

"The wedding must be right away," said Andromeda.

"It is more complicated than that, daughter," Cassiopeia told her.

Andromeda countered, "It is not. Not more than an hour ago you and father had me chained and offered up as a sacrifice to correct your actions. You were going to let that thing *eat me!*" she shrieked.

"What were we to do, daughter? Let Poseidon destroy all we had built?" Cassiopeia shouted, "Are you that selfish that you would put yourself before our people?"

"I know I would not compare myself favorably to gods and their children," retorted Andromeda. "Were you thinking of the people when you angered the gods? Or were you thinking of yourself?"

For the second time in a day, Cassiopeia raised her hand to her daughter...but this time Andromeda did not budge, did not flinch, but instead curled her lip in derision. "Go ahead. Strike me. I suspect my future husband, the monster killer, would have little trouble with you."

"You are disrespectful!"

"You are a boastful fool who would rather see me dead that your precious dowry returned."

Cassiopeia reeled from the retort as only the truly self-deluded can. "I have thought of nothing but your best interests. Phineas is a king! He will give you a secure throne, power, and it will strengthen the whole family. Can't you think about all of us, rather than yourself?"

"Perseus will be a king, and soon...and he fought for me without even knowing who I was! Where was my father? Where was my mother?" Andromeda leaned in toward Cassiopeia, trembling with rage. "Where was Phineas? On the wharf, waiting for the spectacle of my death!"

Cassiopeia recoiled at the last and Andromeda pressed home her will, "Once I am ready, once Perseus has made the arrangements with father, we marry and I will leave this hateful place with him. After that, your next indiscretion will leave you with no one to sacrifice for your pride."

Cassiopeia, never at a loss for words, began to rebut. Andromeda waved her off and turned to her dressing table to make herself presentable. "Leave me, mother. I was dead to you an hour ago, let us leave it that way."

The queen staggered from her daughter's room and stood outside the door, shocked senseless. One of her attendants waited for her to recover, then took her hand and steadied her, guiding her to her own chambers. Without waiting for permission, the maid whispered, "You were right, my queen, to chastise the girl."

"It is not your place to comment," Cassiopeia told her absently.

The servant shrugged, "This is true. This Perseus defied the will of Poseidon, great queen; he prevented justice being done."

"What justice?" Cassiopeia demanded.

"The insult to the Nereids -- however unintended -- was a slight to the Old Man of the Sea," she said, using the description reserved for Nereus. Cassiopeia found it odd that a desert girl, a slave, would have such an insight on the matter.

"I only sought to warm my brother-in-law to her, not insult the gods..."

"Of course, but by slaughtering one of Poseidon's children, Perseus might have brought more harm to us, might he not?"

Cassiopeia stopped short, eyes wide. "Of course! The sacrifice was not completed...Poseidon may yet punish us!"

The maid countered, "But surely, if this slayer of his child, of his beloved Medusa, were himself offered up to the Sea God, that would set things right. Kill the boy and offer his body and the head of Medusa to Poseidon to balance the ledgers..."

Cassiopeia looked on her servant with surprise and backed away from her, terror starting to grip her. The maid rarely said a word, but now was pouring forth the most extraordinary, most truthful ideas. The queen bowed her head to the servant and raced away.

How disappointing, Poseidon thought, *I thought that was rather a good performance, myself.* The maid collapsed to the floor as a puddle of seawater.

Poseidon, relieved of his disguise, flashed away to Olympus. There, in one of the many shaded gardens, away from man, away from nymph and satyr, away from the other gods, Poseidon strolled through the green, pacing a circle until the other he was meeting arrived.

"He bested Cetus. That was not what I was expecting," Hera said.

"I suppose not," Poseidon replied. "You sent him through Phoenicia knowing he would be there when Cetus was...how?"

"That's not important," Hera told him. "Why is. That upstart, that monstrosity that leapt into our company from my *esteemed*, " -- the word dripped with contempt -- "husband's head has gone to war with you, but it is a second-hand war, a war of proxies."

"That is the way our brother wants it, Hera," Poseidon said softly. He had a soft spot for the vitriolic, scheming queen of the gods, but unlike his brother, with Poseidon it was not an incestuous friendship. He would never truly trust Hera, but they were allies -- joined by their hatred of Athena and their disappointment in Zeus.

"I thought Cetus would kill Perseus easily," she said. "I would not have put them together, had I thought otherwise."

"Yes, you would," Poseidon chuckled. Even when mirthful, he sounded angry. "And yes, I would have expected Cetus to kill the boy. However, the matter is closed. Cepheus and Cassiopeia did as I instructed through their oracle: they put Andromeda out to die. The nymphs of the sea can be quiet about Cassiopeia's boast; I do not care to hear more. And if she does as I have hinted and kill the boy, I will have my revenge for Cetus and Medusa. Zeus will be none the wiser and Athena's pet will be taken off of the playing field."

Hera smiled sweetly. Perhaps this would still work out as she intended. "She will suspect we had a hand in it. Cepheus is not a bloodthirsty man."

"But his wife and brother are," Poseidon reminded her. "No matter what Athena suspects, the simple truth is that men kill men all the time, with or without our goading. The matter will end there"

*****

The home of King Cepheus showed signs of damage from the earthquake, but the wave of water that had slammed his town had not reached to the hill on which he lived. Perseus lounged on a couch across from his father-in-law to be, his body aching from the stresses of his battle with Cetus, and retold the story of his quest from his watery would-be grave as a child to his assassination of Medusa. It was a fight not to show how insanely proud of himself he was. Perseus was hoping he was projecting a casual air, but suspected he was coming across as a prideful, silly boy.

The truth was closer to the first. Cepheus could tell the fight had left the young hero tired, shaken, but full of himself. Still, the courage he had showed rescuing Andromeda, and his current attempted humility, impressed the king. Cepheus doubted he would show as much restraint, had he fought and bested the creature. As much as he wanted to honor the promise of betrothal to his brother, to tie their houses back together, he privately thought that Perseus would make a good husband, and eventually a good ruler. He glanced at his brother. Phineas stewed in a corner, his eyes fixed hatefully on the boy-hero.

"It is a good tale, young Perseus," Cepheus said, "and one worthy of a husband to my daughter."

They were all waiting for Cassiopeia and Andromeda to arrive, so that the wedding could be conducted. Perseus asked, "And the ship will be ready to take us to Serifos tomorrow?"

"It is one of the few vessels that is seaworthy after Poseidon's assault on us," Cepheus reminded him, "but it will be ready, as you request. Now I suspect you would like to make yourself more presentable for your wedding. Water for your bath has been set aside, and I have provided suitable clothing for you."

Perseus thanked him and rose stiffly. His left arm was still numb and he had to concentrate to make his hand work. His ribs on his left side spiked pain through him at every breath. Medusa had required finesse, cunning, and speed; it had been little more than murder. Cetus had require strength and courage he hadn't known he'd had, and in the end it was his wits that had kept him alive. It had been a real fight.

The slave led him out to his bath where two female slaves waited to wash him. He gathered his equipment in a corner, hiding the kibisis under his bundle, and behind his shield. He sat in the tub, facing the gear to make sure that it remained unmolested. The brine of the sea was sluiced away, and the women rubbed fragrant oil into his skin, massaging muscle. Cleaned and smelling fresh, he donned the short chiton that fastened over the left shoulder and cloak provided, put on his swortbelt with the scythe, tied the kibisis to it, then threw the shield over his shoulder. They led him out into the gardens of the house, where the town elders, refugees from Poseidon's attack, as well as Phineas and his men were gathered. Somehow, musicians had been secured and they were merrily playing away, while fortifying wine was being poured into jugs for distribution among the guests. Sheep were being driven into the gardens and sequestered near where a firepit was being stoked into life. A few of the guests were already dancing in fits and starts to the music.

At his arrival some of the guests gave a cheer. Phineas and his group glowered and Perseus noted Cassiopeia talking in hushed tones with the man. Cepheus was conducting the last minute preparations for the ceremony. Andromeda's childhood clothing and toys were being gathered near the hastily constructed altar where they would be burned in offering to Artemis, Hera, and Aphrodite. Perseus knew that Andromeda would have, like him, been bathed -- her by children to purify her for the moment -- and would have been dressed for the occasion. That her mother was not part of this process was another warning sign to Perseus...

The trouble started as soon as Cassiopeia saw him. She thrust a finger out toward him and cried, "What have you done?" This caught the attention of the revelers and they turned, stunned to see what was happening. Cepheus was warned and was pushing through the crowd already.

Cassiopeia ranted, "What have you done to us!?! You have killed a child of Poseidon, the god that sought to punish us, and now his rage will be doubled!"

"That's right!" Phineas agreed and he motioned for his crew to lend support. Shouts of derision rose. "Perseus has doomed the city unless this outrage is righted!"

"This assassin has wronged the Sea God: he has killed his lover Medusa! He has slaughtered his daughter Cetus! We will be made to pay for your actions!" Cassiopeia implored the crowd. Some looked confused, others were easily won over by Cassiopeia's charisma, others started to rail at her for her lack of respect to their guest.

"Stop this at once!" Cepheus roared over the crowd.

"I saved this town!" Perseus shouted in response.

Phineas bellowed, "He has doomed this city. He has broken the bonds of hospitality between brothers, he has killed that sent to punish us! Perseus will lead us to our deaths!"

"This is not true," Cepheus whined.

"Perseus must die!" Cassiopeia cried, "The gods demand it!"

"We must obey the gods," Phineas agreed and he rushed forward with his men, toward Perseus. Some of the crowd threw themselves at the Thracians, trying to stop them, and the sailors fought back at them. Cepheus had grabbed a satisfied looking Cassiopeia by the arms and shook her roughly. Perseus couldn't hear what was said, and didn't bother to try.

He drew his scythe and blocked Phineas' sword strike, quickly dancing away from the sword and spear thrusts of his men. Perseus got his shield in front of him, stopping a few of the strikes and slashed desperately at one of the attackers, lopping his arm off. Phineas was back at him, jabbing rapidly and furiously with his sword. The blade could not even scratch the surface of the highly polished shield. Perseus ducked a thrust by a spear at his head, bobbing his head under the shield just in time and continuing to circle the cluster of Thracian sailors until he could gain himself some room to fight and keep them from flanking him.

Cepheus was calling on Phineas to stop, along with other guests. Some of the sailors were fighting the Phoenicians, keeping them from interceding on Perseus' behalf. Perseus sliced and stabbed, injuring several of the men. Blows rained down on the shield and his left arm was losing feeling again. A spear glanced off of his shoulder, cutting shallow; another tore the chiton across his chest but did not puncture skin.

There were too many. Even with those Thracians that had been distracted preventing the townspeople from coming to his aid, there were over a dozen more of them than he. Perseus was brave and strong, but he had not been raised a soldier...he was badly outmatched and knew it. He could see

Cepheus trying to break through the sailors' ranks to aid him, Cassiopeia trying to drag him back from the fray.

Perseus knew what he had to do, but there were too many here that meant him no harm. He broke away from Phineas at a run, drawing the sailors after him, away from the house guests and up into the audience chamber of the house. Phineas was swinging wildly, nowhere near striking the faster boy, but still dangerously close. His men chased after them into the audience chamber and Cepheus and Cassiopeia followed. The people of Tyre hesitated, then rushed for the house.

Perseus ran for the end of the room and the couches that lined the walls. As he ran, he dropped scythe and grabbed the kibisis, pulling the bag open by feel. He reached the far end of the room, cut off from escape by the mass of men behind him, between him and the door. Jumping onto the nearest couch, he laid his back against the wall of the room, raised the shield to protect his face, and pulled Medusa free. He heard gasps, screams, them he heard nothing save for a crackling sound. Keeping the shield between he and Medusa, Perseus peeped around the edge of the shield.

Phineas was stalled in mid-strike, his arm raised back for a tremendous thrust, legs still set in a run. Turned to stone, he toppled over. Others from his crew were frozen, ossified. He could see looks on their faces ranging from anger to surprise to terror. Some stood rooted to the ground like statues, others unbalanced and fell over. The room was filled with the stony dead. Near the back of the room, Cepehus had his hands thrown up, trying to quell the revolt. Cassiopeia stood beside him, her face still smug in the knowledge that Perseus would soon be dead and Andromeda's dowry secure. He could hear townspeople gasping at the sight and he lowered Medusa to prevent the unwary Phoenicians from suffering the fate of the Thracian sailors. Using the shield to see what he was doing, he replaced Medusa in the kibisis. In the reflection, her beautiful face glared at him reproachfully.

"Gods, what has happened!" came a cry. Beyond the field standing and felled once-living statuary, Perseus could see Andromeda. He jumped off of the couch, recovered his scythe and stepped through the ranks of his immobile pursuers. He found Andromeda, surrounded by her people, standing in front of her parents. Near tears, she fought to remain stoic. To her mother, she said, "Now you will remain as beautiful as you ever were." At the sight of him, he could see the conflicting emotions -- anger fighting relief, love fighting hate -- and she fell into his arms, sobbing.

Perseus held her and reflected on the attack. Every leader he had met was filled with perfidy and pride. His grandfather had put his mother and him to sea, intending to kill them to protect himself and his throne. Polydectes assumed the people reigned over were his property, had tried to use his authority to coerce Perseus' mother into his bed, just as his divine father had used his power to seduce his mother. Cassiopeia had nearly destroyed her town in her pride, and had attempted to abuse her right of rule by reneging on their deal and breaking the bonds of hospitality. Even he, Perseus, had misused his influence -- forcing a marriage out of Cepheus in his grief and fear. Power turned a person's mind as surely as wealth or pride. He determined to use caution when it came to its allure. He would do better; he would be better.

Perseus and Andromeda led the rest of the wedding party, now quiet and shuffling, back into the garden. Perseus was shocked to see the number of Phineas' sailors that were injured or killed, lying outside. He had thought, at best, he had injured two or three, but there were nearly half a dozen dead or badly hurt, and just as many lightly injured. These were being guarded by the locals. He had them taken off to be dealt with later, then together he and Andromeda burned her childhood objects, singing praise to Artemis to assuage that goddess for her loss of another maiden, then to Hera in the promise that Andromeda would be a good and true spouse, then lastly to Aphrodite that she might be fruitful from their union.

Instead of a wedding feast, Perseus and Andromeda sat down with the town leaders. With their rulers decorating the palace hall, they were understandably upset and concern...who would rule here? As Cepheus' son-in-law, it was only reasonable that he should take over the role of sovereign here in Tyre, but Perseus cut off this line of argument. He had a kingdom of his own in Argos waiting, his rightful place. He had a pressing need to get to Serifos for reasons he would not explain to them, but would to Andromeda later that night. The town would have to choose among themselves who would lead them, but it would not be him. As for the remaining sailors from Phineas' ships, Perseus decided to follow Athena's example. The goddess would break any deadlock, it was said, by voting for the accused. He told the elders that, while the choice of what to do with them was their purview, he suggested that they be tended to and set free to return home as they could. They were following the orders of their commander and could hardly be held responsible for their actions.

After that, Perseus had the meal prepared and requested Andromeda oversee the food being served to the people of Tyre, while he took only a small amount for himself. With a small group of men, he cleared the palace audience hall of those that had meant him harm. There were dozens of them and Perseus tried to memorize their faces. He personally carried Cepheus and Cassiopeia from the house (with help) and the dead were clustered in a barn not far from the palace.

Later, with the wedding party dispersed, Perseus found the household staff working by candle and lamp light into the night packing up the house. Andromeda was in her childhood room. She was folding clothing, piling it with personal items into chests. When he entered, she paused, then sat on her bed. "I've taken my clothing and some of my mother's...same for some jewelry. I found the money and other presents that Phineas gave my parents..." She trailed off, looking at the boxes that surrounded her.

Perseus had been confronted with various challenges on his travels, but the weeping girl surrounded by the items and memories of her parents was the most befuddling. Tentatively, he advanced and sat beside her, took her into his arms.

"I was ready to be away with you this morning. Between my mother's having brought the wrath of Poseidon on us, and their willingness to give me up to that beast..."

"My mother was angry at my grandfather for a long

time for putting us in the ark and casting us in to the sea, but she always loved him despite that," Perseus told her. "I've never met my father; I may never, but I'd like to think he's watching over me. Yet don't think, no matter what happens between a parent and child, that those ties are ever really fully severed. Your father was willing to risk angering the gods to let me save you. And in her way, I'm sure, your mother still loved you."

He wasn't sure he was saying the right thing, if he should say anything. When Andromeda kissed him, he figured that he had done alright. Later, after they consummated their marriage at length, Perseus lay beside her listening to her sleep fitfully and realized that in the last two weeks he had made his journey from boy to man.

The next morning, Andromeda directed the transfer of their goods to the ship that would take them to Serifos. Instead of the smaller merchant vessel, the Phoenicians had readied Phineas' repaired ship. With all of their belongings moved into the vessel and men aboard to man the oars and sails, Perseus cobbled together a trio of altars and made his gifts to Poseidon first, his prayers mixing a request for a safe passage and a veiled apology for the death of his victims; next he offered up to Zeus, asking his father's guidance, protection, and favor for his works; lastly, he gave thanks to Athena for her continued protection and wisdom. With that he and Andromeda boarded the ship for home.

11. DIVINE INTERVENTION

"He wants you," the Herald said. Poseidon was in residence in Olympus, a rare thing. His palace was near the edge of Olympus, looming over the lip of the realm and the fall to Earth. It was ornate, with Corinthian columns, but Ionic gables and cornices, under which a frieze relating the tale of his birth and deeds, his loves wrapping around the whole of the building. The walls were cool, ocean colors -- blues and green hues that had been washed out to pastel. The god of the sea was reclined on a couch, nereids attending to him, when Hermes arrived.

"And what does my exalted brother want, now?" Poseidon asked petulantly.

Hermes grinned, foxlike, "Events in Tyre have not gone entirely to plan. Your plan, that is."

Poseidon sat up quickly. "What do you mean?"

"You know what I mean," Hermes laughed, "You and Hera have been up to no good."

"You were the one that sent Perseus through Tyre, remember that, Messenger," warned Poseidon.

"I know I did. I knew Hera was plotting something when she asked me to send him through Phoenicia. I've been watching the area since I sent the boy that way." Hermes' humor was starting to grate on Poseidon. "When I saw you sweep the ocean through the town, I knew she had set something in motion. What..? You don't think she had a hand in the insult to Nereus' daughters?"

The nymphs around Poseidon froze and glared at Hermes. Poseidon rose slowly, threateningly to his feet. "She whispers in ears, brother Sea. I wouldn't be surprised if her instigations caused the insult, but then...you were nudging Queen Cassiopeia into action, yourself, weren't you?"

"I don't know what you mean..."

"I hid and watched events in the town, Poseidon. Now, thanks to you, noble Cepheus and his beautiful , proud wife are so much garden decoration. Perseus killed them. And Phineas. And most of Phineas' crew," Hermes said proudly. "And now...Zeus would like to see you."

His brother was in the forum and he was not alone.

Hera sat glowering in her throne, looking dejected; a bad sign. Athena was attempting to look relaxed, but the tension in her limbs was obvious. Her fingers tickled her adamantine spear that rested against her seat. He noted she was dressed for a fight in short chiton, breastplate and greaves, helmet tipped back off her face, but ready to be replaced with a quick nod of the head. Her shield and spear were in reach. Nike, her winged attendant was also dressed fully for battle, and knelt beside Athena's chair.

Apollo sat beside her, casually watching the proceedings and next to him -- lured from her nymphs and women on Earth -- was his sister Artemis. Where Athena was a knot of self-control and suppressed emotion, Artemis was prickly, violent, and capricious. She loved children and female companionship; all others were held in distant disdain. Hermes moved to his throne beside Artemis. Dionysus chair was empty. He was most likely inebriated beyond reason.

Across from them was Poseidon's throne, and next to that Ares loomed in his chair, decorated in images of war. His black armor was chased with red, and he was grinning at Poseidon. When there was strife, Ares was always present to enjoy the show and egg it on. He was impetuous, idiotic, unnecessarily violent, and despite his sunburned, almost black skin, stunning handsome. He was universally reviled by all the company here -- including by his parents, Zeus and Hera. Behind his throne lurked his sister Eris, and their daughter Enyo. Dark and treacherous, they were not even allowed to sit with the Twelve who sat in council with Zeus. A talk with Enyo was like experiencing madness.

Quietly speaking to Ares was the staggeringly beautiful Aphrodite. She practically glowed with health and sexuality. Blonde, blue-eyed, skin like alabaster, fecund, she was dressed to reveal almost everything...but not quite. She and Ares had been lovers for a long time, and everyone knew it continued, even after Apollo and Hephaestus -- Aphrodite's husband -- discovered them in bed together and called on the whole of Olympus to witness their shame. Ultimately, it was the cuckolded God of the Smith, Hephaestus, who could not bear the shame of the infidelity. He rarely could be coaxed to the forum; one had to see him in his volcanic smithy. Demeter and Persephone looked on, nervously. Only Dionysus and Hephaestus were not present.

Zeus swept his hand toward Poseidon's throne, graciously, but the look on his face was dark, angry, and Poseidon noted the clouds circling the forum and the constant rumbling of thunder. Zeus' other hand resting lightly on the writhing, restless, skittering length of pure energy -- his thunderbolt. "Welcome, brother," Zeus said, "You are the last we are waiting on."

The King of the Gods rose suddenly and dashed a bolt into the center of the forum, the blast stunning most of the Olympians with its suddenness and violence. "It has come to my attention that the conflict between my brother, the Sea, and my daughter, Wisdom has grown beyond the initial borders of animosity.

"My son, Perseus," Hera flinched at this, "has been sent on a mission to destroy the man-killer Medusa. Athena and Hermes assisted him in this cause and now the Gorgon is dead. It is my will that this should be so!" Zeus told them. It was a lie, of course; Athena had initiated the quest on her own, enlisted Hermes' aid, but Zeus had not objected. "Now Perseus is the center of our internecine hatred and petty squabbling...Hera engineered him to be in Tyre when the monster Cetus attacked that town, hoping to kill him."

Hera glared at Hermes, knowing he had told her husband about the plot. The Messenger stared back at her, smiling placidly.

Zeus continued, "Poseidon urged the mortal Cassiopeia of that town to break the rules of hospitality, to attack her semi-divine guest -- *My son*! I know that his hand was guided in combat by our daughter Athena!"

The Goddess of Wisdom and War met her father's dark gaze levelly and without a trace of fear. The faintest shrug escaped her.

Zeus turned on Poseidon, pointing the thunderbolt toward him. Poseidon recoiled slightly in his seat, waiting the shock of the attack. "My son returns to Serifos with his bride, there to set matters right. He is fated to continue on to Argos, as prophesied. He will not be harmed. He will not be impeded. Am I clear, brother?"

"You are," Poseidon acquiesced.

Zeus maintained, "If you disobey me, we will have a war here, on Earth, in those dark place our brother Hades inhabits. I will punish *without mercy* any who cross me on this!" He turned slowly, meeting each Olympian's eye to be sure they understood. Hephaestus was above such disobedience, choosing to manufacture an endless array of fantastic creations, oblivious to the world outside of Etna, his smithy. Dionysus might not even comprehend the order, depending on his state, but Athena would be able to secure his vow more easily than even the threat of violence from Zeus could. Those here, however, they were the ones to be watched.

"This fight will end now, or I will cast the next conspirator into Tartarus!" Zeus promised. After a moment's quiet, Zeus returned to his seat. "Once Perseus has reached Serifos, Athena and Hermes will retrieve those divine gifts he was given. In particular, the head of Medusa must be retrieved. Its power is far too dangerous for a mortal to wield. After that, he will continue on his path under his own power. My wife, my brother, my children...you will not *interfere* with his fate, do you understand me? This is my order to you!"

Nods here and there, grudging silence from other quarters greeted him.

"Now get out of my sight!" The Olympians left, Demeter and Persephone practically fleeing the forum. Ares stood cockily and gave Athena a pointed, mocking look, then left with Eris and Enyo in tow. Poseidon flashed out of existence, leaving Olympus for his watery kingdom, Zeus assumed. Hera stalked out, Aphrodite attending to her. Apollo and Artemis left unhurriedly. Athena and Hermes lingered.

"Athena," Zeus called quietly.

"Father?" Athena gripped her spear and shield.

"You guided Perseus' hand in the battle with the Thracians?"

Athena smiled, "Only a little, father. The boy has our instincts. He is already gaining wisdom and *compassion* -- which will serve him well when he wrests Argos from his grandfather.

Zeus looked pleased. "Collect Medusa and the gifts. Leave him the scythe and the Shield of Abas, Hermes."

Hermes bowed slightly.

"And this quarrel with Poseidon..." Zeus began.

Athena answered, "Put aside, father. Medusa is no more, and his daughter Cetus is turning to sand on the ocean floor. I have had my revenge."

Zeus replied, "I am glad to hear it. Now leave me."

When he was alone, Zeus took a deep breath and felt the tension reducing in him. At that moment, Poseidon returned. Zeus launched to his feet, ready for a fight, but his brother put his hands up to placate him. "I have a request."

Zeus hesitated, "Go on."

"Cepheus and Cassiopeia were true to the gods. They sacrificed Andromeda, or attempted to. They tried to appease me by murdering Perseus. I wish to place them among the stars..." Doing this, a constellation of stars would be chosen, and that "image" would be giving the hapless pair a sort of immortality.

Zeus nodded. "Athena has declared herself satisfied in this matter. And you, brother?"

"Nowhere near satisfied, but I will honor your command concerning her."

"That is all I ask," Zeus told him. "I would have the two of you cease this pointless competition, Poseidon."

"That is unlikely to happen, brother," the Sea God told him, "but anything is possible." With that, Poseidon left Olympus for the sea. Eventually, Zeus knew, their rivalries would help end the rule of the gods. Their fates were not written beyond a certain point in time, but Man would continue to spread across the world and thrive, and even the Fates did not know why, but the future was unclear beyond that.

12. THE HERO RETURNS

They reached Serifos two weeks and two days later, pushed along by a favorable wind and a surprisingly mild sea. The sailors (and Perseus) were surprised at this -- a woman aboard a ship was considered bad luck. Perseus' years at sea with Dictys came in handy as he captained the vessel, piloting them along the most direct course he could figure from the excellent charts that the Phoneician navigator had brought with him. The first leg of the trip was the longest, setting out for Cypress, then turning west northwest to Rhodes, and on into the Cyclades group. They found Thira almost by chance, then turned north. He knew these seas, and they wound their way past Ios and Sifnos before finally arriving at their destination. As the ship sailed past vessels of the fishing fleet, Perseus hailed friends on the other vessels, asking after *Okeia* and her master.

    Phida, one of the boat captain heaved alongside the much larger vessel Perseus commanded and jumped aboard. "Much has happened since you went away, Perseus. Not a day after you sailed, Polydectes called for your mother with the intent of her marrying him. With her as his wife, most believe he thought would have a claim to Argos. Dictys protested, but his brother ignored him, and ordered him to bring Danae to him.

    "Instead, Dictys took her into the hills to the Temple of Zeus, where the priest has given them sanctuary." Phida paused at the sight of Andromeda approaching, "Polydectes assembled some of the men of town and went to recover her, but some of us convinced him that raiding the house of the highest god would be unwise. So soldiers wait outside of the temple for a chance to snatch Danae."

    "She is safe?"

    "She is well..." Phida told him.

    "Dictys?"

    "He returned to Serifos to persuade his brother to stop his pursuit of your mother. For his efforts, Polydectes has him locked away in his house, under guard. It has been this way for a month."

    Perseus nodded, "Thank you, old friend. I will see

you tonight, I'm sure."

"What will you do?"

"I will do as I promised and bring Polydectes the head of Medusa."

Phida reeled, "You did it?"

"I did it and more," said Perseus, putting an arm around Andromeda. "It will make for a good symposium tonight. Tell the others: Until tonight, stay clear of Polydectes' home."

Phida debarked and Perseus ordered the ship into port. To Andromeda, he said, "Stay aboard with the men and do not go ashore until I call for you." To his first mate, he instructed, "You will obey Andromeda as you would me, understood?"

As the ship pulled up to the beach, men jumping from her to drag her onto the sand, people of Serifos came down to the sea to greet the new arrivals, recognizing the markings on the sails as Thracian. What they hadn't expected was a tanned, armed Perseus to leap over the gunwale. Scythe on his belt, Shield of Abas gleaming, a large leather sack hanging from his swordbelt, and uncharacteristically clothed in a short chiton, he marched up the beach to the townspeople. He could hear them exclaiming at the sight of him. Merchants, women, fisherman that had been ashore for one reason or another, gathered and followed him through the town to Polydectes small palace -- a shade of a place compared to the massive home Andromeda had grown up in.

The commotion of the approaching crowd had drawn the attention of the house servants and as they reached the stoop, Polydectes stepped out. The older man stopped short, his face a mixture of anger and surprise at the sight of Perseus.

"My lord," Perseus called brightly, "I am sorry to have been away so long..."

"You were instructed not to return without the head of Medusa, Perseus," Polydectes called haughtily.

"I have done just that!" Perseus retorted. He laid his hand on the bloodstained kibisis. "She is here."

A collective gasp went up from the crowd. Polydectes

looked uncertain, "Then show it to us, young man," he ordered.

"The face of Medusa is not for the average mortal to see. This is *your* gift, my lord. This is for your eyes alone."

Polydectes smiled craftily, then motioned for Perseus to enter. Perseus had no doubt that once they were inside and away from the crowd's eyes, Polydectes would have his men set on him. Trying to look unsuspecting and at-ease, Perseus stepped into the house. He kept his shield on his arm, but let the limb hang casually. He followed the king into his audience room, where some of the local toughs were enjoying his food and wine. They reacted at the sight of Perseus, but seeing Polydectes -- calm and unconcerned -- they relaxed a bit.

"Perseus has returned from his journeys, my friends! And not a moment too soon!" Polydectes said.

"I understand that you have besieged the Temple of my father, with my mother inside," Perseus responded, "and that you have locked Dictys -- my father in affection, if not in blood -- away in his house."

Polydectes snarled, "It is true. You mother agreed to be my bride -- I could not wait for you to return with my bride gift for Hippodamia, and with a princess of Argos here under my protection..."

"If she agreed, why is she shut up in the temple?" Perseus inquired.

"That is enough from you," Polydectes cried. "You have been a thorn in my side for too long, pup. I could have had my heirs by now, were it not for you."

Coldly, Perseus swore, "Danae will never be yours, Polydectes."

The king motioned to his soldiers and they rose as one, collecting their gear. Perseus opened the kibisis, reached in and took a hold of the wriggling horror inside. "That is where you are wrong, boy. Dictys can't protect you; he's not a fighter. Your mother is in hiding and couldn't protect you anyway. And your alleged father doesn't appear ready to strike me down..."

"I don't need my father, tyrant. My father did not help me slay Medusa, or Cetus -- the sea monster -- in Tyre. He didn't help me slaughter the men of Phineas of Thrace, who sought to murder me to prevent my marriage" Perseus smiled viciously, "There's no 'boy' here, Polydectes. I am a man, and more of one than you. Dozens are dead at my hand for trying to stop me from having my bride; a priest and a temple stay your hand."

"Enough! Take him!" roared Polydectes. The men grabbed their weapons and began to advance. Perseus raised his shield in defense and fixed his eyes on his enemy.

"You haven't received your present, yet, old man." He pulled Medusa free, turned his head and shifted the shield to see Polydectes and the others reaction.

Shock, horror, and dismay crossed Polydectes face before his eyes calcified, his face froze to stone. His hands were half-raised to protect himself, but the effects had already petrified him. The soldiers were converted, as well. Reflected in the shield, he could see Medusa surveying her handiwork with complacency. Perseus pushed her back into the kibisis and tied it closed. He was not a moment too soon, a servant entered to wait on the company. At the sight of the horror in the room, she screamed and fled the room. Perseus turned and walked out into the street where the people were gathered.

"Polydectes is no more. He saw the face of Medusa, as did his men." Perseus saw the surprise in their faces, and fear. It was empowering. Perseus could claim Serifos as his own, but he recognized the lure of entitlement and pushed it down. "Dictys is the rightful leader now. Is there any here that oppose my will in this?"

Perseus left the stoop of the once-king and walked through his home town to the house where he was raised. Guards set themselves, ready for a fight, as Perseus approached with a mob behind him. "Polydectes is dead. Dictys is ruler now," he told the guard -- Aramos, a young boy he had grown up with. "You are relieved."

The boy hesitated, saw Perseus' hand on his scythe, ready to draw, then stepped aside. A cheer went up from the crowd behind Perseus, who stepped forward and opened to the door. He found Dictys in the center courtyard. The old fisherman jumped to his feet at the sight of his adopted son and ran to embrace him.

"I'm fine, sir," he told the old man, "I'm just back from Polydectes."

"You know what's happened, then?"

"I do and he is no longer a threat," Perseus informed him.

Dictys shied away, "What did you do?"

"I protected my family. You, my mother...my wife."

"Wife?" Dictys blinked and Perseus grinned.

"She is on my ship on the beach, waiting for word from me that it is safe to come ashore. Is it safe...my king?"

Dictys looked distraught, "He is dead, then?"

"He is, and his soldiers, as well. His charge is now yours."

"I do not want it," Dictys told him. "You killed him, you should rule."

"This is not my kingdom," Perseus said. He jerked a thumb vaguely northwest, toward Argos. "My kingdom is over the water. And it would be inappropriate for me to rule here, considering..."

Dictys regarded Perseus carefully. The boy had changed sharply in a short period of time. He was confident and subdued, and there was an easiness to his words and actions that the fisherman found both comforting and intimidating. Perseus suggested to him, "Don't be a great king...be a *good* king, father."

The old sailor nodded slowly. "I should talk to the town elders and explain the situation."

"I will call for Andromeda." He saw Dictys' querying look, "My wife...then I will go up the hill and bring my mother home."

Together they walked from the house to the applause of the people. Perseus left Dictys there to address them and headed back to the beach to retrieve Andromeda and give his men permission to disembark and set up camp along the shoreline. A few were tasked with transporting their belongings to Dictys' house and when he returned to the home with the blue-painted doors, he found the townspeople had dispersed, and Dictys had gone with them. He left Andromeda with the servants, instructing them to set her up in his boyhood room.

Then, alone, he marched up into the hills to the Temple of Zeus, where it all got started. He could see the simple building with the pinax on either side of the entrance.

There was a small contingent of men camped outside of the temple. They barely reacted to Perseus' approach, until it was obvious that he was coming toward them, specifically. The leader was a farmer in the hills that Perseus knew only by his face. "I am Perseus, son of Danae, whom you have trapped inside. I am here to take her home."

The leader explained, "I was instructed to return her to Polydectes, should she come out."

"You would have to walk to Hades, then. That is where you will find him."

"The king is dead?" another guard asked, stunned.

"Dictys is your lord now, and I have come for my mother."

"You are brave to come alone," the leader remarked.

Perseus shrugged and hefted his scythe, "I am not here for a fight, but if one presents itself...I have prevailed over worse foes than you." He proposed, "I am simply taking her back to town. You can follow and ascertain that I have told you the truth. No one gets hurt, no one is inconvenienced, and it gets you out of the hot sun."

This last bit seemed to sway a few of the boys in the picket and their leader grudgingly nodded. Perseus walked past them and entered the small temple. Right now, Danae was alone, sitting on a blanket in front of the altar to her divine suitor. Zeus' eyes stared out past the temple opening toward the skies to the west. Food was in a basket by her and the smell of urine told him she'd been making her toilet in a jug in the corner.

"Are you ready to go home?" he asked her. Danae jumped at the sound and turned to see her son in the doorway, smiling at her. She launched herself at him and hugged him tightly.

"You have no idea what has been going on here!" she said.

Perseus peeled her loose. "Polydectes is dead and Dictys rules Serifos now."

"Dead?" she asked

"Yes. And there is more: Your daughter-in-law waits at the house to meet you."

"Daughter-in-law?" Danae cried, eyes wide.

"Andromeda, daughter of the Phoenician king, Cepheus. It's a long tale, and an entertaining one." He saw the priest emerge from his apartment behind the altar. Perseus put out a restraining hand, "I am her son."

"He's returned!" she confirmed. "I am going home."

The priest nodded sagely. "I will gather her things."

"My thanks," Perseus told him. After a few minutes, her bundle was put together and they exited the temple. Perseus went first, hand on his scythe, in case the guards had had a change of heart. Danae blinked in the late afternoon sun and watched her former jailers packing up their belongings to leave.

Perseus saw the owl a moment later. It was watching him from the olive tree, blinking slowly at him. It flew off a distance and waited, turning to watch Perseus. "Wait here a moment," he told her.

"Where are you going?"

"To meet my sister, I think..."

Perseus followed the owl, which flitted from tree to tree, drawing Perseus far enough away from the others that they would have privacy. Athena stepped from behind one of the olive trees, nibbling at one of the fruits. Her helmet was pushed back, to reveal her handsome face. Her shield and spear were leaned on the tree. "You have done well," she said.

"Thank you, divine sister," Perseus replied.

"That bit with Cetus...that stirred up quite a row at home," Athena stated, "but you did alright for yourself."

Perseus bowed, speechless.

"However," she continued, "your use of the Gorgon's head has become dangerous."

"It is a weapon far too powerful for mortal men," he agreed. "It is too easy to kill with it. It's intoxicating," he admitted. Anticipating her requesting, he added, "That is why I humbly ask you to accept Medusa as a gift, my offering of thanks for your aid and instruction."

Athena chuckled, smiled crookedly. Perseus undid the kibisis and handed it to the goddess. She indicated his feet. "The sandals, as well. Your need for them is done."

Perseus hesitated, then began to strip them off. As he did this, Athena opened the sack and looked in. She sighed slightly, with a look of distaste, and closed it again and set it down with her shield. She took the proffered footwear, the wings flapping fitfully, and hung them from her spear.

"That's it, then?" he asked.

Athena laughed, "Of course not. You have a long and interesting life ahead of you, I suspect. The next part of your journey doesn't require toys like this. That scythe and that shield will serve you well. Your mind will serve you better. You still have a destiny to pursue."

"My grandfather?"

"The very same," she affirmed. "Don't worry, my little mortal brother, I will be looking in on you during your travels. I might lend a bit of wisdom here, help your sword arm there."

"The events at Tyre...?" he started.

Athena nodded, "You were being used as a tool by greater forces to...*annoy* one another. It could have cost you your life."

"It cost several dozen men theirs. As well as the creature, Cetus."

Athena looked at him inquisitively. "You think this was wrong?"

"It's not my place to remark on the actions of gods," Perseus said contritely.

"No, it is not," she agreed, "but I find your concern for the others -- the ones that would have done you harm -- curious."

"As you said, they were manipulated. As was I."

Said Athena, "Yes."

"Some were doing only what they thought best."

"Of course." The goddess asked, "If you were to replay those moments, would you do it differently?"

Perseus thought about this. "I don't know. I don't think so. Maybe I could have handled the matter of

Andromeda's parents better."

Athena shrugged, "Then things turned out for the best. In the end, you cannot allow doubt and conjecture to rule your life and your decisions. You will make good ones, and you should always try to do that. You will make bad ones; learn from them."

"Will I see you again?"

"Perhaps. I will see you, however," she assured him. Athena shooed him away and began recovering her gear. Perseus walked back to where his mother was waiting, surrounded by the guards. Together they all went down into Serifos.

*****

Perseus told his tale. He stood on a table, one of many that had been dragged from people's homes and arranged in the town marketplace. Dictys had declared a feast in Perseus' honor -- celebrating his return and his wedding. The new monarch said nothing about celebrating his rise to command the town, nor did he mention his brother, who remained in his audience hall, frozen for eternity in fear and loathing. The people had brought lamb, fish, fruits, beer, wine, and other things and much of the town now ate, drank, and caroused in the cool of the late evening.

The women of town had been curious about his new bride, and there was certainly a great amount of gossip and comparing of Andromeda's beauty to the local lights. His mother had received her new daughter enthusiastically, but with the usual wary eye of a mother not quite ready to let her baby go. Most of the people would admit that Andromeda was certainly beautiful, almost without compare. She was out of her element, among new people, introduced to a mother-in-law of her husband -- a boy turned man whom she had known for all of a few weeks, yet her cool confidence, her polite manner, and her frank speech made her attractive to many at the festival.

Danae watched her son and his bride together and was happy. The girl was stunning, no doubt, but she had been pleased to learn Andromeda was smart and courageous -- an excellent match for her young hero. And what a hero! Danae listened to Perseus shouting his tale over the crowd -- how he was given gifts from the gods to complete his divine mission. His encounter with the crones was dark, menacing, and dangerous (more so than the actual events in the cave.) His visit through the scrying pot drew wondrous exclamation from the audience. He talked about Cerna, the island beyond the edge of the earth and Medusa's garden of statues, all heroes and victims that were unlucky enough to view her visage.

At this Andromeda wept slightly, and through the chapters of the tale wherein her parents died. Perseus made them the dupes of cunning gods working to cross-purposes, minimizing her mother's perfidy and her father's weakness. Dictys also dashed away a tear and hid others behind his drinking jug. Only a few hundred yards away, his brother had suffered the fate of those unfortunates on Cerna, in Tyre.

Perseus told the fight with Cetus without much elaboration, playing up his fear and pain, so as to make the battle that much more amazing. He explained his movements, and those of Cetus, using his hands, dancing carefully on the table as he told the adventure. His report on how he gained Andromeda's hand from her parents elicited gasps of surprise at his boldness, and some of the girls cast a knowing eye at the sacrificial daughter. The gods were, indeed, cruel.

He finished with his return to Serifos, playing up the difficulties of the journey -- mishaps of navigation, trouble with islanders that hadn't been anywhere near as cagey to Andromeda's mind, and finally the showdown with a duplicitous Polydectes. Here Perseus did not pull punches in his story, instead letting his years of mistrust and hatred for the man come forth, painting him as a villain.

The crowd loved it. Her son had always been good with a story, Danae knew, but his relation of the past month was superb. When he was finished, Perseus bowed to the people, then leapt off of the table to join his wife and mother. When he was done, Dictys stood slowly, sadly.

He raised his wine and spoke quietly, so that the people had to *listen* to what he was saying, "My brother was not perfect, and his lust for Danae was that of a man seeking more -- more money, more power, more opportunities. Pride and greed were my brother's flaws, and from Perseus' tale we can see that it is an error in character that is cultivated by authority. I promise you that I will not fall into the same trap!" This brought applause from his people. Dictys continued, "However my brother ruled us, by and large, fairly over the years. For all his failings, he was beloved by me, and many of you, as well. We shall not forget the good he did, we will not discount the evil, and we will view him as the whole man he was and hold him in the esteem he deserves!"

    Perseus felt heat on his cheeks and ears -- not anger for the veiled correction his adopted father had just faulted him with, but shame. He hated Polydectes, and he hadn't stopped to think about those who loved the man, and those that had been helped over the years by him -- his mother and himself included, who had been allowed to stay in the town. He met Dictys' eyes and nodded by way of apology. That good man that had raised him nodded back in forgiveness.

    The revelry went on for a while longer, but Dictys and a few others retired to the beach to set up an altar to Hermes, to beg him to take the soul of Polydectes to Hades. Perseus did not attend. As the murderer, it was not appropriate. As the moon rose, Perseus went home with his family. Once in the house, his mother turned in for the night and Dictys snuck off to his nightly delights. Perseus and Andromeda returned to his far-too-small bed and made love, as they had every night since leaving Tyre.

    The next morning, at Perseus' insistence, Dictys took his warship out to fish, so that Perseus and a few others could clear Polydectes' house of the dead and remove them. He dumped their rocky corpses in the ocean as an offering to the Sea God. When the captain-turned-king returned from the sea that afternoon, he called Perseus and others from the town to meet and discuss the future. They gathered in the central courtyard of Dictys' house.

    The first matter was the planning and announcement of funeral games for his brother. Dictys ordered that their merchants and fishermen would head out to those towns and kingdoms that frequented Serifos to tell them of the event, and ask them to send athletes to compete in Polydectes' honor.

The second order of business: Dictys would not move into his brother's place, but instead ordered it turned it into a granary for storing food and wine. He chose to remain in his old home, even though the townspeople thought it too humble for a king. Some of the masons, the shipbuilders thought that the leader of Serifos should have a home to command respect from visitors and in the end Dictys lost the argument when Perseus sided with the elders. He would have a house that was appropriate to his station, and the locals would build it.

With that business concluded, Dictys dismissed the others, bidding Perseus to stay. The two men sat on the lip of the pool in the center of the courtyard, alone. The old man sighed heavily, "I cannot cleanse you of your guilt in this matter, my son. While I agree you did what you felt you had to, you must find expiation elsewhere."

Perseus nodded, but he could feel his chest tighten with sympathy for the hurt he inflicted on his adopted father. He would have to go into exile from Serifos, find someone to cleanse him of his wrongdoing. He realized in that moment that by saving his mother, he had lost his home. Dictys might forgive him, he might find absolution from a monarch or a priest, but in the end he would not be able to remain here on the island. He added, "And I still have penance to do for Cepheus and his brother."

Dictys nearly remarked on the tally of rulers' heads Perseus had racked up, but though it uncharitable and held his tongue. He loved the boy, but the pain and anger he felt toward him surprised and depressed the new king.

"You will leave with as many provisions as we can spare," Dictys told him. "Where will you go?"

Perseus considered this, then realized there was only one destination. "Once the ship is victualed, I will take my mother and wife and we will depart for Argolis. Perhaps my grandfather or his brother will see fit to hear my penance."

"You know the pronouncement of the oracle," Dictys warned him.

"I do," Perseus acknowledged, "but after a month of slaughter -- men and monsters -- I've had my fill of killed, father." The boy had grown quite a bit in his labors. He was more mature, even more thoughtful than he had been before, and there was perhaps not guilt, but an understanding of his actions and their consequences. "I will not offer my grandfather violence."

"Fate has a way of ruining our pledges," Dictys reminded him.

"If it is my choice, father, I will hold to it."

*****

When it came time for the ship to leave, Dictys had her stocked with provisions galore. Perseus had convinced some of the Phoenicians that had sailed from Tyre to remain with the ship, and a few of his friends from Serifos volunteered to complete the crew. They had taken a few days to prepare the vessel, giving sacrifice of cattle to Poseidon to bless the vessel, repainting her, renaming her to propitiate the superstitions of the sailors that an unnamed ship was an unlucky ship...they would be taking their chances with women aboard, as it was. Her name was *Gorgoneion* and her destination was the lands of Argos.

It was midmorning by the time their preparations were made to cast off, and many of the townspeople had turned out to see Perseus off. Andromeda noted with some amusement how many of his well-wishers were women; she would have to keep a ready eye on her handsome, heroic husband.

Dictys said goodbye to Danae, who was like a sister to him after all these years and -- had he bothered to ask -- would have been his wife, and fought desperately not to weep as Danae did. He embraced his son, Perseus, and wished him well. He reserved a bow to his adopted daughter-in-law and after the women were aboard, put his shoulder to the aft alongside Perseus and his crew, pushing the vessel into the sea. With one last clasp of hands between them, Dictys retreated to the shore and Perseus clambered up into his ship. The men rowed her a few stadia from the beach, then set the sail. He could see through the cloth where some of the crew had painted a terrible, stylized head topped by snakes on the canvas.

Some of the island's fishing vessels escorted her out to sea, including Dictys' very own *Okeia*, and the vessels exchanged taunts, jests, and good wishes. He doubted Perseus would ever return to Serifos, and he wasn't certain that it would be right for the boy to do so, but Dictys found he was already missing the boy and his mother -- his family for a decade and a half.

The new king stood for a good two hours, the surf lapping at his feet, and watched the vessel sail away until he lost her in the haze near the horizon.

13. THE MUSINGS OF A GOD
Zeus daydreamed as he looked down from Olympus -- if "down" was the right way to put it. Olympus was a location of the mind, mostly, displaced from reality but still connected to it. He watched, and he dreamed the unfolding story of Perseus. His mortal son who had already achieved great things, closing on that moment fated to him. Destiny, the lord of the gods thought, was a funny thing. Many people had some moment in their lives around which the rest of their days circled. For most mortals it was a simple thing: the realization of love, the birth of their children -- the only real function that any mortal thing had, Zeus knew; a poor immortality -- a moment of heroism, or of loss. It was to and from that moment that all things led inexorably.

For Perseus, that moment was the oracle's prophecy that he would end Acrisius' rule. Medusa, Cetus, the rest of it would make his name and legend, but it was this one moment in time that Perseus was truly "born for." It would make him the man he would be, it would set the stage for Perseus' decedents to do small and great things. Zeus knew something of their fates, if he didn't actually know their future.

He sometimes dreamed of these future people and events, and was only partially surprised when they came true. For Perseus, the cast off turned sailor turned hero turned king, there were several moments of his life that were unavoidable. He would kill Medusa. He would defeat Cetus. He would kill his grandfather. There were variations to these themes that Zeus dreamed of. Or did he remember them?

Memories were events no longer manifest; the past was as ephemeral as the future. He could remember dreams. He could dream memories. Zeus wondered if there was really any difference between the two. If he dreamed the future, did he remember the future? Was time that malleable? He knew it could be stretched and contracted by mass or speed, or perception of time. It could be linear; it could be curved.

Zeus' dreams (or memories?) of the future were imperfect, as were his memories of the past, dulled by time. Things would happen and while he anticipated the overarching flow of events, it was the minutiae, the extempore on a theme the participants crafted, that caught him by surprise. He remembered Perseus traveling to Larissa -- not the hill outside of Argos, where his grandfather was currently attending the *Hecatombaia* celebration to Zeus' wife and sister Hera, to Athena, and to Hermes -- but the city of Larissa, far to the northeast in Thessaly. Perseus attended funereal games in that set of memories, killing Acrisius with a discus, or with a quoit -- the poor man's discus; conflicting memories of the future Proteus, Acrisius' brother, had finally driven him off the throne and Perseus killed him to reinstate his grandfather to the throne in the vain hope of avoiding fate. He would kill his grandfather by accident with a discus at the Hecatombaia. There were other versions of this memory -- almost like Zeus has watched this story play out over and over again, each time the players doing things differently, each time leading to those fulcra of events -- Medusa, Cetus, Acrisius' death.

Was he experiencing different versions of the same story, until the multiplicity of events distilled down to the one possibility that was happening? Had he witnesses this tale repeatedly? If the latter, why wasn't he aware of this repetition? If he was the one telling the story, how was it that he, the author, was unable to control the outcome of the tales?

Zeus' gaze followed *Gorgoneion* as she plunged through rough seas and an unfavorable wind, taking almost four days, instead of two to reach the shore of Argolic Gulf. The ship landed before noon in Nauplia, the main port of eastern Argolis and an hour's travel through the verdant plains to Tyrins, the capital of Perseus' great-uncle, Proteus.

14. THE ORACLE FULFILLED

The arrival of *Gorgoneion* might have gone unremarked through Argolis. There were at least a dozen vessels her size drawn up on the shore, and there were plenty of ships from other ports visiting. However it was the disembarking of the young captain and his two stunning female companions -- one older, the other still girlish in her figure -- that attracted the attention of some of the town's officials and local sailors. Before they could engage Perseus in conversation, they were astounded to see the famed Shield of Abas over his back. Some of the older men had seen the shield in the *megaron*, the great hall, of Argos' ruler, Acrisius, the son of Abas. None, however, had ever seen the shield polished to such a fine sheen.

"I am Perseus," the young captain answered their queries, "son of Zeus and Danae, the daughter of King Acrisius," he indicated his mother and earned gasps of surprise, "slayer of the Gorgon, Medusa, and the sea monster, Cetus. I have come back to the land of my birth to seek out my grandfather and his brother and reunite our family."

"If you've a mind to see Proteus," one wiry old man opined, "you have best hurry. Our leader, it is said, is near death." A murmur of grief went through the crowd that had assembled as word of Perseus' arrival spread.

"Is there anyone that would be able provide us with mounts so that we might reach Tiryns more quickly?" Perseus asked around. One local owned a stable, and after some negotiation, horses were bought for himself, Andromeda, and Danae were secured, and a pony-drawn cart for their belongings would follow with a few of his trusted lieutenants. The rest of the crew would remain behind with the ship to assure its safety.

Mounted, the eighteen stadia trip to Tiryns took less time than the haggling for the horses had taken. They wound through fields of grain, groves of orange, lemon, and olive trees, passed the hovels of local farmers, spotted goat herders watching them. The acropolis of Tiryns rose above a clutch of houses on a curve of rock that jutted out of the surrounding plains. The walls of the city protected the complex of buildings: temple, palace, and the apartments of the king's relatives, servants, and officials crowded the southern end of the hill. As they approached the thick, impressive walls that the city was so famed for, Perseus could see that they were expected. Guards and other functionaries crowded the gates to the citadel, and the square before the palace.

There was a subdued, somber, and expectant air to the people, but they turned their attention to the visitors riding through their midst -- Perseus, his shield over his shoulder catching the sunlight and flashing brilliantly over the people; the stunning Andromeda in her purple and lavender dress, long and lustrous black hair tied back to reveal her face; and the more matronly, but still very beautiful, Danae. They dismounted in front of the palace, and while Perseus was helping the women from their horses, a powerful-looking young man, perhaps a few years older than Perseus, appeared in the antechamber of the palace, dwarfed by the columns that supported the front of the home.

Danae stepped forward, smiling hopefully, at him. She asked, "Megapenthes?"

"I am," he confirmed and he stepped down the few stairs to the courtyard. "You are my cousin, Danae?"

She nodded, "I am!"

"We thought you dead, although there had been rumors you had survived Acrisius' attempt to drown you." Megapenthes had turned his attention to Perseus, sizing him up. "You are Perseus?"

"Your cousin, yes. I have returned with my mother and wife," he motioned to Andromeda, "to pay our respects to my great-uncle, King Proteus."

"You should come in," Megapenthes said, and he motioned for them to follow. They went through the anteroom of the megaron and through to the great room. Proteus' throne was against the right wall, and the far wall was dominated by a massive fireplace, bounded by tremendous Doric column made of burnished wood. More mourners were lurking here, waiting for news. Megapenthes suggested to Perseus that the ladies be given a chamber to make their toilet and freshen up from their journey, and once they had retired from the all-male company in the great hall, the two cousins sat facing each other.

"What has happened here?" Perseus asked.

"My father has taken ill. The great healer Melampus has been called and pronounced my father to be dying."

"Could he be wrong?"

Megapenthes replied, "This is the man that cured my sisters of their madness after Dionysus cursed them. He is unquestionably the greatest man of philosophy today."

"I had come to pay my respects and to seek his aid..."

"For what purpose?" inquired his cousin, suspiciously.

"I have, in my travels, assassinated rulers." There was a gasp from those around them that could hear their conversation. "All in self-defense, but it is still manslaughter and I hope to repent for my acts."

"My father is hardly in any condition to expiate a supplicant..." Megapenthes said, "But I will take your request to him. Now tell us about these travels of yours."

Perseus stood and began to tell his tale, starting with his unlikely birth, the attempt by Acrisius, Megapenthes' uncle, to drown Danae and Perseus, and their rescue. He told of Polydectes' attempts to woo Danae, and his ruse to get Perseus out of the way by having him hunt Medusa. His story of the gods and their aid in his quest to murder Medusa drew gasps and some unbelieving shakes of heads, but the denouement of his hunt had everyone entranced. He related his return to Serifos, with the stop in Tyre when he spotted Andromeda, left to be sacrificed to Cetus. His marriage and the attack by Phineas and his men, and Perseus' dispatching of them drew rapt attention, and by this time Perseus had warmed to his subject weaving an arresting tale. He finished with his confrontation with Polydectes and the rescue of his mother. Once done, Perseus sat and was plied with a flurry of questions, but Megapenthes raised a hand for silence.

"That's quite a tale," he observed.

Perseus countered, "All true, although I admit, had I not experienced it I would have been skeptical. There are witnesses to the deeds, however."

Megapenthes asked, "And you wish to find absolution

for these manslaughters?"

"I do. I acted to save myself or others, but I find that a small comfort for having taken away all my victims would ever have or have been." The crowd responded favorably to this.

His cousin nodded, thoughtfully. "I will take your request to my father. For now, though, enjoy the hospitality of our home."

It was a grand home, much like the palace of Cepheus in Tyre, and Perseus and the ladies were installed in a large apartment with a porch on the roof of the lower floor. Below, the jumble houses and temples of the acropolis filled the south end of the hill, some of the buildings piled atop each other. From the porch, Perseus could make out Nauplia from here, across the plains of Argolis, along the curve of deep blue that was the Argos Bay.

Servants brought water basins to wash and a plate of fruit and bread for refreshment, and Andromeda and Danae retired to the room set besides his. After cleaning up, they relaxed on the porch until an aide from Megapenthes came to them. The women were directed to where Stheneboea's entourage were dining, Perseus was escorted to the bedchambers of Proteus. At the last moment, considering his luck with other leaders he had visited, Perseus strapped on his scythe before leaving, but forwent the armor.

There were soldiers and courtiers loitering in the antechamber to the Proteus' room, and the aide swept aside the curtain over the doorway and Perseus entered. Megapenthes was here, but Stheneboea was absent. Perseus found the queen's absence curious, but did not pry. On the bed, the dying man was wheezing arrhythmically. He was an old man, but not as ancient as the boy-hero had expected. His hair was still mostly black, but his beard was gray; his nose was blotchy with broken blood vessels -- the signs of hard living -- but the rheumy eyes regarded him sharply.

"You will have to stand close to hear him," Megapenthes instructed Perseus, who moved to the bedside and knelt to hear the ruler of Tiryns.

"You are my brother's grandson?" whispered Proteus.

Perseus nodded and Proteus continued, "I am happy to lay eyes on you. Rumors that you had survived had reached my ears, but I gave them little credit. Your mother survived?"

Perseus knew this man had nearly ruined his mother when she was young. "She did. She is with my wife."

"Wife, eh?" Proteus looked pleased. "I am not long for this life, Perseus, and I find that -- as I face death -- I wish to...atone for some things."

"I had a similar wish," said Perseus. He thought, perhaps, the old king had misunderstood the request, had thought Perseus was here to hear his expiation.

Proteus sighed, "Perhaps we can help each other."

"Of, course, great uncle."

"When I die, there will be games for my funeral. I wish these to be in Larissa, the acropolis outside of Argos..."

"In Acrisius' kingdom," Megapenthes reminded Perseus. "I have sent my request to my uncle and he has accepted it. It is my understanding he will be there, as well."

"He would not have honored an appeal from me, out of spite...as I would have done were our situations reversed..." Proteus smiled a bit at this. "While I know I cannot let go of my hatred for my twin, I do regret that I have not the will to change, even now." Perseus did not know how to respond to this, so he nodded slightly, trying to look deep in thought. Proteus added, "I would like you to attend and compete in my memory, Perseus...and express my regret for my intransigence toward that brother of mine. As a way to bring our families back together."

As a way to get in one last dig at Acrisius, Perseus thought.

"Do this, and do the proper sacrifice for those you have wronged here in our city," -- Perseus knew this was to bring favor (hopefully) to Tiryns -- "and I absolve you."

"Thank you, sire."

Proteus closed his eyes and drifted off to sleep.

Megapenthes related, "Melampus says that he will not survive the night."

"What can I do to help?" Perseus asked.

"You, your mother, your wife will be in the funeral

parade to Larissa," It wasn't quite an order, it certainly wasn't a question. Perseus accepted.

Again, others sought to use him as a weapon against their enemies.

*****

After Megapenthes left the room with Perseus, Proteus opened his eyes and found the figure in the darkened corner of his room. Thiro had been an attendant to the king for a long time, but Proteus somehow knew Thiro wasn't who he appeared to be.

"I have done as you asked," the dying man said weakly.

The figure stood and moved to the bedside, the flickering lamp light reflecting from the gray eyes that regarded him. Thiro's eyes were brown, Proteus thought. "You have done well, old mortal," the god disguised as Thiro told him. "Your brother will meet the fate written for him, Perseus will ascend to his throne, and you will have your nemesis beside you in Hades, as you wished."

Proteus inquired, "What do you receive from this?"

"My son plays the part that he was destined to," Proteus was told, and he could feel cold fear sweep through him as he realized he was in the presence of the King of Gods.

*****

Proteus, King of Tiryns, survived just over another two days.

In that time, Perseus had heard some of the stories about the great man's last days, including the curious tale of a young Corinthian hero named Bellerophon, who had come through Tiryns looking -- like Perseus -- for absolution for the accidental (he claimed) murder of his brother. This apparently handsome and strapping young man caught the eye of Sthenoboea, or so one of the women of her court delighted in relating to Danae, who tried to win the boy over. When he rebuffed her advances, she claimed he had tried to violate her.

Proteus did not want to break the bonds of hospitality, so he sent Bellerophon off to the court of King Iobates...Sthenoboea's father. All in Tiryns knew what should have followed next, but at last word, Iobates had sent the boy off on a labor: to kill the Chimera in Caria.

To Perseus, it was a familiar theme. He hoped the hero would succeed.

Proteus passed late in the evening, and after Megapenthes announced his father's passing and his assumption of the role of ruler, the body was prepared and wound in purple fabric that was to have been a gift from Perseus and Andromeda for the trip to Larissa. A cart carried the corpse the 40 stadia to the holy acropolis above Argos, and the procession followed along, some lost in silent reverie, but most getting into the spirit of the upcoming festival -- feasts, games, enjoyment were the order of the day, despite the grave reason for them. Forty leagues through olive, orange, and lemon groves, past fields with grain, past sheep and goats and cattle, small farmers' houses scattered through the rich valley.

Argos was a sprawl of buildings -- houses, markets, temples, the palace complex of Acrisius sitting higher on the hill, but not so high as Larissa, where there were temples to Athena, Artemis, and Hera on a terraced hump of rock. The mountains that ringed the valley of Argolis were a hazy pen around the scene. He noticed his mother's gaze, directed toward her former home on the hill. Andromeda was intrigued, but Tyre was easily a match for the city in size, beauty, and was much wealthier he presumed...

Other mourners and well-wishers were streaming from the city as word of their arrival spread. Megapenthes, rather than going into the city, took them along a winding track to the acropolis, where the games would be held. As they reached the uppermost tier of the temple mount, they met with the royal contingent from Argos, ready to receive them. Acrisius had dressed in a knee-length chiton, sandals, and a simple crown. His retinue, like Megapenthes', were armed and armored. In the center of the plaza between the temples of Athena and Zeus, there was a bier made of wood waiting for its resident. Megapenthes signaled a stop and for a moment, all was quiet, save for the buzzing of the bees looking for the last bits of pollen before the weather began to turn cold, and the cry of an eagle somewhere overhead.

Then Acrisius, Perseus' grandfather, spoke in a strong, clear baritone that carried out over the masses assembled. "Nephew! I welcome you and you fellows from Tiryns. I am sorrowed to hear of the death of my twin brother, Proteus" -- not King Proteus, Perseus noted -- "and we are honored that he would choose our kingdom for his funeral and games in his memory!"

Acrisius' words brought forth a wave of applause from the crowd -- Tiryns and Argos, alike. Acrisius moved with his men to meet Megapenthes. Perseus, only a few ranks behind, was studying his grandfather. He was much like Proteus, and he could imagine what the corpse might have looked like when healthy. Strong, tanned arms were starting to show signs of age, the skin wrinkled at the elbows, a bit loose where old muscle had disappeared. He kept his hair and beard close accentuating the balding pate. His eyes were brown, like Danae's, and looked used to laughing. He was smiling now, but Perseus could see him eyeing his nephew warily; Megapenthes was a young man and very fit, and had been raised since childhood to view his uncle as perfidious and hostile. A misstep on either side could lead to violence.

Next to him, he could feel his mother tense as he approached. Perseus said, "Remain calm, mother."

"I will be discrete," she told him.

Andromeda whispered, "I do not see the resemblance..."

Megapenthes was speaking to Acrisius, "Uncle, we are ready."

"Of course," the older man responded and motioned for the cart and pallbearers to move to the bier of wood. They moved forward and as he passed his grandfather, their eyes met. There was no recognition in Acrisius' eyes. Perseus followed with the other bearers to the funeral bier and helped lift the former king onto his final resting place. While Megapenthes retired from the tower of wood to offer his father to the gods, Perseus and the others waited with lit torches for the moment to send Proteus on his way. Megapenthes gave thanks and supplication to Zeus and Athena. Then, when he had finished, the pallbearers lit the pyre and jumped back as the brittle kindling took immediately. Within minutes, the entire construction was alive with crackling flames and smoke took the last remains of King Proteus into the air.

While the invocations were being made by Megapenthes, his uncle at his side with a perpetual bemused look, preparations were being made by the court and the temple's acolytes to feed to the crowd. Bulls and sheep were slaughtered ritually, baskets of fruit and bread were heaped on tables, jugs of wine watered appropriately with prayers to Dionysus...a god that had been at odds with Proteus in the past. When the bier had collapsed into an explosion of sparks and a burst of flame and smoke, King Acrisius took the opportunity to address the crowd and declare the feast open to all. This spurred a cheer and a mad rush for the tables of food. The honored guests and their host retired to a group of couches set aside for them on the steps of the Temple of Hera and there food and wine was brought to them.

Sometime during this period, as people were settling, Acrisius' eyes found a handsome woman in Megapenthes' retinue -- one he did not know, but there was something in her countenance that was familiar...she reminded him greatly of his wife, Eurydice -- recently passed beyond to Hades' care. She had the same strong chin and nose, same confidence. With her was a young couple, still adolescent to Acrisius' mind. The young man was strong looking -- sunburned and his dark hair sun-bleached just a tad. He had intense gray eyes and seemed particularly interested in Acrisius. The girl was stunning, almost-black eyes, thick, wavy black hair with just a touch of red in the highlights...a Phoenician girl, he would bet. All were dressed with in rich white and purple cloth. The older woman had been studiously trying to avoid his gaze, but occasionally would shoot Acrisius a glance. Her expression was peculiar -- somewhere between terror and longing.

He had to know her. To Megapenthes, he inquired, "My nephew, now that we have had time to conduct the necessary business that brought you here, I would meet my guests."

The boy dropped his head a bit, eyes narrowing. He was a brave one, Acrisius could see, and there was a hint of arrogance to him. The older woman jolted and tried to look anywhere but at him. King Megapenthes smiled broadly -- what was he playing at? -- and gestured to his contingent, naming them off and giving a brief synopses of their achievements...some were his soldiers, others merchants, and Acrisius could feel impatience starting to take hold of him. Megapenthes purposefully left the three for the last. The unidentified boy seemed to be enjoying the show, and they locked eyes from time to time. Finally, his nephew got to them.

"...and finally, my uncle," Megapenthes stood and moved to the trio, resting his hand on the older woman's shoulder. She finally looked at him with something between hate and pity. "I introduce my cousin, your daughter, Danae!"

Megapenthes shouted the last, catching the attention of those nearby. The crowd reacted with amazement, and much of Acrisius' court started. Acrisius struggled to keep the false smile on his face, but all saw that moment's hesitation, the battle of emotions that ended in recognition and a sudden understanding. Megapenthes' hand swung toward the boy, who stood slowly, purposefully, "Her son, Perseus -- slayer of the Gorgon Medusa, and Cetus the sea monster, slayer of Polydectes of Serifos, and your grandson! His wife, Andromeda, daughter of King Cepheus of Tyre."

The ground seemed to fall away from under Acrisius, but he kept his wits and his calm. Having composed himself, the king rose quickly and addressed the assembly, "This is an auspicious day, my people! At long last our daughter has returned home to us, and she brings with her a son; a strong, young hero to defend Argos from her enemies!"

The crowd roared its approval, but he could see his nephew and grandson were regarding him with amusement, his daughter with contempt, and his granddaughter-in-law with reserved curiosity. Megapenthes made to speak, but Perseus called out with a clear voice that was still a bit boyish, higher than his grandfather's baritone, but clear and supple, "Thank you, grandfather, for your warm welcome after all this time in exile! My family and I arrive much as we left Argos -- with the protection of my father Zeus and the good graces of my uncle, the mighty and benevolent Poseidon!" Perseus figured it couldn't hurt to lend a complement to the Sea God after having caused Poseidon so much trouble of late. "We come to honor the great King Proteus, and we have no intentions other than that."

"We are pleased to hear it," Acrisius responded, "It would seem we have much to celebrate at these games." To the crowd, "Eat! Drink up, my friends! This is truly a day to celebrate!"

The collected peoples of Argos and Tiryns shouted and applauded, and quickly settled into merriment. While they did, Acrisius strode to meet Perseus, who -- along with Megapenthes -- stepped away from Danae and Andromeda, shielding them from the king. "He is my guest, as well as yours, uncle," pointed out Megapenthes. "The rules of hospitality are clear."

Acrisius sized Perseus up. The young man was strong, fit, and there was intelligence in his eye, and a wariness. He would not be easily deceived. "Indeed they are, and no harm will come to my grandson or his family while he is here."

"I know about the oracle and the prophecy, grandfather," stated Perseus, "and I want you to know that I have had a belly full of murder -- monsters, dozens of men...kings. Prophecy be damned, I say; I will not raise my hand against you, save to protect my mother and spouse. If you can accept this, then I am your humble grandson and subject."

Megapenthes looked surprised, then disappointed. Acrisius knew his treacherous brother's blood was not to be trusted: he had planned for Perseus to murder him, as well. More surprisingly, to the aging man, he believed Perseus has spoken the truth. Unlike the boy, however, Acrisius knew that where fate was set, no mortal's will would be enough; the gods would conspire to make sure that, when the time came, Perseus killed him. The only way to stop it would be to kill Perseus...but that would be thwarting his fate, as well. Acrisius had tried that: he had shut up Danae to prevent her getting with child and Zeus had thwarted him; he tried setting his daughter and grandchild off on the ocean, intending them to die, but even there the gods had interceded, he was sure of it. Now Perseus was *here*...in Argos, a hero at such a young age, a slayer of monsters.

Acrisius looked at the boy, so earnest in his statement that he would not harm the old tyrant, and saw the face of his executioner. No matter what happened now, the close of King Acrisius story was coming and he was powerless to stop it.

*****

The games began that afternoon with wrestling matches. Acrisius did not participate, but instead left his various soldiers to represent Argos. Megapenthes and Perseus participated and did well, although one of the Argos men was a beastly creature -- large and muscular, and worse, fast. He easily won most of the wrestling matches. He had a hard time pinning Perseus, who was able to slip his grasp repeatedly, but in the end, he lost. Megapenthes fared better, winning once out of three matches with the "beast." The new ruler was also able to best Perseus, more from brute strength than subtly; Perseus was faster and more flexible, but Megapenthes had the muscle.

The night, the men of Tiryns camped in Larissa, while most of the people or Argos retired to the city. Midmorning, however, found the revelers back on the acropolis and the next set of games were played. Foot races dominated the morning and Perseus showed an advantage here -- he was young, enduring, and able to hold his speed for longer than many of the other runners. In the end, he won the sprints and the distance run.

In the late afternoon, after a break for lunch, archery displays, some sword exercises, javelin and discus tosses were planned. Throughout the day, locals meandered into the acropolis to witness some of the festivities, so no one took particular note of an older man -- a shepherd or mountain man, perhaps -- who was escorted in by a young, almost girlish, boy with longish red hair. There was a family resemblance, mostly around the eyes, which were a deep, unnatural gray. They took up a position on a boulder that had a decent view of the games field, where men and boys were shooting their arrows at target bales to the applause of the audience.

"And now?" asked the boy. He surveyed the athletes with interest, but like the older man, his attention returned often to the seated King Acrisius and his nephew, and the their favored competitors. Perseus was here, naked like the others, just finished with his javelin throw. He was a good hand with a spear, near the best of the field.

"Now, we wait for the moment for fate to take hold," the old man replied. "You heard his pledge when he was revealed to Acrisius...he will do what he can to avoid to culmination of his destiny."

"Fate will attend to itself. Isn't that what you've told me before?" the boy asked, eyes sparkling.

"Yes, but sometimes fate needs to be helped along."

The boy laughed, "That would seem contradictory."

"Don't laugh about destiny, daughter," he said lightly.

The boy, in actuality Athena, shrugged dismissively. "What were you thinking?"

"An accident. Something Perseus can live with. Something that will satisfy the Fates."

Athena looked unconvinced, but continued to survey the field of competitors. She was itching to show off, to hurl the walking stick that was in truth her spear across the distance, easily besting the men throwing the javelin. This was not her moment, however; her father had designated this her brother -- Perseus' -- time.

Unaware of the divine observers, Perseus was preparing for the next round of competition: the discus. This was one of his worst events -- he had never had a discus on Serifos, instead having made do with the poor man's version, the quoit. He was better at trying to put the modified horseshoe on a particular point than throwing for distance, like the discus. The quoit was not a weapon of war, where a well formed discus could crack a skull or break a neck at tens of yards, if thrown well. He had watched some of the men practicing and was itching to best them in this last event, as he had not in the wrestling and archery tests. Instead of shining, as the son of a god should, he had done well in everything, but excelled only in the javelin throw. He was determined to win the discus, and was limbering up, practicing his spin and release.

Finally, Acrisius announced the next event and the athletes began to line up for their throws. They would be throwing (or try to) the discus the length of the acropolis. The crowd lined the playing field to either side, and the royal entourages sat elevated on the steps of the temple of Athena. One by one, the men threw the metal disc. Some did quite well, a few were nearly disastrous for the onlookers, throwing wide and nearly injuring the observers.

Megapenthes was stepping up for his throw, and as he did the old man that was Zeus disguised turned to the boy Athena pretended to be and said, "When Perseus throws, be quick and make it happen, daughter."

Athena frowned at the command, but she turned her attention to Perseus, who was picking his discus and stretching his back for the throw. Megapenthes cast his disc long and true. As the King of Tiryns stepped off of the field, he shook his head at Perseus.

"It was a mighty cast," Perseus pointed out.

Megapenthes responded, "I could have thrown farther. I have thrown farther."

"Still, you have the win, thus far."

Megapenthes brightened, "I do at that."

Perseus stepped up to the circle, faced away from the target zone. He began to sway his upper body, gaining momentum, preparing for the spin. One and a half times counterclockwise, he turned, quick as a flash, arm arcing around for the throw. In that split second before he released the disc, Athena crossed the distance -- to all observers seeming like a flash of light off of the metal disc -- and gave Perseus just the slightest nudge. Her supernatural eyesight and sense of form gave the young hero just the extra bit of energy needed.

To the observers, it looked like his foot had slid just a

bit in the gravel, and in correcting his balance, Perseus had thrown a fraction of the moment too late. The discus flew from his hand, spinning across the acropolis, forty-five degrees off target and high. It misses Megapenthes by inches, flying over his head, zipped past Danae's surprised face, and ended its flight when it impacted Acrisius' throat, crushing it. The discus rolled down the steps of the temple, as Acrisius lurched to his feet, clutching his collapsed trachea, and toppled after the weapon down the stairs.

The crowd was still reacting to the hit when Perseus finished his recovery. He saw his grandfather topple from his perch and bounce down the steps. His mother was screaming and chasing after the body, all anger over her father's betrayal all those years ago gone for a moment. Andromeda had her hands over her mouth in shock and Megapenthes was looking about, trying to understand what had happened. Perseus bolted toward Acrisius, stunned at what had happened, quietly cursing the gods for what had transpired.

"That was a mean thing. Cheap," Athena informed her father.

Zeus nodded in agreement, "It had to be done. Now your brother can go on to found his kingdom. He will be a good ruler, I think."

"Better than some," she opined.

"Careful, daughter," Zeus warned her. She met his gaze steadily and without fear.

One day, Zeus thought, *this goddess will be the end of me.*

He would have been surprised to know his daughter, usually so loyal, was thinking the same thing. The pair rose and walked away from the scene below, where Perseus had dropped to the side of his grandfather in time to see the panicked, knowing look on Acrisius' face give way to the slackness of death. His mother's cries hammered home the enormity of what had happened, and Perseus did his best to console Danae, although he could not quite understand why, after all he had done to her, his mother should mourn this man. Megapenthes, standing off to one side, was both pleased at the death of King Acrisius and worried. Perseus had convinced him that he would not harm the old man, yet with one throw, the boy-hero had ended his grandfather and become the King of Argos. A monster slayer and a demigod, he knew that -- eventually -- he would have to deal with this Perseus.

All eyes were on the death scene of the king. No one noticed the old man and the young body simply vanish into thin air.

15. THE HERO A KING

"You are ruler now," Megapenthes observed. Perseus had been watching his mother directing the priests of Athena in their work, washing and wrapping the body for his burial fire. They were in the *cella*, the main chamber of the temple.

Perseus raised his eyes to the face of the statue of Athena that loomed over them, spear in hand, shield resting on her hip, an owl in her offhand. "I didn't want a crown. Certainly not this way," he responded.

"Nevertheless..."

"I know." Perseus turned to Megapenthes. "I know, but it is...unseemly."

Megapenthes asked, "What do you mean?"

"I killed my grandfather. Patricide is a grievous crime."

"It was an accident. You said so yourself. Others in the crowd saw you slip." Megapenthes laid a hand on Perseus' shoulder. "Still, if you feel you need to go away to cleanse yourself..."

You would like that, Perseus thought. *Have me out of the way while you steal my kingdom...* "There is a way. One that would satisfy propriety, that would absolve me of the crime, and that would suit us both, I think..." To Megapenthes' questioning look, Perseus suggested, "You will reign in Argos. I will take Tiryns. Consider it a final swap, as Acrisius and Proteus were supposed to have done during their rule. You have the greater section of the valley and its fields, I have access to the sea that I had worked since a boy."

You would do this? Why?"

"I cannot rule here. I would be consumed by shame. This way, I will pay a price -- the larger share of Argolis -- for my grandfather's death, and you will know that I do not wish for there to be any reason for us to distrust one another," Perseus said. "You can make a show of it, that the price of my expiation of guilt is the abdication of Argos...but as a rightful heir to the throne, we agree to give me Tiryns."

Megapenthes had not expected this and it showed in his face. Perseus had judged correctly that the young king would see him as a threat, and after the manslaughter of

Acrisius, would view Perseus as a constant threat. With this proposal, Perseus strengthened the illusion that he was a simple boy, more interested in right than power (and in that Megapenthes would be right); he would seem less a threat, less likely to want to fight his cousin for the rest of the kingdom.

In the end, Megapenthes could see no danger, no loss to his accepting the offer. After resolving a few of the details, they called in their counselors to witness their deal. When it was time to bury Acrisius under the evening sky, Megapenthes announced to all that he, and not Perseus, would be King of Argos; and that Perseus would succeed him as the King of Tiryns. Afterward, Perseus and his mother led the prayers to Zeus and Athena, Poseidon and Hera, to look after the soul of the dead monarch. Sparks and ashes flew into the star-filled sky and Danae could have sworn that a few of them fixed in the heavens, marking her father's passing.

*****

The days flew by. While Andromeda slowly grew larger with their first child, Perseus learned his new trade, that of ruler. He found he was good at it, and he always strove to treat his subjects as people, with kindness and honesty. The allure of power was as great as he expected, for many expected him to lord over them, and many sought favor by playing to his vanity. Sometimes it worked and he favored those he shouldn't have; often it did not.

Months after ascending to his throne, Perseus received an envoy from Serifos, a friend and sailor from the old days who brought congratulations and a gifts from his adopted father. A year later, Dictys visited Tiryns for a few weeks to see how his old family had settled in. He was pleased to see that they were all well, and played enthusiastically with Perseus' infant son, Electryon. The two men fished together from the deck on one of Perseus' warships.

Hoping to emulate the kindness Dictys had shown him, Perseus attempted to throw himself into the role of father. He taught Electryon not just the finer points of athleticism and war, but how to rule well and fairly. Perses followed, another son, and then a daughter that they named Gorgophone[5], partly in honor of her father's achievements, and partly as an honor to his sister Athena. She would ever be a challenge to her parents, being highly intelligent and strong-willed. In time, Gorgophone would marry not one, but two Spartan tyrants and her offspring would play important roles in the politics of the Hellenic world. Alcaeus, Cynurus, Heleus, Sthenelus -- all sons -- would distinguish themselves little, nor would their sister Autochthoe, but Alcaeus' grandson would loom large over his world as another son of Zeus -- the mighty Hercules.

All of them were well-loved, knew they were loved, and never had to worry about their father shutting them in an ark and tossing them into the sea.

*****

His relationship with Megapenthes was always a tense one. His cousin never fully trusted Perseus, but trade between their states because strong and regular, so there was little danger of attack. Despite this, Perseus would tramp the valley and the hills of his lands, getting to know the terrain, how it could be used to attack or defend, should it be needed. He came to know many of the farmers, shepherds, and mad men of the hinterland, and developed a network of common people loyal to him and willing to act as his eyes and ears.

One day, several years later, while out exploring one of the canyons through the hills to the north with some of him men, Perseus stopped at a spring for a drink near a hill called Mycenae for the people that lived nearby. While they rested and quenched their thirst, Perseus noticed an owl sitting on a nearby olive tree. The bird intently watched him, then flew off a few trees away and continued to observe him. Giving his men instructions to wait there for him, he followed the bird, which flew from one tree to another, always allowing him to get close, but not too much so. Eventually, he found himself on a hill overlooking the Argolis Valley, Tiryns and Argos both

---

[5] "Gorgon Slayer" in Greek.

visible in the distance.

"Excellent lines of sight," a voice noted from behind him. It had been years since he had heard that mezzo-soprano, and he wheeled excitedly. Athena sat on a large stone, owl in hand letting the bird nuzzle her face. She was dressed simply, white muslin with a red and gold shawl. "You've done well for yourself, brother."

Perseus told her, "I never thought I would see you again!"

"That was never a certainty," she admitted. "My role in your life is mostly finished."

"But why?"

"You shouldn't look for our intervention, Perseus," the goddess warned. "Mortals rarely fare well from our meddling."

"Why are you here now?" he inquired.

"A simple visit. I've kept an eye on you, from time to time," she confided, "and I must say you've done better than I might have expected at the outset. You rule fairly, with wisdom and compassion. That makes you an exception to most."

Athena threw the owl into the sky and it fluttered away. The goddess rose and joined him, looking over the land. "Good lines of sight. High ground, so it's more work for those coming at you, and you have the advantage. Lines of escape -- back through toward Nemea, or flanking the road from Argos to Tiryns. Good land and fertile -- plenty of food. The spring might suggest an underground cistern..."

"You think I should fortify the hill?" he asked

Athena responded, "It would be an excellent location for a city, don't you think? Well-defensible, a wealth of resources..."

Perseus glanced at her and asked casually, "Why the concentration on defense?"

"All cities should be defensible, don't you agree? Tiryns is build with the sturdiest of walls, on a hill...why?"

"Point taken," Perseus told her. He surveyed the ground and realized she was right. It was the perfect place for a city. When he turned to speak, Athena was gone.

A year later, construction on Mycenae was well under way. Within three years, the walls were up and Perseus and his family had moved from Tiryns to Mycenae. Many of their court made the journey, as well.

The importance of the move was not lost on Megapenthes, who was aging and worried about the succession of his children. Tiryns and Mycenae were tempting targets, and despite years of peace and friendship, Mycenae began to look on Perseus' kingdom with increasing desire.

*****

Mycenae had been founded when Electryon was a toddler. By the time he was the age his father had been when he had undertook his Medusa adventure, Mycenae had grown to become the largest, most wealthy city in Argolis, rivaling Sparta and Athens. Argos, still powerful, still important, was nevertheless losing prestige and revenue to the new city. Megapenthes had not been personally affected by the rising mercantile and military power of Perseus' kingdom, but many of the older interests of his court had been. They were losing trade to Mycenae as ships came to Nauplia, rather than Kios, Argos' port. Farmers, craftsmen, and shepherds found more work and better prices in Mycenae than Argos, and prices of goods rose as they had to be bought from Mycenae or Tiryns.

Personally, Megapenthes believed that Perseus meant his lands no harm, but his cousin also made little effort to stem the flow of goods and wealth from Argos (and, if he had bothered to note it, Perseus' own Tiryns) to Mycenae. The wealthy in Argos wanted to "adjust" the balance of power, his warriors ached to take on this "hero" Perseus' army, and his son Argeus -- only a few years older than Perseus' Electryon -- would soon need something to distract him; the boy was anxious to prove himself in battle and, not content to wait for his father to die, to build himself a kingdom. For almost two years, Megapenthes managed to fend off the calls for war from his rich friends and his avaricious family, but in the end there was nothing for it...he would have to bring a fight to the walls of Mycenae.

For years, these martial threats reached the ears of the courts at Mycenae and Tiryns, and hoping to defend their homes and profits, the people of Perseus' court started to press for a preemptive campaign to stop the aggression of Argos. Perseus, for his part, had been kept apprised of the burgeoning push for war in the Argos court. He and Megapenthes had traded missives for the better part of a year, trying to find a way to quell the lust for blood that was sweeping the people of Argos and Mycenae. Ultimately, the two rulers knew that the momentum in their courts was with the warmongers. The God of War, Ares, it was said, was always attractive and often stupid -- the very definition of the war that was overtaking them.

To avoid looking weak, to avoid internal strife, the two kings conspired to give their folk a short campaign -- something to ease their lust for war, but that would be limited enough to avoid too much carnage. So it was that when the envoy from Argos brought the declaration of war, Perseus was not surprised. He called together his captains, including the young Electryon, and set about readying the city for the impending attack. For the first time in over a decade he took down the dazzling Shield of Abas and the scythe that had not tasted blood since Tyre. He put on new leather greaves on his legs and arms, a new bronze breastplate with leather skirt -- never worn, tightly uncomfortable, and humorously creaky.

Electryon, tall and strong, with his father's tanned skin and deep gray eyes and his mother's red-tinged black curly hair, was similarly dressed. His shield was hammered bronze over wood with a spiral of pictograms retelling his father's deeds -- the murder of Medusa, the fight with Cetus, the marriage to Andromeda, and the deaths of Polydectes and Acrisius, as well as the founding of Mycenae. In the center was a highly stylized Gorgon's head. He carried a spear and had proved himself an exceptional talent with the javelin, whether thrown or wielded in close quarters. Like his father, he was a smart, conscientious man, but -- having a monster killer and hero as a father was a powerful legacy to live up to -- he was more aggressive than Perseus was. He knew the war was idiotic, but he was eager to test himself in the field.

Mycenae was well positioned to withstand siege or attack. The people of the town and the surrounding hinterlands were ordered inside the strong walls, or to scatter to Tiryns or elsewhere. Food was bought into the city, the gates were secured. Water was no problem; the spring that had refreshed him so many years ago, when Perseus last saw his divine sister, was safe inside the fortifications. Battle plans were made -- Perseus would draw the forces of Argos up close to the city, where their archers could soften them up, while his army pincered Megapenthes between the Mycenae forces and the reinforcements he had sent for from Tiryns, which would be on his cousin's right flank. They were ready when word came out of Argos that Megapenthes was leading his army across the plains of Argolis to the northeast and Mycenae.

Megapenthes has a captain named Kiros. He had not shown himself excessively talented in the area of tactics before, but Argos had not gone to war for the last decade, either. Kiros understood that the large city and its strong walls dominated the valley and the passes into those hills, that it was a weak position: Tiryns was on their right flank, requiring Megpenthes to push his forces further north, closer to the hills than he wanted, so that grand city and his forces would not be at his back. His scouts returned with reports of the garrisons at Tiryns moving to meet him. While it was part of the plan, Megapenthes was starting to share Kiros' worry that Perseus might use his advantage to crush Argos' army and take his kingdom.

It took a day for Argos to move to the field of battle, and Tiryns had mobilized and was on his right. To protect his flank, Megapenthes set up his forces in a curve, facing Mycenae and Tiryns. It was a strong defensive position, but weak for advancing. He kept his forces back far enough from the walls of the city to avoid a barrage of arrows from the men on the walls. Perseus would have to come out to meet him.

The next day, the cousins met for *parlay*, each with a couple of their aides at their side. Perseus had his son Electryon and a captain named Nerus; Megapenthes had his son Argeus and Kiros. Perseus once again offered peace, that they could negotiate some kind of deal that would satisfy the merchants of Argos, but he knew after a few minutes that it was futile. Megapenthes had been listening to Kiros all morning as he skillfully explained the need to strike hard and fast.

Megapenthes did not know that Kiros had been asleep in his tent that morning, that the advice he received fell from the lips of Eris -- the Goddess of Strife and perpetual companion of Ares. Even now, the God of War was disguised in the army of Argos, hoping for the opportunity to slay a few men, but mostly longing simply to see Athena's pet, Perseus, perish. Kiros, for his part, only dimly remembered having counseled the king, some of these memories whispered into his ear by Ares' son Phobos. That minor god, along with his twin brother Deimos, were even now spreading fear throughout the army of Argos and Mycenae in advance of the fighting.

If you don't strike now, Fear murmured in Megapenthes' ear, *Perseus will win the day and you will lose Argos.* "I fear, my cousin, that there can be no peace between our lands while we both live," Megapenthes stated simply.

A personal challenge had not been part of the plan and Perseus cautioned, "Think this through, cousin...there's no turning back from this, once we begin. I had hoped that we could work together to find a solution."

"My army is outnumbered and out-positioned, Perseus," Megapenthes said. The implication was clear: Perseus meant not a sham fight, but a real battle. "I can only hope to win in direct combat..." Louder, so that he could be heard by the two forces, "I am Megapenthes, son of Proteus -- sworn enemy to Acrisius, your grandfather. Our houses have been opposed to each other for years, and even now. I challenge you, Gorgon killer, for the honor of our ancestors and the fate of our armies!"

Perseus hesitated then replied in kind, "As you wish, cousin!" He shooed a concerned Electryon and Nerus away. Argeus retreated with Kiros, who was wondering how this farcical fight had become a actual challenge.

Perseus readied his shield and scythe, pulled his helmet low over his face; Megapenthes drew his sword and set his shield. Between the two lines of soldiers, the cousins circled each other, testing each other's defenses with feigns and jabs. Megapenthes was repeatedly driven to the defensive and Perseus used the brilliant reflections off of his shield to dazzle his opponent. Megapenthes moved to have the sun in front on him, so Perseus could not continue to use the shield to blind him, but Perseus was pressing the advantage, and used the curve of his scythe to trap Megapenthes' blade between his shield and the weapon. Frustrated, Megapenthes gave a cry and rushed his cousin. Perseus tried to back up and shift, to let the men pass by, but their shields clashed and both were thrown to the ground.

Electryon had started forward, only to see Argeus matching him, spear ready. The princes faced off, trying to both watch their fathers battle, and each other. The armies stirred and cheered their respective leaders. Ares, hidden among the warriors, could feel the heat of battle flushing through the men around him, felt the rush in the golden ichor that ran through his veins. Soon the bloodletting would start! Across the field, he could see one of the people of Mycenae staring at him. An older man, the soldier was armed with a spear. There was something off about the man, and with a start the god realized that he was looking at an Olympian, like himself; he could *feel* the other god and knew that this creature wanted him to know it was there. It shook its head at him, in warning...only one god would be here to warn him off, but ready to fight. Ares knew her now: Athena. He grinned manically; he had longed to pit himself against this supposed "greatest" of the Olympians...the one all the others feared.

But not him.

Perseus rolled to his feet quickly, across Ares' line of sight to Athena and broke his concentration on her. Older and slower, Megapenthes followed suit and had to immediately defend against a series of slashes from Perseus. He blocked them with his shield, but one found its way past and clanged off of his helmet. Megapenthes shoved out and up with his shield, smashing it off of Perseus' and knocking him back, then jabbed not at his body, but hacked toward his arm. The blade missed, but Perseus stumbled slightly and Megapenthes pressed the advantage, pushing Perseus back toward the line of

Argosian soldiers.

Ares has lost Athena in the crowd; she had disguised herself once more. The god turned his attention to the kings fighting. Perseus was stumbling back toward him, Megapenthes slashing and stabbing at the man. Ares readied himself, considered striking the fatal blow if the hero-king came too close. Zeus would be furious and Ares would pay the price, but it was so tempting!

Perseus threw himself to the left, using the shield to tumble past Megapenthes and gain a few precious seconds to set himself against assault. Swords clashed, shields pounded against each other and all could see that Megapenthes had the strength advantage, Perseus the speed. A stray slash and Perseus had laid open his cousin's forearm. Megapenthes' sword cut along Perseus' shoulder, having glanced off of the Shield of Abas. Both men were sweaty, bleeding, tired, but well matched.

That was when, driven to boredom by the minutes of combat, Ares revealed himself. Just for a moment, and just to Perseus. The king of Mycenae was facing him and saw one of the soldiers in the Argos lines shift and change to present a terrifying vision -- a warrior taller than any man on the field, staggeringly power in build, tanned to almost black skin, bright blue eyes flashing with hatred, his armor black with red trimming, red horsehair crest over his helmet -- before turning back into just one of any unremarkable spearmen. Less than a second, but just enough.

Megapenthes had been in mid strike and Perseus had flinched. The king of Argos slipped past the shield and into Perseus armpit, severing nerves, muscle, arteries. Perseus' sword arm went limp and the scythe tumbled from his grasp and blood showered the ground. The hero that had killed Medusa, bested the tremendous sea monster, Cetus took a few short, staggering steps and collapse to his knees, dazed. Around him, all could tell from the blood flow that it was a fatal hit. Megapenthes was equally stunned -- he had not meant to kill Perseus, merely wound him. Electryon, with a cry of despair, launched himself at Megapenthes, but Argeus was there and the boys were squaring off.

The spell of single combat was broken by the peal of lightning and thunder. Megapenthes was shaken from his moment's shock to see one of his soldiers disappear, blown from existence by the bolt. In the Mycenae lines, there was something like a piece of the sun, flashing among the men, crackling with energy. The men near the thing shrank back, the heat of the god singeing them. Some dropped to their knees in surprise and terror. The battle that had been about to rage had been nipped in the bud by the god in their midst.

KNOW ME! The command was felt, more than heard, and the soldiers felt back from Athena. Argeus and Electryon were falling back as the goddess advanced into their midst, moving to Perseus' side. Megapenthes saw the hero was still on his knees, still bleeding copiously, his shield dropped. He raised his face and smiled weakly at his divine sister. Athena slowly raised her helmet so that Megapenthes could see her handsome, strong face. Grey-green eyes like storm clouds regarded him with open hostility and Megapenthes felt himself go cold, seized with terror.

"Now what?" Perseus asked.

Athena smiled sadly, "Now your memory lives forever."

"But not me," Perseus responded.

She confirmed, "Not you, no."

"Father!" Electryon cried and felt to his knees, taking Perseus in his arms. He glanced to the goddess imploringly

"Say goodbye, nephew," she told him, "while you can."

Perseus was bleeding over Electryon's breastplate, the sheen of the bronze making his blood look like the golden ichor of the gods. Quietly, he told him, "Be a good king, my son, not a great king. Be a good man, not a great one."

Unseen by the men on the field, hovering above Athena, was Hermes. The trickster god smiled benevolently, "It's time to go, brother. Elysium awaits."

"Elysium..." Perseus muttered, unheard to all but the gods. The afterlife was a sad place for most, but Elysium -- the island where the heroic, the virtuous resided -- was a place of joy and light, and as Hermes took his hand he could see it:

light from everywhere, illuminating the fields of Elysium with an otherworldly glow. There was the palace of Kronos, released from Tartarus by his son Zeus, to rule over the souls of the good and brave. He could feel himself detach from his body.

Then he was gone.

Electryon fought back his tears and holding the lifeless body of Perseus, turned his attention to Megapenthes. "I must bury my father with the appropriate honors due a son of Zeus. And you...Leave. Leave with your army, now, or we will crush you. I will press on to Argos and murder every one of your sons and daughters. I swear this by the goddess standing here, by my father's memory."

Megapenthes blinked and looked to Athena. She ignored the man, resting a hand lightly on Electryon's head. "He will be remembered. His image written in the stars above alongside Cetus." With a last glance at Megapenthes, she flashed away.

Electryon lowered his father's body to the ground and stood, taking the Shield of Abas on his arm and lifting the scythe that killed Medusa. To Megapenthes, he asked, menacingly "What do you say, cousin?"

Megapenthes stepped back from the boy and nodded slightly. "The war is over, Electryon."

EPILOGUE

Zeus and Athena watched the flames from Perseus' funeral pyre leap into the evening sky, watching the sparks fix themselves in the sky. A new constellation...one that would mark Perseus' passing for all time. The assembly of family and subjects of Perseus were singing his praises, and those of the gods, and Athena could see they were pleasing to her father.

"A stupid death," she observed.

Zeus chuckled, and thunder rumbled across Mycenae, "Aren't they all? But that is the lot of mortals." The two gods observed the revelry from a distance, unseen by the men and women. "Both you and Ares ignored my injunction not to meddle in the affairs of Man."

"Ares ignored it. I stopped him."

"And in no way did you coax your mortal brother to construct a new city in a location that is ideal for resisting a siege or attack."

"You know I did," she told him, "and you know that the rest of us have continued to play with the lives of these people. Yourself included, father." Both knew she was referring to his continued preference for mortal women. "You cannot expect obedience for a law which you yourself flaunt."

"It is a dangerous precedent," Zeus told her.

The goddess inquired, "Why? What is it about this fraternization that worries you, father?"

"Man is filling the world quickly, they are learning too fast," he glared at Athena, "and for that you and Prometheus are to blame..." Before she could respond, he continued and his voice was heard across the Peloponnese was grumbling of a storm coming, "And among these men are the semi-divine. Men like Perseus, men who are paragons of their race. Perseus was just the beginning. One day, they will become a threat to us..."

"That seems unlikely," she responded.

"You do not know the warp and weft of Fate, my daughter," Zeus reminded her. *And that will have to be rectified*, she thought. He told her, "If we are not careful, there will come a day when Man will become a threat to themselves, the world, and ultimately, us."

Athena quipped, "Perhaps a bit of discretion from the Lawgiver would act as an example..."

"Do not forget yourself, Athena. You are my favorite of my children -- we both know this -- but these acts of rebellion, small as they are, only compound your prior crimes against my rule."

Zeus was privately unnerved by her lack of fear in the face of his ire. She said, "Perhaps you should have let Poseidon kill him when he was put into the sea with Danae...or kept our aid from him when he went after Medusa. Why keep him alive, if he was the vanguard of a new, dangerous breed of humans?"

"Even I have to follow the fates," he said huffily.

"What is it that has you so scared?" she asked.

"You are too shrewd, daughter," he countered.

"There is something, isn't there? Something in the future the Fates revealed to you..?"

Zeus looked away, watching the end of the prayers and the beginning of the feast to celebrate the life of his now-dead son. He remembered the vast tapestry of time and space, showed to him only once by the Fates, but burned into his mind. The strands of individual lives, decision trees and probability spread across their works, creating patterns both elegant and puzzling. Zeus had marveled at the vista, and his mind had instinctively, selfishly sought out the strands of the gods, watching them wend their way through the history of the world...then disappearing into a whorl, an eddy that seemed to pull them out of the universe itself. How could they simply cease to be? They were immortal, the Fates acknowledged that, so how could they stop being? No matter how persuasive he had been they would not reveal the truth to him. They claimed they could not.

There was but a short time to figure out the puzzle, and Man seemed at the heart of it -- the Titan Prometheus' greatest and worst creation, favored of the Olympians, and soon masters of the world. Zeus had seen how the gods' children would weave through the next few centuries, coming together in two massive events in which the gods were tied.

"Even I don't understand it," he told her.

Athena let the subject lie, but it confirmed her belief that Man was more important than she or Prometheus had believed. They would have to be counseled, taught a way better than that of the gods. Despite her father's rule to the contrary, she intended to help them come into their own.

CPSIA information can be obtained at www.ICGtesting.com
Printed in the USA
LVOW121854081112

306497LV00019B/32/P

9 781479 259649